# HORIZON

## KEITH STEVENSON

First published in paperback in Australia in 2022

by coeur de lion publishing

www.coeurdelion.com.au

© Keith Stevenson 2022

www.keithstevenson.com

Print ISBN 978-0-6481975-4-6

Also available as an ebook from HarperCollins Publishers
Australia

Ebook ISBN 978-1-4607046-5-3

 A catalogue record for this
book is available from the
National Library of Australia

FOR CALLUM
FOR FREYA

# 1 THE VOID

WE TERM SLEEP A DEATH, AND YET IT IS WAKING
THAT KILLS US.

1

Something was stuck in her throat, hard and unyielding. Her gullet closed painfully around it. Her stomach convulsed. Hot puke welled up and sprayed from her mouth. It stuck to her face, running down her neck and breasts. Her teeth clamped around some kind of tube, but it was too tough to bite through and her hands seemed locked to her sides. She called for help in the darkness, an incoherent rasping that she hoped someone – anyone – would hear. She was fighting for breath.

A keening siren pierced her consciousness, and Cait knew where she was.

Flexing her fingers, she heard the gauntlet seals pop and thrashed her arms back and forth until they were loose. Her fingers felt weak as she wrapped them around the flexible pipe and pulled it free. She pushed her head through the webbing that supported her, vomiting again as soon as she was clear. Her abdomen cramped painfully with each sobbing retch.

'Phillips!' she screamed hoarsely and prised the

rem-pads from her eye sockets. Darkness became a greyish blur. Tearing at the leg bags, she spat out the last of the bitter bile and slapped her calf and thigh muscles hard.

'Come on, come on,' she urged, rubbing until hot pins and needles spread from her toes. The catheters were still in place and she allowed herself a breath, willing her hands to stop shaking as she drew the tubes slowly from her body.

Her surroundings began to resolve.

The siren still wailed loud enough to wake the dead. The command port was only a few steps away, squeezed against the wall between her harness and Sharpe's. But she knew better than to try to walk there.

'Lights,' she shouted above the din, but the dull illumination of the wall readouts persisted.

The harness webbing criss-crossed around and over her to the support strut above. She quickly shuffled along to the command port end and pushed her way through the straps, reaching up and hanging from the overhead webbing as she felt for the seat back. She didn't dare fall now. Bones could become brittle in prolonged deepsleep, and she'd been under for ... how long? Her fingers closed on the seat, and she eased herself down into it.

The cold plastic was a shock to her skin. Firing up the monitor, she killed the siren and brought up the lights, rubbing at the sudden pain in her eyes.

Sharpe lay wrapped in his webbing beside her, oblivious to her struggle. Onscreen, computer and life support were flagged in red. She punched for deepsleep and read the figures scrolling across the display, then focused on Sharpe once more.

She grabbed for his harness, pulling herself up and pushing through the wall of webbing. His body jiggled in the cradle like a marionette, and his eyes were open, staring through her. She would have fallen backwards if the straps hadn't held her from both sides. As it was she let out a cry and black spots swam before her eyes, threatening to swallow her. She waited for the dizziness to pass before forcing herself to look again. He'd pulled his left hand free of the gauntlet. The clenched fist lay across his chest, the tip of the rem-pads poking out between his fingers. His pallid face shone in the light of the single overhead. He looked terrified and alone.

Tentatively, she reached out a finger to touch his cheek. His skin felt dry, but it was still soft and warm. She couldn't tell how long he'd been this way. The harness had lubricated and massaged his body, fed him and siphoned his waste, monitored and scanned and adjusted his chemistry when it needed to. But it hadn't stopped him dying.

Sluggishly, her mind recalled mission protocol. In the event of crew death, Phillips – the integrated ship-control persona – should have woken her. Where the hell was he; why wasn't he responding?

'Sharpe!'

The sound came from above, startling Cait. Pulling free of the webbing, she looked up towards the far side of the habitat ring.

Bren stood naked, clinging to her own harness webbing. Her gaze was locked on Sharpe's body, ignoring Cait completely. Even from where she stood, Cait could see Bren's every muscle was taut, as if her whole body was locked in some kind of epileptic spasm. And then the woman's head rolled back and she slumped to the deck.

Cursing, Cait dropped into the port seat and scanned the display again. The sensor log was clear of proximity warnings. That would have to do for now. She keyed in the wake-up sequence and cut back the habitat ring's spin, sliding from the chair onto her hands and knees as soon as she was done.

The deck curved up and away from her, and her wasted muscles protested as she crawled towards Bren's body. Slowly, the strain eased as the ring's spin rate decreased and the faux gravity reduced, so she covered the last few metres in a long, low bound. There was a whirring noise from above and she looked up to see her PAL, the tiny sphere recording every move with its single blue eye. At least some things still worked as they should.

Bren looked like a starved waif. Her flesh had an unhealthy yellow cast and her ribs poked out beneath her small breasts. Cait pressed an ear to her chest and heard a strong heartbeat and slow, steady breathing. Catheters still trailed between the younger woman's legs, and Cait drew them out and pulled a shift from the floor locker to keep her warm. She grabbed a one-piece for herself, wiping at the sweat and puke still clinging to her body, then grabbed another and quickly dressed.

She still had no idea how long they'd been in deepsleep, and Phillips wasn't around to tell her. She looked closely at Bren, trying to detect any signs of ageing. The mission was scheduled to take fifty-five years by Earth's frame of reference, or slightly more than forty-five years' ship time. On average, deepsleep slowed physical processes by a factor of seven so the whole journey should see them age by a little over six years. Bren's bleached buzzcut had grown out to a shoulder-length, mouse-brown cloche with a wistful frizz of blonde at the tips. But apart from that and her sickly condition, she looked pretty much the same. Hell, they might be no more than a couple of years out from Earth for all Cait knew.

She heard movement from the next harness and hauled herself up, her arms shaking with the strain. Parting the webbing, she pulled the rem-pads from Lex's eyes and helped him free the tube from his throat. He turned his head quickly and she moved awkwardly aside as a stream of bile surged from his mouth. It splashed onto the deck, globules breaking away and rising slowly only to fall to the floor again, trapped by surface tension.

Lex blinked rapidly and focused on her. 'I feel like you look,' he croaked.

'You look like I look,' she said. 'Get up. I need some help here.'

She slid one arm under his shoulders and, leaning into the harness for support, lifted him to a sitting position. His muscled body was surprisingly light, even in the reduced gravity, and his pale skin felt cold and dry. She undogged the leg bags while he pulled out the catheters.

His brown hair hung lankly past his shoulders. He swept it back out of the way and asked, 'What's happened?'

'Sharpe's dead,' she said, looking for some strength in him that she didn't feel in herself, but seeing only sudden fear. 'And Bren's collapsed. I need you to look after her while I see to the others. Can you manage?'

Lex pushed his legs through the strapping to sit on the side of the harness and saw Bren. A retort froze on his lips and he nodded slowly.

The faux gravity was all but non-existent now as the ring continued to decelerate. Cait pushed off from Lex's harness and flew across the deck, bringing her arms and legs forward to push away again as she came into contact with its surface. She sailed past the main control interface, covering fifteen metres in three strides, and bent her knees deep on the last to kill her forward momentum.

Harris was leaning over the webbing when she reached him. He pushed himself up and wiped at a trail of spit necklaced across his beard.

'You okay?' Cait asked.

The lines of his face pulled together to form a humourless smile. 'Ask me in five. I just need a bit of time.' He coughed, and reached over the side of the webbing to pull a shirt from the floor locker to wipe his face.

'Harris,' Cait said and hesitated.

'Trouble?' he asked, shifting his bulk to sit more upright.

'There's been some kind of malfunction. Phillips isn't responding … and Sharpe's dead.'

'Sharpe? But –'

'I don't know any more than that,' Cait said, waving a hand. The pressure to get to work on some answers was becoming unbearable. 'Bren's hurt too. Give Lex a hand when you can.'

She moved on shakily. Her body was beginning to betray her, but she pushed on through sheer willpower.

Nadira was already pulling on a one-piece when Cait got there. Winded from her exertions, Cait took a slow, deep breath before speaking. 'You okay?'

Nadira's eyes flicked towards hers for an instant then focused on her fastenings again. 'Fine,' she said, her tone decidedly unfriendly.

Cait felt like she'd been slapped. The petty bickering they'd endured before deepsleep came flooding back, along with a surge of anger. She wanted to shout at Nadira that Sharpe was dead and next to *that* nothing else mattered. But Nadira didn't know what had happened, and Cait didn't have the energy.

She'd checked Nadira was okay; that was all she had to do.

'Help Harris and Lex when you're dressed,' she said.

She turned and kicked off, coming full circle to the command port and sinking gratefully in front of the display. She was hot, sweaty and smelt of vomit. Her body was one unrelenting ache. If not for the harnesses, she knew she'd barely be able to crawl so fresh out of deepsleep, but that wasn't much consolation.

Sharpe lay beside her, almost mummified in the harness webbing, and she angled away from that side of the seat. Where was Phillips, and what the hell had happened to Bren?

Thinking about Sharpe brought her close to tears. Somewhere deep inside she recognised she was in shock. She just wanted to curl up and make everything go away. But she had a ship and crew to look after.

Her PAL latched onto the wall track above the port and lowered itself to a position just above the display.

'Address intra-ship,' she told it. 'Briefing in ten.'

She could hear tiny echoes of her voice around the ring as her image was relayed to the other PAL screens. 'Just as soon as I figure out what's going on.'

The port still flagged computer and life support. She cleared the screen with a wave and began checking internal sensors, bringing up a schematic of their craft. *Magellan's* familiar stubby cone flashed up in cross-section and she worked the sensors from stern to stem. First came the thickest portion, the massive hold containing the zero-point drive, partially open to the vacuum. Next the aft storage area, hard up against the revolving drum of the main habitat ring. Nothing. Hull integrity, atmosphere, ambient temperature, servos, relays, all okay. Ahead of them was the fore access tube and the six segmented bulkheads of the forward section tapering towards the nose: auxiliary command, clean room and lander lock, bot tubes and launcher, computer core, environment plant, and long- and short-range sensors and communications – each segment lined with additional storage bins wherever clearance allowed. There was nothing out of the ordinary. Which meant whatever had gone wrong was outside their ability to easily define.

Ten minutes later, the *Magellan's* crew sat around the main control interface: a long, matt-black, waist-high slab inset with ports and relays that curved gently in parallel with the deck. They all looked like shit. Harris, normally stocky tending to fat, had lost a fair amount of weight. Even Nadira, whose skin colour hid the pallor evident in the others, showed black circles under her eyes. Cait didn't feel much better, and smelled worse, despite her tightly shut one-piece.

She, Harris and Lex were at one end of the table, huddled together as if for mutual comfort, but Nadira chose to sit at the far end and eyed them all with cool reserve.

The implications were obvious. Nadira, the sole representative of the Compact of Asian Peoples, had done little to fit in with the predominantly Pax crew. But to be fair, there had been transgressions on both sides during the slow journey to the edge of Sol System. Harris was a dyed-in-the-wool Pax nationalist and set in his ways. Lex was from the European Union, which was supposedly neutral, but it hadn't stopped him airing his opinions either. Cait and Sharpe had tried to keep a lid on things, but it had been a relief when they'd finally locked the systems down and entered the deepsleep harnesses.

Interpersonal problems were the least of her worries now. It seemed an effort just to think. She looked at the flimsy spat out by the command system. Time to get on with it.

'There's good news among the bad,' she began. 'We're on course, and the drive appears operational. But we're still a long way out from Iota Persei. Roughly six weeks from scheduled wake-up, which means five from the V-dump cascade. We're lucky we woke up when we did. It gives us that long to get the AI up for the burn.'

'So we're close to Horizon,' Lex said. 'We made it.'

'*So far* we've made it,' Cait corrected. 'We have to work out what happened during deepsleep before we can start patting each other on the back.'

'If the Phillips persona was down and out, the fail-safes must have tripped your wake-up,' Harris said.

'That or Sharpe's death. Or both depending on the timing. Something's obviously gone incredibly wrong.'

'Do you know what the time delay was?' Harris asked.

'No. I don't have access to the log yet. Even though the back-ups are functioning, we don't have integrated control.'

Harris took a sip of coffee and sat back in his seat, swirling the hot liquid in its bulb. 'I wonder what things are like back on Earth.'

Lex glanced towards Nadira at the other end of the bench and folded his arms. 'Why bother about them? We've been away for over half a century. I can't see there'd be anybody left who'd care about five people blasted thirty-four light years into space.'

'We're not all like you,' Cait said. She'd heard this before from Lex. It was a pet topic, but not a debate she wanted right now. 'Some of us do care. And we're looking forward to going home after the mission.'

Lex smiled. 'All I'm saying is, don't be surprised if all you find is a smoking cinder. Pax Americana might have tolerated the Compact when we left, but sooner or later they have to revert to type. Overfarming, rising salinity – I don't care how good genetech gets, you can't grow crops on salt pans. That means a growing pressure for fertile arable land. Sooner or later something's got to give. It all comes down to *Lebensraum*.'

Harris scowled. 'The Pax government is not Hitler.'

'Hey, I'm not singling out the Pax,' Lex said, raising his hands. 'Any government's going to feel the pinch and act on it. Even the EU, if we had the military muscle. Besides, how would you know what the Pax government is like these days?'

'And how would you?' Cait interrupted. 'In those fifty years, progressive governments could have solved the problems of our time. Don't forget one aim of our mission was to study the planetary environments we encounter to better understand our own. And that was only one of a raft of programs the UN sponsored with the full support of the Pax, the Compact, the EU and the UNS. There's no reason to expect that progressive approach hasn't survived for the past half century and prospered as a result, unless you have a pessimistic take on humanity.'

'Yeah,' Harris chipped in, 'don't judge others by your own low standards.'

At the other end of the bench, Nadira was ignoring

them. She'd accessed a terminal on the tabletop and her fingers were moving across the inset keyboard.

'What about you, Nadira?' Lex asked. 'What are your views?'

'Lex,' Cait warned.

The Compact scientist ceased her steady tapping and regarded them coolly. 'My views I'll keep to myself, until airing them serves some constructive purpose. I'm waiting for the briefing to continue.'

Harris gave a low whistle.

Lex just smiled. 'That's me told,' he said, and sat back in his seat.

'We're looking at three main problems,' Cait said, focusing on the job at hand. 'First, we need Phillips up and running to integrate ship's systems and operate the drive. Second, we have to find out what killed Sharpe – if it was the harness, that spells trouble for the V-dump. I don't want to think about how long conventional braking and backtracking will take.'

'Third is Bren, I take it,' Lex said. 'I've only managed a cursory examination. She's got bruising from the fall. Nothing serious. There are some odd readings in the EEG though.'

'It'll be that bloody computer link,' Harris said. 'I told them it wasn't a good idea having her on board.'

'You're jumping to conclusions,' Cait said. This was another long-running argument from before deepsleep. 'I'll come take a look after we're done here, Lex.'

He shrugged. 'Whatever.'

'And I'll need you to start an autopsy on Sharpe as soon as you can.'

'What!' Lex sat forward so quickly, he floated off his seat. He pushed against the benchtop to settle himself again. 'I can have a poke around, but I'm not exactly qualified.'

'You're the most qualified person in thirty-four light years. It's important we know what happened to Sharpe and when, if we can.'

'I'd like to start a physical systems check, drive to nose,' Harris said. 'For peace of mind, if nothing else.'

'I agree,' Cait said, 'but after we get cleaned up. There's one thing that can't wait, however. I think we should check out the core. That's your job, Harris. And Nadira …' Nadira looked directly at her for the first time. 'I'd like you to help him. I know it's not exactly your line, but with Bren –'

'I'll try to cope,' Nadira said frostily.

Cait felt her tension levels rise in response. 'Okay,' she said, drawing the syllables out. She didn't want to deal with Nadira's attitude in front of the others, but it couldn't wait much longer. 'If there's nothing else, we all know what we're doing.'

They stood awkwardly, and Nadira and Harris made for the access ladder against the wall. Cait followed Lex, copying the rolling gait he'd adopted for the low-g in the ring.

'I don't know what I'm going to be able to tell from a post-mortem. It'll be pure guesswork at best,' he said as they bounded slowly past the resistance gym.

'Humour me. It's my job to keep you all busy.'

They entered the med lab, which wasn't much more than a collection of lockers and wall screens clustered around a broad ledge built into the wall that served as a bed. Bren lay there now, her body plastered with sensor patches.

Lex perched on a stool, took a small penlight from his pocket and pulled back one of her eyelids, shining the light into her eye.

'Is she going to be all right?' Cait asked.

Lex took a deep breath and smiled unconvincingly. 'I don't know. I'm not much more than a glorified GP, you know. I didn't think I'd have anything worse than a couple of broken limbs to treat on the whole trip.'

'I know. We've all been caught by surprise. I can't really believe Sharpe's dead.' She hooked a leg around a nearby stool and sat down. 'I've tried to imagine how he felt in those last moments, coming so far and then dying alone. I feel responsible.'

Lex grunted. 'Well, you're not.'

'I know that. But I'm also mission leader, which means I am responsible, just in a different way. My confidence has taken a beating in the last half-hour. All I see is questions and I haven't any answers.'

She looked down at Bren. The woman's chest was

rising and falling steadily.

Lex reached for the pull-down screen overhead, pointing at each scrolling graph line and naming them for Cait's benefit. 'Heart, respiration, core temperature, lymphatic system – all fine. It's this one, the neural readout that has me stumped. The electrochemical activity's very low.'

He prodded the screen and Bren's skull appeared in outline. Blood flow and tissue were clearly visible, tagged in a rainbow of colours.

'Even when you're asleep, the synapses are ticking over with a steady stream of neurotransmitters, but right now there's next to nothing. I've run an MRI – there are no lesions, no tumours. I've seen something like this in coma cases, but there's usually an obvious cause.' He pushed the screen away. 'It's as if her brain's on standby, not sending or receiving.'

Cait thought for a moment. 'Can you access her implant?'

'It's not that easy. It responds to her thoughts directly, keyed in to a specific firing pattern. There is an access link close to the surface behind her left ear, but I'm not sure I can kickstart the built-in fault-finder.'

'If you tried, would it harm her?'

'It shouldn't. These systems are triple redundant on fail-safes. They have to be. But then it shouldn't let her stay in a coma either. I'd rather wait and see if she comes out of it herself.'

Cait shook her head. 'We can't afford to do that. Bren was the only other person awake when I found Sharpe. She may know something about what happened.'

'It's not worth risking her life for, is it? Sharpe's dead. Whatever she may know can't help him now.'

'This isn't *for* Sharpe.' Cait tried to keep her voice level, but her frustration was starting to get the better of her. Was she the only one looking at the bigger picture here? 'There's five other people on board and *we're* still alive. As long as we don't have a cause for Sharpe's death, we're all in danger. Look, you said the risk is low. Hook her up. You can blame me later if anything goes wrong.'

'I hope I won't have to,' Lex said, stony-faced.

He palmed a drawer open in the bench and scrabbled around for the right equipment. He pulled out a small cube and bent over Bren, sweeping the hair back from behind her ear.

'I see a good sleep hasn't improved Nadira's mood.' He looked up when Cait didn't respond. 'I mean, I can understand how she feels, but –'

'You've got enough to do. Let me deal with her, okay?'

'That's just it.' He stood and rested a hand on her shoulder. 'You don't have to. You're not alone, Cait. There are others here willing to share the burden. Me, for one.'

She was sure he meant it, or thought he did. But his actions betrayed him – like trying to provoke Nadira at the briefing, and the run-ins he'd engineered in Sol System.

Of course, she'd seen Lex in a very different light then. He'd been self-assured naturally, but also attentive, supportive, willing to listen to her worries – let's face it, her fears – about the mission. Sharpe was a good 2IC and a solid friend, but Cait had never been physically attracted to him. Lex was intelligent, funny, different. He'd filled a need. Then the friction began between the team and he'd waded in with both feet. That's when she saw how childish and self-centred he could be, and things had cooled between them, at least from her side.

He squeezed the tense muscles of her neck. 'You need to relax. I can handle Nadira for you.'

She shrugged off his touch. 'When it comes to pouring oil on troubled waters you have a tendency to fuck things up.'

He stared at her for a second, the muscles along his jawline flexing. 'And what about you and me?'

'I don't know. Things are different out here.'

Lex flushed, but he didn't get the opportunity to respond. Harris's voice sounded from above. Cait looked to where her PAL nestled beside Lex's on the wall track. Harris's face, ruddy and slightly bloated from the freefall near the core, stared at her from the screen.

'Cait? We're at the computer core now. I think you'll want to have a look at what we've found.'

'On my way,' she said, grateful for an excuse to

leave Lex to his work.

She pushed off the floor and sailed towards the wall, grabbing a rung on the access ladder and pulling herself up towards the hub.

'Let me know if you find anything,' she called back.

Lex didn't reply, but she could feel his eyes on her as she climbed.

2

The negligible pull on Cait's body fell away as she reached the access tube into the forward part of the ship. Her PAL followed her ascent. Drifting free of the wall track on its tiny fans, it hovered above her, watching with its single cheery blue eye. She clung tight to the top of the ladder and the scene around her seemed to flip one-eighty degrees. Unlike her PAL, she hated freefall. It always took too long for her to adjust to the loss of 'up'.

She pulled herself over the lip of the access tube and glided towards the lazily revolving spider's web at the other end, reminding herself as she went that *she* was the one revolving. Grabbing a thick strand of web, she lost her own spin and the tube continued to turn around her. She pulled herself closer to the wall until she could swing her feet free of the tube. She was hanging dead centre in a small, disc-shaped chamber. Web strands offered hand and foot holds to six separate openings into different segments of the hull.

Cait started to climb towards what she continued to think of as 'down' by virtue of the fact that her feet were in that direction. She passed through the opening and into a large, shadowy chamber. A ladder extended beneath her. The shape of the outer hull was clearly visible below in the way the floor raked steeply towards the front of the ship.

Harris and Nadira were tethered to the core itself – a huge pylon hanging from the central spine of the hold and extending well forward, tapering off into darkness. Their PALs orbited around them like tiny satellites.

Running out of ladder, Cait took a line from the bottom rung, attached it to the hip ring on her one-piece, and kicked off towards them. Harris was braced against the access hatch and he caught her by the elbows, absorbing her forward momentum. She reached towards the hatch and pulled herself down to the computer interior.

The outer skin was only a few centimetres deep, encasing the clear perspex core, which was separately pressurised in case of hull breach. A maddening network of wires ran through the interior, linking at junctions in a seemingly random pattern. She couldn't have picked any damage in all that jumble even if she knew what to look for. Nadira watched her, perched on the outer casing, her face unreadable.

'So what am I seeing?' Cait asked Harris.

He grunted. 'There's no damage as far as I can tell. But I can't get anything sensible out of the thing – at least not through the on-site interface.' He indicated the scat board set into the hatch. 'If Bren were here ...'

'Just tell me what you've found.'

'Not much. None of the nodes are damaged, and all the connections seem to be up, but there's no contact between them. You know how the system works: the nodes are hardwired but the firing between them's modified by a gas algorithm program –'

'Mimicking the action of neurotransmitters in the brain,' Cait said. 'I feel like I've just had this conversation.'

Harris looked at her quizzically, but she didn't feel like elaborating.

'I thought that if the hardware was fine, the fault must be in the software, but I can't find anything there either,' he said. 'As far as I can tell, the whole system's inwardly directed. It might know we're here. It might know what's happening. But it's not doing anything about it.'

'Another marvel of Pax technology,' Nadira said. 'If I'd known there would be so many problems, I wouldn't have agreed to come.'

Cait ignored the remark, but she saw Harris beginning to bristle. 'If we tried to re-initialise, would that kickstart a response?' she asked, distracting him.

'It wouldn't leave us any worse off than we are now,' he said. 'A dead system's a dead system.'

'Wait till I get back to the ring. I want to monitor things from the command port.' She glanced at Nadira, still sitting hunkered on the core. One thing Cait didn't need was Harris distracted during the restart. 'Do you need Nadira to help?'

Harris hid a smile as he scratched at his beard. 'I think I'll be able to manage.'

Cait hauled on the line and floated off towards the ladder again. Nadira had no choice but to follow.

Cait waited until both of them were climbing before she spoke. 'We need to start observations on Horizon's system and make a comparison with our baseline data from Earth. Sharpe would have done it normally, so it falls to you as second stringer for that function.'

'Fine,' Nadira said without enthusiasm.

The clearance reduced sharply as they entered the accessway to the hub tube. Cait stopped when they were both inside and out of earshot. Nadira made to push past her, climb up the webbing and head into the tube, but Cait placed a restraining hand on her shoulder.

'Give me a minute. We have to talk.'

The woman floated back, keeping one hand on the webbing. Her eyes focused on Cait's boots.

Cait marshalled her thoughts. 'Look, I know you're not happy. And I know why.' Nadira's expression when she finally looked up indicated Cait didn't know anything of the sort, but she pressed on. 'Earth, the Pax and the Compact are light years away now. There's only us, and we need to depend on one another, because at any instant our lives can turn on what each individual does.'

'Spare me the pep talk. I don't need you to tell me how important I am.'

Cait felt her cheeks flush. 'We're all important. So long as we're all putting in. But you should know I won't allow anyone or anything to jeopardise the team or the mission. If you're not one hundred percent behind that, then we all have a problem and it's not one I'm going to ignore. That's my job, Nadira, and there's nothing I take more seriously.'

For an instant, Cait felt she saw something behind Nadira's aloofness. A hint of vulnerability perhaps, but it was gone as soon as it showed itself.

'I'll do my job,' Nadira said simply.

'Okay. I know.' Cait relaxed a notch. 'And I'm here to help. We can talk any time you want. About anything.'

'Can I go now?' Nadira's voice was as cold as before. Then she added in what Cait took to be a more conciliatory tone, 'I need to make a start on the observations.'

Cait nodded and stepped aside, watching as Nadira climbed the webbing and sailed through the accessway.

Cait waited a moment, then launched herself into the tube, reaching out as she moved along to acquire some spin. Nadira disappeared from sight, tumbling over the lip at the far end in one graceful move.

It had been obvious from the start that Nadira's last-minute inclusion on the mission was going to be problematic. The nukes that took out targets in the

Middle East and Asia, and prompted the Compact's formation, had been followed by fifty years of bitter and protracted Pax-led sanctions. Nadira's presence on board was meant to herald a new era of détente between the Compact and the Pax Americana. But while politicians made and broke alliances almost without thinking, the wounds history inflicted on individuals took longer to heal.

Cait swung herself over the lip of the tube, feeling her internal organs settle as she descended the ladder and stopped halfway. On the floor below it was easy to forget where you were, but from this vantage point the curvature of the drum was more obvious. The layout inside clustered the harnesses, med lab, gym, ship controls and so on against the fore and aft walls, leaving a broad walkway running around the midpoint. Lighting and colouring were muted and shadows minimal, giving an illusion of space, but it was still just the inside of a large can. An odd place to spend the best part of a century.

She took a breath, feeling oddly separated from the others below. She realised that up until now things had been easy, despite the bickering. Lex's attentions too had been part of a game they'd played on the out-system leg. But now it was very different. Out here they could be sure their bodies would never be found if disaster struck. There would be no one to mourn them, no marker to show how far out they'd come. Sure, this had been the case when they were mere light days from Earth. But it *felt* more true out here, in the space between the stars. The hard, uncaring void, as Sharpe would say before pulling some stupid terror-stricken face and doubling up with laughter. Cait just wasn't sure how far she should go in adapting herself to that difference. She couldn't quieten the nagging feeling that she was pushing too hard just to keep up the illusion of moving towards a solution – forcing Lex to wake Bren early, ordering the reboot without a more considered study of the situation. Her head hurt, and she wanted to sleep. How could that be when she'd only just woken after forty-five years?

People reacted differently to emergency situations – herself included. Under the circumstances, perhaps Nadira's continued aloofness was understandable. Cait wondered what reaction was the right one for *her*?

She felt dizzy again and clung to the ladder, closing her eyes and breathing deeply. The drum servos hummed through the wall, maintaining the spin. Inside there was light, air, everything was quiet. It was hard to believe they were in the midst of an emergency, hard to keep focusing on that. But the emergency was real. And that was why she had to keep going.

Holding onto that thought, she finished her descent and made her way back to Lex. He looked up from his monitor as she came close and shook his head.

'No change. The implant's hooked up but I haven't

been able to influence it. I don't even know if it's functioning.'

'Keep a close eye on her,' Cait said. 'We're going to reboot the main computer.'

'What difference will that make?'

Cait frowned. 'I don't know. Just watch her, okay?'

She glided over to the command port again. Her PAL was settled above the port, already linked to Harris's.

'I'm in position, Harris. Ready when you are.'

'It'll just take a moment,' Harris said over the link.

Cait began setting up her screen to monitor the key systems simultaneously.

'You have to stop her! Don't let her do it!'

Cait turned at the noise. Bren was trying to get up; Lex was struggling against her.

Bren stared at Cait, eyes wild, as she forced Lex's hands away.

'Don't reboot Phillips, Cait! You'll kill us all!'

Cait turned back to the port. 'Halt the reboot, Harris. Do not proceed. I repeat, do *not* proceed. I need you back in the ring. Now!'

3

The mission's systems specialist perched like some flightless bird on a med-lab stool, a foil blanket draped across her shoulders. Lex fussed around Bren, removing sensor patches and checking readings, and Harris leaned against the bulkhead in half-shadow, watching the proceedings with a grim look on his face. Nadira was off somewhere, preferring to 'get on with some real work'.

The *Magellan* fell steadily towards Iota Persei and its retinue of planets. Its hull was coated in a thick mantle of water-ice. Cait knew the interplanetary 'vacuum' was anything but empty. At 0.6 light speed, even a tiny fragment of rock crossing their path could cause major damage. So far, statistical probability had been on their side. But serious collision was only one of a million things that could kill them without warning. She'd been appalled at first and then finally bored by the seemingly endless catalogue of hazards laid out in the mission pack. Looking at Bren now though, she couldn't shake the feeling the list may not have been as exhaustive as she'd thought.

'I think you're going to be all right,' Lex said, offering Bren a bulb of coffee. 'Your scans are back to normal, but I'll want to run some more tests just to make sure.'

He moved the bulb closer when she didn't respond, and she finally took it from him. Bren didn't look so okay to Cait. She seemed distracted, worried.

'Can you remember what happened?' Cait asked her. The question was a simple one, but so much rested on the answer.

Bren's eyes darted around the ring as if cataloguing their world would make it somehow more real for her. 'I had a bad dream ... I think. Sharpe was dead.'

'I found him that way, yes,' Cait said. 'You were out of the harness. You collapsed.'

'I don't remember anything. Just images, thoughts. Until I went online.'

Harris grunted from the shadows. Cait knew what he thought about transhumans, and Bren in particular.

'When was that exactly?' Cait asked.

Bren blinked rapidly and looked directly at Cait for the first time. 'What?'

'Cait, she's tired,' Lex said. 'She needs some rest.'

'I'm just trying to get the run of events straight in my head. When did the link start functioning?'

'I'm not sure,' Bren said, hesitantly. 'After I dreamed about Sharpe, I guess. The first real memory I have is being in the ring with Phillips. I knew that wasn't a dream. The texture was too vivid. I tried to talk to him but he wasn't answering. He was floating in the hub. Kind of staring at his hands, rubbing them together over and over, like he was washing them.'

Her words drifted off and she was silent for a few seconds.

'Usually he's juggling the subsystems,' she said, more animated now. 'But the icons were just floating around his head. So I grabbed for comms and dived in. I thought I could get him to respond through the dedicated line. But when I got inside, his mailbox was gone.' Her sudden smile looked out of place. 'I guess you'd have to see the environment to understand it. I call it the sorting office. I templated it from an old picture I used to have. It usually works pretty well, but where his box should have been there was nothing – a blank wall. Then I saw the parcel sitting on the floor, right in front of where his box should have been. It was large, wrapped in brown paper, with thick string around it, sealed with blobs of that red, shiny wax they used to use. It had Phillips's name on the top.' She shook her head. 'I don't know why really, but I didn't like the look of it. Maybe I was feeling jumpy from the dreams.'

Cait could see that Bren was totally immersed in the memory now, seeing the virtual environment as she spoke. Her hands reached out and downwards.

'I went to pick it up. Then something made me

bend down instead and listen. It was ticking,' she said, almost laughing at the absurdity. 'Just like in the old flat-vids. I touched it very lightly, and it felt like cold death, like we didn't want any part of it. I knew I had to tell someone. I had to wake up.' She focused on the others again, hands still outstretched. 'And then I was here, in med lab.'

'You said rebooting Phillips would kill us all,' Cait told her.

The corners of Bren's mouth turned down. 'If Phillips went online, his postbox would open and the parcel would go through. Whatever it was, I didn't want it getting into our system.'

'It wouldn't get through the protocols, no matter how damaged Phillips was on reboot,' Harris said.

'I didn't want to take that chance. You don't know what it felt like, Harris.'

'Yeah, right,' he said, folding his arms.

'What do you know about Phillips's condition?' Cait asked.

'What?' Bren pulled the blanket tighter around her and shifted on her stool.

'Why wasn't he reacting?'

'I don't know,' Bren said, hesitating. Her eyes focused on Cait then darted away again. 'I was too distracted by the package to register much else.'

'You didn't get anything from him over your link?' Cait asked.

'No,' Bren said emphatically. 'I was worried about the parcel, okay? I didn't want to waste any time.'

'Okay,' Cait said. 'It pays to be circumspect. Can you go back in and isolate it before we reboot?'

'I think so. I –'

Lex broke in. 'I can't tell what interfacing again's going to do to her. She might end up in another coma.'

'I'll be fine,' Bren said, shrugging off the foil blanket. 'I'm sure that package is dangerous.'

'You can monitor Bren while she's linked, can't you?' Cait asked Lex.

'Yeah, but I can't reach in and snap her out of it if she starts going under. It's –'

'Lex,' Cait said and nodded towards Bren, who was sitting very still with her eyes closed. Her head jerked to the side and Lex reached out to catch her.

'I've got it,' she said, coming round. 'It's in my vault.' She looked at Lex, still crouched ready to support her. 'Back off, will you? There's nothing wrong with me. Or the link.'

Lex took a step back as Bren slid from the stool and pushed past him and Nadira and out of med lab.

'Bloody hell.' Harris rolled his eyes. 'I'm off to reboot Phillips, if that's okay with everyone. Call me when she's making sense.'

Cait followed after Bren, past Nadira's harness and into one of the two shower stalls in the ring. The door was locked and she hesitated to disturb her, but she couldn't let this wait.

'When can you tell me what's inside?' she asked.

'I'm in the vault now,' Bren called over the running water. 'It's totally partitioned. There's no way anything can get out. The package is open. There's just one box inside. I'm going to try and access it. Uh –'

'What is it?' Cait asked, expecting the walls to crumble around her.

'No encryption. Whoever sent it wasn't expecting it to be intercepted. Standard codes, file protocols. It's Pax Space Admin, or a very good copy. Seems to be course data and – shit!'

'What's wrong? Bren, are you okay?' Cait pulled at the door handle.

The water stopped running and Bren opened the stall door and stepped out, ashen-faced.

Before she could speak, Harris's voice called over Cait's PAL. 'Computer's on restart. All readings nominal.'

There was a shimmering on the deck in front of them and a holo-image began to scan in layer by layer, building shoes, legs, a torso, until an older man stood before them dressed in smart Space Admin fatigues. His skin had a healthy tan that contrasted with the shock of white hair swept back from high temples. His eyes were deep-set and gleamed with cold fire as he registered their presence.

His left hand stretched palm upwards towards Bren, still standing naked in a puddle of water. 'You have something that belongs to me, Thurgood. For everyone's sake, I suggest you give it up.'

Logically, Cait knew Phillips couldn't and wouldn't harm them, but something about him made her uneasy all the same. She moved to stand in front of Bren.

'Harris!' she called to her PAL. 'What are you reading?'

'Nothing unusual here. It's a clean restart.'

Bren was unfazed. 'Relax, Phillips. What I've got, you don't want. Believe me.'

Phillips turned his attention to Cait. 'Mission Leader Dyson, Systems Specialist Thurgood is withholding a communication from launch control. This message may hold mission-critical data. I must be allowed to access it immediately or I cannot guarantee the safety of this ship and crew.'

'This is *about* the safety of the ship and crew,' Bren told Cait. 'Believe me, we can't release these files. Not yet anyway.'

Cait was torn. Phillips was adamant but weird, and she needed to understand why the package had worried Bren so.

'Phillips,' she said as calmly as she could manage, 'the communication will be withheld until we can be sure it's safe. On my authority.'

'As you wish,' Phillips said, nodding curtly. 'But in so doing you may be compounding the danger to this vessel.'

'That's my responsibility. I'm more concerned right now about what made you shut down.'

Phillips's image seemed to stutter, slowing and freezing in mid-motion, then stabilised as he cocked his head to one side. His teeth bared in a predatory grin. 'Why nothing ... and something.'

Cait shivered despite herself. It was Phillips, no question, but somehow not Phillips. Something had changed.

'I don't like this,' she said. 'Harris, suspend integrated control.'

The image of Phillips froze again then vanished.

Cait crossed to her command port, Bren following behind. She pulled herself into the chair and activated the scat board. Her fingers flew across the pads.

'Let's get to the bottom of this,' she muttered and hit the send key.

<access log>

The cursor flashed a line and a new set of characters appeared, confirming her query.

<log>

<query integrated control>

<integrated control> the cursor complied, the commands progressively tunnelling through the system linkages to the main core diagnostics now back online.

<query shutdown> Cait typed, and pressed send.

<nil shutdown> the cursor stated.

'Bullshit there wasn't,' Cait hissed, biting her lip for

a second before typing again.

&lt;query internal clock&gt;

&lt;internal clock&gt; the cursor replied.

&lt;query gap&gt;

The cursor blinked at her for a few seconds as if pondering how to break the news. It finally settled on a direct response.

&lt;nil gap&gt;

Cait slapped the keyboard in disgust. 'This is getting us nowhere.' She looked up at her PAL. 'Address intra-ship. Attention, everyone: take some time out to get cleaned up. The computer's going to take longer to fix than we thought. We'll meet in the mess in one hour. End.

'And now,' Cait said to Bren, 'why don't you get dressed and then you can tell me exactly what you've found.'

4

Cait waited for Lex to cross back to his harness from the showers. Bren was with Harris at the core, and Nadira was still off somewhere, so Cait had a little time to herself. Her own shower had done nothing to relax her, and her neck felt stiff.

What Bren had told her about the package presented a whole raft of new worries. But right now it was Bren that was causing her the most anxiety. There had been a lot of hidden bigotry towards the woman before lift-off, from the top ranks of Space Admin down, and Cait had pushed hard to get her on the mission. Not just because she was a remarkable talent in the field of systems interfacing, but because Cait knew firsthand how hard it was to escape the post-deluge Florida Ghettos.

Cait was seven when her father had won the employment lottery and they'd moved to the space-tech conurb in Sub-California, old enough to remember the squalor and hopelessness of the place. It had created a bond between the two women; Cait had felt they really trusted one another. Now she wasn't so sure.

She'd put Bren's behaviour in med lab down to the effects of prolonged deepsleep, but the systems specialist had shown no signs of residual disorientation once she'd gone online to recover the package. She'd been lucid and precise in explaining to Cait what she'd found inside. But when Cait brought up Sharpe's death, Bren's responses had become vague and hesitant again. To Cait it felt as if she was trying hard *not* to remember something.

Lex was still towelling himself dry as he loped towards the harness. He tossed the towel at the webbing and shook his head, droplets of water cascading lazily away in the low-g.

'What's up?' he said.

Cait folded her arms and leaned against the ring wall, looking away as he grabbed at the harness straps to steady himself and bent to open his floor locker.

'I've been thinking about Bren's link. Did you notice when it came online?'

He shrugged, standing as he pulled on the one-piece and pressed the adhesion surfaces together. 'I didn't see any kind of change at all.'

'What about when you hooked up to her fault-finder?'

'There was no change,' he said, eyes narrowing. 'What are you getting at?'

'Well, if you didn't observe a change in her

responses, we can't be sure the link wasn't functioning before Bren woke up in med lab.'

'Apart from the fact she said it wasn't.'

Lex leaned against the harness and sized Cait up. 'Has Harris been planting ideas in your head? You know what he's like about enhanced humans.'

'I haven't spoken to anyone else about Bren.'

'So what's your motivation for doubting her word? I thought Bren was your friend, or does "things being different" extend to her too?'

Cait straightened. 'Why are you insisting on making this personal? We had some fun together; it was nice. Now it's over. But I'm still your commanding officer, and our situation is serious. As medical officer you oversaw Bren's treatment in med lab. You were monitoring her EEG. You said she was in a coma. How do you explain her suddenly waking if there wasn't any change in the readings?'

'I suggest you ask Bren about that – she's the expert.'

'I'm asking you.'

'I don't know what's gotten into you, Cait.' He picked up the wet towel and balled it in his fists. 'I'm telling you what I saw. If you think something's going on, *you* work it out.'

Cait pursed her lips for an instant. 'Okay. I will.' She pushed off the wall. 'I'll see you at the meeting.'

She sailed over to the central walkway, twisting in

mid-air to rebound and put some distance between her and Lex. She hadn't thought he'd be the type to act like a jilted lover. Childish and self-centred – there it was again. She should never have become involved. And she certainly didn't have the mental space to deal with any fallout now. If he was moping over her, he'd have to work that one out on his own.

'We're going to have to go over the whole bloody thing component by component,' Harris was telling Lex when Cait walked into the mess section thirty minutes later. The space looked almost homely; this was the one part of the ship where utility gave way to comfort. The walls were painted in warm earth tones instead of the 'restful' mushroom of the rest of the ring, and the seating was well-padded couches arranged around low wooden tables.

Everyone had taken the opportunity to shower and fix something to eat. The smell of food made Cait realise how hungry she was. She pulled a bulb of broth from the wall store and flopped into a chair, watching as Bren climbed down from the access tube to join them.

'If only your Pax engineers had run proper checks while we were still Earthside,' Nadira said, reaching for more coffee.

'There was nothing wrong with the ground checks,' Harris said, his voice tight. 'And I'm still not convinced it's a malfunction.'

'What then?' Nadira asked. 'Divine intervention?'

'No,' Harris snapped. 'But it's not a closed system. Bren was affected by the shutdown. Perhaps –'

'What do you mean I was affected?' Bren halted on her way to the servery.

'Well, you don't jolt out of deepsleep for no reason,' Harris said. 'I assumed you sensed the malfunction.'

'Well, don't assume. I had no link. The implant was off. You think I've got nothing better to do than twiddle my virtual thumbs for forty-odd years?'

'So what – you sleepwalked your way out the harness?' Harris looked at Cait and smirked. 'Must have been one hell of a dream.'

'Look, Harris, I don't know what the fuck happened. And neither do you. So keep your suppositions to yourself.'

Cait frowned. 'But you did link with the system before you woke up in med lab.'

'I've got no recollection of that either,' Bren said.

'You said you dreamed Sharpe was dead.'

'So? That doesn't mean I was linked. I could have heard you talking about Sharpe when I was out cold. My subconscious could have woven it into my dreams. And it was Lex who hooked up my implant to the diagnostics.'

Cait glanced at Lex. She could tell he was thinking the same thing. 'And that initiated the link?' she asked, feeling a cold lump form inside.

Bren turned back to the servery and pulled out a tray. 'Well, I didn't do it.'

It took an effort of will not to look in Lex's direction again. So there it is, Cait thought. She's covering something up. Unless Lex was totally incompetent, or asleep on the job, activating the link would have shown up on his scans. So Bren's link must have been running before she arrived at med lab – which could explain why she and the computer were suffering similar symptoms. But why lie about something like that? It was easy to jump to conclusions, especially with a dead body on board. No, Cait thought, that's being ridiculously melodramatic. But if whatever Bren was hiding didn't concern Sharpe, what on earth was it?

Cait desperately wanted to confront Bren, but couldn't do it here with everyone watching, and it might not be the best approach even in private. Bren was already prickly because of Harris. Perhaps she'd gain more by tackling the situation obliquely, putting Bren at her ease and observing her reactions. It was worth a try anyway.

She tore the seal on her broth and took a sip. 'In any event, we have some things to discuss,' she said. 'Let's start with the message you intercepted.'

'Okay,' Bren said, still annoyed. 'You're not going to like this. The message I found was from Pax Space Admin. All the coding checks out. It was set to load through Phillips and change the ship's course before wake-up.'

'Shit!' Lex said around a mouthful of pasta. 'Why?'

Bren shrugged. 'Who knows. They didn't give a reason. But the drive would be running hot now if Phillips hadn't been offline. And there was something else in the message. A nasty little protocol to keep a direct channel open to the navigation and drive sections.'

Harris's brow furrowed. 'For what purpose, for God's sake?'

'Beats me,' Bren said. 'But if the channel was detected and closed, the protocol had a wyrm back-up. Basically it was set to cause an instability in the drive that would build until it went critical.'

'Totally destroying us,' Cait finished. 'Bren's isolated comms so there'll be no more surprises, I hope. But this new course would have brought us in-system direct to Horizon. We'd miss the close fly-bys of the outer planets and a lot of valuable telemetry as a result. As things stand, we can't change course even if we wanted to. But we're still far enough out that we can make the correction later. I guess I wanted to get your initial reactions.'

'Bren couldn't have made a mistake?' Harris asked.

'No, she couldn't,' Bren snapped.

'And you've scanned the files too?' he asked Cait, unperturbed.

'Yes,' Cait said, feeling irritated on Bren's behalf. 'They're exactly as Bren described.'

'What's your point, Harris?' Bren said.

'Nothing.' He pushed his tray away. 'I just wanted to check if you could be positive you knew who sent it. I mean the codes might have checked out but they're fifty-five years old. It's possible they could have been broken, or stolen.'

'I guess,' Bren said, somewhat mollified. 'If you put it like that, I have no way of telling if the wyrm protocol was part of the original message either. It could have been piggybacked on.'

Lex tossed his fork onto his tray. 'Oh, great. Suddenly I'm not hungry. I don't know who I'd rather be killed by – a complete bloody stranger or a supposed colleague.'

'The only way to clear this up is to contact Space Admin,' Harris said. 'Ask them to confirm the broadcast.'

'That's going to take too long. And why bother anyway?' Lex said. 'I didn't travel all this way to put up with this sort of bullshit. I say we ignore the whole bloody broadcast. Earth's too far away to bother about now.'

'If it wasn't for the generosity of the Pax,' Harris said, his voice rising, 'you wouldn't even be on this mission.'

'There is,' Cait said quickly, 'another reason not to query the broadcast. Going on how far out we are, the message was only sent five months ago. If someone in Space Admin did send the wyrm, they're likely to still be there. Querying it will tip them off that we found it. We're supposed to be asleep, remember?'

'Is this how you intend to run the mission from here on?' Nadira asked. Her voice was quiet, but it cut through the conversation like a stone through water.

'Go on,' Cait said, trying to ignore the obvious challenge in Nadira's words.

'As far as I can see, there may be a perfectly valid reason for the course change. Some unforeseen danger in our flight path, or something else we can't even guess at. You say the message appears to be legitimate. And from what I've heard, no proof has been advanced that would bring that legitimacy into doubt. Yet here you all are debating whether or not you should obey it. In the Compact, we know our duty is to follow orders.'

Three pairs of eyes shuttled back towards Cait. She could almost hear them wondering how she was going to handle Nadira.

She sipped her broth, letting the silence stretch. Finally, she placed the bulb down in front of her. 'I guess I wouldn't have put your point quite in those terms. But, like you, I'm concerned that we don't fail to follow a lawful directive. The fact that there wasn't an explanatory file attached is cause for concern. That's SOP.'

'Even with all of us in deepsleep?' Nadira asked.

Cait nodded. 'Even then. And there's the presence of the wyrm too. One interpretation is that while the codes may be correct, the action itself wasn't authorised by the launch director. Where legitimate doubt exists – and I think you'll agree that's the case here – my primary duty is the safety of this ship and its crew. We need to proceed with caution.'

'Look,' Lex said, leaning forward and breaking the tense atmosphere, 'I don't want to upset anyone, but I think it's safe to say we've all got a massive personal investment in this mission. Some of us have left loved ones behind, and we know they'll most likely be dead by the time we make a round trip. This isn't a question of loyalty or duty or anything like that. The fact is, altering any aspect of this mission without the consent of the crew is quite simply an outrage.'

'I can always count on you to give us one more thing to think about,' Cait said. 'We'll talk about this again when a course change is feasible. In the meantime, we scan as far ahead as possible and make sure we're not about to collide with something big.'

She looked around the group. No one seemed to want to add anything. Bren, slumped in the armchair beside her, looked bored by the exchange. Perhaps if they moved on to something a little closer to home ...

'Okay, next is the computer. Found anything in the log, Harris?'

'Only more questions,' he said. 'The main log's useless, but I did some digging in the subsystems. One registered a controlled core shutdown two hours and forty-three minutes before you woke up. But don't ask me who or what initiated it.'

'What about a time of death for Sharpe?' Lex asked.

Harris shook his head. 'There's no record of that anywhere, even on his harness system. I'd say that information's been erased.'

'Is that possible?' Cait asked.

'Well, it shouldn't happen of its own accord,' Harris said. 'But anyone who knows what they're about could do it. Particularly if they had remote access.' He glanced at Bren.

She slammed down her drink bulb. 'Get fucked, Harris. For the last time, I'm not responsible for the computer, for Sharpe, or the message from Earth for that matter. Why don't you try using your brain to solve some problems instead of looking for scapegoats?'

'Okay,' Cait said, rising and placing a hand on Bren's shoulder. 'Harris, if you have some proof of wrongdoing, lay it out.'

Harris glared from Cait to Bren and back again, then his gaze fell to his food. 'I've got no proof,' he said quietly.

'We all have things to do,' she said. 'Harris, you're on hardware faults. Bren, once Lex has checked you out I want you on software. Nadira, you're on systems watch after me so get some rest. Let's start acting like a team.'

•

Lex grabbed a couple of sensor patches from a nearby drawer and turned to Bren, who was sitting on the med-lab bench. He held them up but didn't come any closer.

'You're not going to bite *my* head off, are you?' he asked.

'Not unless you think I'm some Frankenstein freak too.'

He smiled. 'Where I come from we're not phobic about transhumans. But then there weren't many in the EU when I left.'

'Chipheads, they call us.' Bren said. 'And that's when they're being polite.'

Lex pressed the patches to her temples and flicked the monitor into life. He picked up a metallic wand. 'You shouldn't feel any discomfort. I'm just going to send a range of harmonics through the soft tissue and see what the sensors pick up.' He touched her chin and turned her head to the left. The wand hummed in his hand. 'What's it like anyway, the link?'

Bren snorted and Lex saw a smile spread across her face.

'You don't know how many times I've been asked that.'

'Then you should have a good answer.'

She turned towards him and he gently moved her head back into position. 'A lot of people can't get used to it. There's the increased cognitive capacity, of course. You're totally aware – of everything. When you're linked, you can instantly understand concepts, complex equations, programming, the works. You access information, formulate solutions, in the blink of an eye. But the perception change can really get to you. Some things you encounter are actual representations, like when I saw Phillips in the ring. Some things you can template and construct yourself. But every now and then something will come at you that's totally figurative. Like the interface has tapped into your subconscious imagery and selected something that embodies completely what you're experiencing intellectually, emotionally, and even spiritually. It can freak you out if you're not used to it.'

'Like that package ticking?'

'Yeah, but that's a simple example.'

'Look to the right, please,' Lex said and swapped the wand to his other hand.

'Anyway, it's helped me become more than I ever could be,' Bren continued. 'But Harris and people like him will never understand. And they'll never trust what they don't understand.'

'Okay, we're done here,' Lex said, peeling off the patches. 'I can't find a thing wrong with you now.'

'You say that like it's a bad thing.'

'Sorry. I'm just worried I might be missing something.' He placed the patches in the bench drawer and closed it slowly. 'And a little upset about what you found in the subsystem.'

'You mean the wyrm?'

'Yeah, the wyrm. But the other stuff too. I meant what I said, Bren. I've come too far and invested too much to drop everything because someone on Earth wants things done differently. I noticed you weren't saying much back there.'

'That's because I don't have an opinion.'

'Rubbish. Everyone's got an opinion. Come on, this is important. If this mission's to have any meaning at all, no one, not even Cait, has the right to change it unless we all agree.'

'That's not what we signed on for.'

Lex saw she was getting ready to leave, so he leaned close, blocking her.

'Cait's been asking about you, you know. About your link,' he said quietly, watching for a reaction.

'Asking what?'

'Whether it might have been functioning before we brought you to med lab.'

Bren made to say something but he held up his hand. 'Don't. I don't need an explanation. Unlike Harris and Cait, I trust you. But things are changing. And I'm pessimistic enough to know they usually change for the worse unless people are very clear in pushing for what they want. You may not have an opinion now, but sooner or later you're going to have to decide which way to jump.'

5

The laser cut deep, parting skin and muscle. Cait hadn't anticipated the smell of burning flesh. The incision ran from Sharpe's left shoulder to join another that ran from the right, above his sternum. Lex's hand moved deftly, guiding the beam down from the breastbone to the pubis. Cait wanted to plug her ears to the sound as Lex peeled back the skin and muscle.

'Is this really necessary?' she said. She felt sick to her stomach to see Sharpe cut up like meat.

Lex regarded her unsympathetically through the clearplas mask he wore. 'You wanted an autopsy. There's no substitute for direct physical examination. I'm hoping it'll tell me something different from the scans.' His tone was all business with none of his usual warmth.

They'd hardly traded two sentences since yesterday's meeting. At least it wasn't affecting his work, but Cait hoped he'd be back to normal soon. Opinionated as he was in full flow, she valued his ability to look at things from a fresh perspective.

He moved the beam to cut through the ribs on either side, and lifted the ribcage off. Cait tasted bile and looked away, swallowing hard. Lex's PAL hung directly above the body, suspended from a bracket attached to the side wall and recording the procedure.

'There's no blood in the pericardial sac. That bears out the scans. The aorta's intact.' He slid both hands partway into the body cavity. 'I don't feel any tumour encasing the lungs.'

'What did the scans say?' Cait managed.

'That there's no reason he shouldn't just get up and walk around. All I've found so far are by-products of increased levels of adrenaline. But there has to be something else. Hearts as healthy as Sharpe's don't just stop.' He shifted position, withdrawing his hands slightly.

'By the look of him,' Cait said, moving closer and glancing at Sharpe's clenched teeth, lips pulled back over gums, 'he was awake when it happened.'

'That's the only other thing I'm sure of: he was out of deepsleep when he died. His metabolic rate was close to normal, but whether or not he was conscious ...' Lex shrugged.

'So the computer initiated a wake-up?'

'Or the localised harness system, reacting to something. If he was suffering a heart attack, say, the harness would attempt to revive him fully, bring his heart rate back to normal. But that kind of activity would be logged on the subsystem.'

'He looks terrified,' Cait said, folding her arms around herself. She'd seen Sharpe laugh so hard he cried. He'd loved to laugh. But this would be the memory of him that stuck.

'He could have been scared,' Lex said, 'or in pain. Your guess is as good as mine at this point. I've taken the whole harness apart, but I can't find anything wrong with it, or the deepsleep system.'

Cait passed a hand across her forehead, feeling the beginnings of another headache. 'This is getting ridiculous. Look, we need to verify a cause of death if only to prove the harnesses are safe. We don't have the reserves to make it all the way without using them again.'

'I'm doing everything I can think of.' He sounded tired and more than a little irritated.

'I know. I'm sorry. How long till you finish up here?'

'A couple of hours. There's nothing obvious. I'm going to have to dissect the heart, maybe even attempt a cardiac conduction systems dissection – check the heart's electrical pathways,' he added when Cait looked blank. 'I'll seal him back up when I'm done. And then we're going to have to do something with the body.'

'Let me know if you come up with a good, hard fact I can use.'

She turned awkwardly, feeling as if she was carrying a sack across her shoulders, and left Lex to his carving. She'd taken his advice to crib the spin on the ring up to one-fifth-g to start rebuilding their muscles and stamina. The increased physical effort made the problems she faced seem even more insurmountable. Her mother had always chided her about taking on too much, but she couldn't help feeling responsible – for the crew, the mission, Sharpe, everything. They were hurtling through space at 0.6 c, closing on an unavoidable deadline to dump velocity or overshoot their destination, and both the computer that controlled the drive and the harnesses that protected them from picopulse deceleration had large question marks against them with no obvious answers.

She hadn't underestimated what it meant to be mission leader, but living it was very different from anticipating it. She'd always been prone to self-doubt. It was something she'd realised early on and worked hard to defeat. You couldn't hold a command if you didn't believe in yourself. You had to trust your instincts. But you also had to realise your own limitations. It was a difficult balancing act, and in times of stress her old fears resurfaced.

The seventy-two hours since wake-up had been crammed with a jumbled series of emergencies and frustrations. The temptation to second-guess herself was almost irresistible, but she couldn't afford the luxury. It was stressful enough without a nagging inner censor reassessing her every choice.

What she really needed was someone to confide in. As her offsider, Sharpe would have provided that sounding board. Likely replacements were thin on the ground.

She walked into the control area and stopped. The lighting here was subdued, but she could make out Nadira sitting in front of the sensor bank, a lone figure outlined by the spill from the readouts. She seemed totally absorbed in her work. Cait considered leaving her to it, but she knew she had to start building bridges. Her own feelings of isolation showed how quickly things had deteriorated for her over the past few days. Nadira's situation must be even worse.

She walked up to stand by the Compact scientist's shoulder and read the telemetry coming in from the long-range sensors. A grid overlay of Iota Persei dominated the main viewer. Even corrected for red shift, the image of the type G star glowed warmly, reminding her of their own sun so far away.

'It's beautiful,' she said.

Nadira turned and almost smiled. Her eyes were alive with the same sense of magic and the unknown that Cait felt.

'It's mother sun for us,' she said, mirroring Cait's thoughts. 'At least for the next few years. A precious commodity in all this darkness.'

'How are the readings coming?'

Nadira turned back to the console and manipulated

the displays, shrinking the image to take in more of the surrounding star field. 'I've just finished corroborating the baseline data. I'm showing position consistent with linear motion and radial velocity from the ISS scopes.'

Lines appeared between Iota Persei and a number of the larger stars in view. Two sets of identical figures sat beside each of the stars, showing ISS plots and Nadira's own observations.

'And we have a positive on the photometry. Look.' She magnified the target sun again, and pointed to a small fingernail of black on the edge of the corona. 'We've just missed a partial occultation by one of the outer planets. From the apparent size and position, I'd say it was Iota Persei F, just over two Jupiter masses.'

'It's nice to know something's going right.' Cait sat on the stool next to the station. 'Look, about our meeting yesterday,' she began.

Nadira blanked the display and clasped her hands in front of her – withdrawing into herself again, Cait thought.

'I just want to say, I didn't take any offence at what you said. You were motivated by a genuine concern for the mission. And I want to thank you for that.'

Nadira regarded her with a calculating look. She seemed about to say something, but instead she turned back to the console and punched up the display again. 'We should be in position to begin direct spectroscopy of Horizon in a couple of days.'

Cait stood, pushing back the feeling that she'd failed again. She wasn't going to win any of them over that easily. She just hoped she had the reserves of patience to get through.

'That'll be your next job,' she said. 'There's not much else for you to do right now.'

Nadira smirked. 'You mean Harris doesn't want my help any more.'

'In a way,' Cait said, choosing her words carefully. 'But I wouldn't take it personally. He's not being particularly sociable to anyone at the moment. In any case, what you're doing here is important for our main mission – which we'll all hopefully be able to concentrate on soon.'

Nadira began calibrating the sensor inputs. Apparently the conversation was at an end.

'Okay,' Cait said. 'See you later.'

Her feet started moving without any conscious decision about where to go. She rounded the control banks and found she was heading for the gym. She still had an hour before it was her watch. Perhaps a workout would help.

Bren was already there, sitting in a rowing machine, pumping with her legs and pulling with her arms. Cait wasn't sure she was ready to talk to Bren yet. She certainly wasn't up to some kind of verbal chess game where she waited for Bren to make a mistake and reveal her deep, dark secrets. It wasn't her style.

She took a position at the pull-down bar and dialled her usual setting. But it was too stiff in her depleted state and she had to crank it down by half before it grudgingly moved for her.

The two women exercised together for a few minutes, until Cait broke the silence. 'I was hoping you'd come for a talk.'

Bren glanced up but kept rowing. 'You know how it is. We've all been so busy there hasn't been much time for chitchat.'

Cait pulled the bar down and held it at full extension. 'That's not what I meant. There's something you haven't told me. Something I didn't want to press you about in front of the others.'

'You're going to have to enlighten me,' Bren said, rowing harder.

Cait let go of the bar and it snapped to the top of the frame. She knelt down and grabbed the younger woman's arm, forcing her to stop. 'Come on. Your link was working before you came to med lab. Maybe even before you collapsed in the ring.'

She broke off, caught by a sudden vision. She'd been looking down at Sharpe's body. There'd been a shout. She'd looked up and seen Bren. What had she called out?

'Shit! You shouted his name. You knew something was wrong with him. I've got a dead body on my hands, and from the look of him he was terrified before he died. If you know anything, you owe it to all of us to tell me about it.'

Bren pulled her arm away but kept silent.

'The more you stay quiet, the more I'm inclined to believe Harris.'

That got a reaction at least. Bren glared at her.

'I mean it, Bren. We've got a controlled computer shutdown and a deliberate log erasure. No one was in any state to use the access port before me. How do you think that looks? Your interface makes you the prime suspect.'

'I didn't do anything,' Bren snapped. 'I saved the fucking ship from that wyrm. Why would I want to jeopardise the mission?'

'You tell me,' Cait said.

Both their voices were raised, carrying possibly as far as med lab.

'Look,' Cait began again, quietly, 'maybe it was the interface, functioning outside your control. When Lex checked you out, your brain scan mirrored the computer's output signal. It's possible there was some kind of negative feedback, something affecting the computer that affected you too. Something you might not be aware of.'

'Lex said he couldn't find anything wrong with the implant.'

'But he's no expert.'

'And neither are you. You're just going to have to

take my word for it. Sharpe's dead, and I'm sorry about that. But I'm not responsible.'

'There's more though. Isn't there?' Cait pressed. 'More you're not telling me.'

Bren leant forward and unclipped her feet from the rowing machine. She stood and walked past Cait to the 'mouse wheel' dogged onto the ring wall: two circles of tubular steel held together by crosspiece rungs. She pulled it from its mooring and positioned it facing along the central walkway.

'I've said all I'm going to say,' she told Cait. 'Just leave me alone.'

She stepped inside the wheel and reached up to a spar an arm's length above her head, simultaneously lifting her legs off the deck and pulling down. The wheel began to move forward, and she stepped on a descending rung and pushed. She took another step and the wheel sped uphill/downhill around the central walkway.

Cait watched her move off, wondering what more she could do.

Lex had sewn Sharpe's chest back together after the post-mortem, filed an inconclusive report, and now drifted in the hold with Harris as they guided the body into the small airlock. Cait, Nadira and Bren, tethered separately some way off, watched. Sharpe's remains were, thankfully, Cait thought, wrapped in a foil blanket and unrecognisable.

The tension between them all was unbearable. They were like floating islands, remote and unconnected. That was how Cait felt anyway. Sharpe, her command confidant, was well and truly beyond her reach now. Bren had been a friend once, and Lex a lover. Harris was hard to get close to at the best of times, and Nadira ... she'd always been apart from the rest, but how much that was down to choice or circumstance, and how she really felt about it, Cait couldn't guess. Six humans. Alone with each other, and further removed from the rest of humanity than anyone else in history. If they didn't start working together, they'd be lucky to reach Horizon alive.

With Sharpe inside the lock, Harris moved to the cycle control and hesitated.

'I'd like to say something.' Cait's voice rang out louder than she'd intended. The others waited in silence. 'I've known Sharpe the longest out of all of you. We graduated from flight school in the same year.' A smile came to her lips. 'He never let me forget how much better his grade average was than mine. But he was the first to congratulate me when I landed this mission.

'He wasn't a religious man. He said he didn't need a god. But there was one photograph he'd had for years – he carried it with him wherever he went. Where it came from I can't remember – some crypt in the Southern Pax, Australia maybe. He said seeing the real thing was the closest he'd ever come to a religious experience.'

She pulled on the line and slowly rotated towards the others, but it was Sharpe's picture that filled her mind. She saw it so clearly, saw him holding it out to her and smiling.

'It showed part of a mosaic floor – very simple. At the top was an enormous sun – our Sun – so huge that only a part of it was visible. Bands of sunlight raced away from it into space – life-giving energy spreading out across the void, filling it with warmth and light. And basking in that glory, taking strength from it, was a small blue-green planet, so tiny it was almost lost in the brilliance.

'He said that when he first saw it, it struck him what a fortunate planet it was, and how lucky the people were who lived on it, to have light and warmth and the knowledge that the sun would be there for tens of thousands of years to come. But the mosaic showed more, and that was what fascinated him: beyond the small planet, the sun's influence paled and faded into nothingness, and the true void began to assert itself. The sun was vast and brilliant, but what lay beyond made even it seem insignificant, as insignificant as the Earth. The darkness was so terrible in its indifference that any sane person would want to turn their back on it, and push the cold emptiness from their mind.

'But Sharpe told me it was the darkness that called to him, not the sunlight, because within it he saw not the end of life but endless possibilities. As he stood in that crypt, he knew above anything else that he wanted to enter that void, push back the boundary, push back the fear, and make sense of the unknown.'

Cait blinked and focused on the others again. Her eyes were wet. 'That's what drove him. It was the single defining aspect of his life.'

She turned slowly in the zero-g. Harris and Lex were waiting patiently. Nadira was watching her from the same position as before, but Bren had floated closer to the access ladder, her arms wrapped around her knees, hugging them to her chest.

'Those same feelings are what drew us together in the first place and made us into a team. And, ultimately, they're what makes sense of our lives.' Silence descended as Cait let her words sink in. 'If this mission's going to be a success, that's what we have to focus on now.'

Her throat suddenly felt thick as she gave the order. 'Do it.'

Harris punched the button and the inner door closed over. The body was still visible through an oblong porthole. The outer door opened. The stars outside seemed crowded together. Sharpe's body was carried out in the last of the expelled air, surrounded by a cloud of ice crystals. It cleared the outer hull, cartwheeled into the darkness, and Sharpe joined with the void at last.

Harris hooked Bren with a glare. 'Satisfied?' he snarled.

'Haven't you heard a word I've said?' Cait asked, dumbfounded.

'Haven't you worked it out?' he countered. 'Lex couldn't find a thing wrong with Sharpe, and I can't find a thing wrong with the computer. She has to be responsible.'

'This isn't going to –'

'No, leave it,' Bren said, hauling on her line and floating towards Harris. 'I can fight my own batt– Uh!' She twisted, breathing in sharply, and began to flip over.

Cait pulled on her own line and grabbed hold of Bren, drawing her close. 'Are you all right? Bren?'

Bren's eyes snapped open. 'We've got another message.'

6

'Welcome to the twenty-second century.'

A tall, thin man stood backlit in front of a large picture window with sunlight streaming through it; it looked incongruous in the ring. There were no buildings visible through the glass, only sky. The room was hung with rich tapestries dyed a deep red and decorated with intricately intertwined lotus blossoms. The holo-image panned as the man walked towards them and sat behind a large mahogany desk decorated with an unfamiliar insignia. He was dressed in a severe black frockcoat and suit trousers, with white starched collar and cuffs accentuating the paleness of his skin. Fine blond hair swept back from a high forehead and fell to his shoulders, and his features were pinched and dominated by an aquiline nose. But it was his eyes that drew Cait's attention. They had a fatal intensity to them.

'My name is Enoch Bowen,' the image said, 'your launch director. And this message has been sent in preparation for your scheduled wake-up.' A humourless smile assembled itself on his lips. 'Firstly, I'd like to extend heartfelt congratulations from all of us here at Space Admin for safely traversing such an inconceivable distance.'

'Is he for real?' Bren asked.

'It's probably for the globecast to the "folks back home",' Lex said scathingly.

'Quiet,' Cait said.

'What I have to tell you may be difficult for you to understand. But there is no easy way to break this kind of news.' His brows knitted together as he stared sightlessly at the crew. 'The Pax Americana as you knew it no longer exists as an independent entity. This mission and the majority of the former Pax territories are now under the direct control of the Compact of Asian Peoples.'

'What the hell?' Harris said, drowning out Lex's objection.

'Freeze!' Cait ordered, and the image halted mid-sentence.

'Where'd this come from?' Harris was white with shock.

'Same place as the other message,' Bren said. 'Same protocols, same codes. And before you ask, the transmission was clean. Data only.'

'This is bullshit. There's no way this could have happened.'

Cait glanced at Nadira. Their sole Compact citizen was sitting poker-faced at the end of the table.

'There's a massive history file attached to the transmission. That's why the datadump fazed me for a second.' Bren sounded distracted. By the way she paused briefly before continuing, Cait could tell she was flash-scanning the documents. 'It's not very useful,' she said, focusing again on Harris. 'Most of it reads like a political manifesto. The "Popular Invasion", as they call it, took place forty-four years ago – Earth time, that is. If you can believe it, the Compact armies took over without a shot being fired, supported by a large contingent of the Pax citizenry –'

'There's time to look at this stuff later,' Lex said, sounding irritated. 'I want to hear what else this creep has to say.'

'Okay, resume,' Cait ordered.

'We understand how disoriented you must all feel by this news,' Enoch Bowen said, 'but to us it is almost ancient history. I have sent separate files that will give you much of the background to the change. I understand you will need time to discuss this and come to terms with it. I can assure you that no civilians were harmed during the conflict. And apart from a change in administration, life within the former Pax has continued much as you might expect.' Bowen stood again and walked around from behind his desk, unbuttoning his frockcoat as he went. He perched on the desk's edge and folded his hands easily in front of him. 'I would hesitate to tell you anything else at this point if our need was not so great. But you must have noticed by now that there was a course correction during your sleep.'

'Wrong,' Lex said.

'We apologise for that. In the normal course of events, we would not have considered changing anything without consulting you beforehand. But I ask you to understand the urgent necessity that drove our actions.' He turned towards the window behind him. The last rays of a setting sun were streaming through it now, accentuating the deep red of the tapestries and spilling out into the ring. 'The situation here is desperate. The biosphere that sustains us is approaching total collapse and there is nothing we can do about it. Our own short-sightedness and petty bickering has seen to that. The only option left to us is to leave Earth. While you slept, we have been searching the heavens for a suitable planet. A world where we might transplant as much of humanity as possible before life here becomes totally untenable. The system you are approaching contains the only potential candidate we have found.

'Our course correction will bring you into orbit around Horizon as quickly as possible. Once there, we need you to assess its suitability for colonisation and advise on any necessary terraforming. I understand this goes beyond the original purview of your mission: to explore the planet but leave it essentially untouched. Given the crisis we find ourselves in, I trust you will understand the desperate need that drives this change and comply accordingly.

'The schematics attached at the end of this message will allow you to assemble a new form of hypercaster so we can establish instantaneous communications. Our techs believe you can cannibalise the necessary parts from your auxiliary systems.' Bowen pushed off the desk and walked towards them until his face dominated the holo. 'The situation here is very tense. We are facing a breakdown of civil order if we cannot offer some hope of resettlement soon. All of us are relying on you. Please open communications with us as soon as possible. Message end.'

The hologram shrank to a pinpoint and disappeared and a tense silence settled over the ring.

'Biosphere collapse?' Harris said. 'What the hell's that all about?'

'It looks like Earth's governments took the last fifty-five years and kept doing what they do best,' Lex said. 'Fighting wars and making land grabs. It was all about oil in the early twenty-first century. Now it's viable living space. There must be precious little left on Earth if they're willing to travel thirty-four light years to settle on another planet. Do those history files tell us what the "ecological disaster" was, Bren?'

She shook her head. 'No. Just the takeover of the Pax, nothing more recent.'

'Well, that's convenient. Maybe it's all some kind of elaborate hoax.'

'If it is, it's hard to see what reason there could be behind it,' Cait said.

Nadira slapped the matt-black surface of the main control interface, startling Cait. She was trembling with anger.

'God, you people have a talent for avoidance! Is it so difficult to believe your mighty Pax could be brought down by the lowly Compact? That you're no longer in control?'

Cait expected Harris to react, but he seemed wrapped in his own thoughts.

'This isn't about the Pax or the Compact, Nadira,' she said.

'Damn right,' Lex said, leaning forward. 'It's about the mission. *Our* mission. I came here to study an alien biosphere, not work out how to change it so we can move in wholesale.'

'I think you're getting ahead of yourself,' Cait said.

'Bullshit! We'd be halfway there by now if it wasn't for the computer.'

Cait tried again. 'I agree we need to discuss this. But we need to discuss it calmly and sensibly.'

'Oh, yes,' Nadira said. Her voice was low and hoarse, and the tendons on her neck were sticking out. 'You Pax types are good at discussing things sensibly. And taking your time to look at "all the options". How much food should we give the Compact so not too many die of starvation this year? How much medical aid so the death rate in their hospitals isn't too embarrassing? How much do we really give a shit? Do you know how often your delegates stalled our aid requests through the UN? And all because we wouldn't allow your biggest companies access to our markets.' She bared her teeth in a vicious smile. 'Well, things are different now. There's nothing left for you to discuss. The Compact is in control and I suggest you start doing what you're told.'

'Jesus!' Lex said.

Cait met Nadira's gaze steadily, but her hands were clasped tightly beneath the bench. 'I'm still mission leader. I'm mindful of the request we've just received, and I'm taking it very seriously. But the ultimate authority on this ship lies with me. Until I hear otherwise, I'll continue to discuss all the issues before us with every member of this crew. You might be comfortable with what Bowen's told us, but there are others among us who'll need a little time to come to terms with what's happened and get some more details.'

She looked around the table. They were watching her so closely, ready to praise her for her reason or pounce on her for her folly. This message had thrown everything into disarray. She was in a room full of strangers, none of them willing to offer their support. As much as she wanted time to consider the message, she needed some space to analyse the crew's reactions too. There was too much to think about, too much to do, and too much depended on making the right choices.

'We can't rush into something we're going to regret later,' she said. 'We'll reconvene tomorrow. In the meantime, we'll need the computer back online just in case. Can you handle it, Harris?'

'Huh?' Harris focused on Cait's face. 'Sure. I'll get right on it.'

He pushed himself up with some effort despite the low gravity, and shuffled off in the direction of the access ladder.

'Go with him, Lex, will you?' Cait asked.

Lex nodded and followed Harris.

'And I'll start calibrating sensors for a close fly-by on Horizon,' Nadira said, standing. 'For when you all come to your senses.'

'I don't think that'll be any time soon,' Bren said wryly as Nadira walked off towards the forward access tube.

'This isn't a game,' Cait said. She felt sick and angry. 'Nadira's reaction I can at least understand. Yours on the other hand …'

The smile slipped from Bren's lips and her pale cheeks flushed. 'My reaction is quite understandable, Cait. I'm being accused of something I didn't do by someone I thought was a friend.'

'And I'm getting the run-around from the only person who might shed some light on Sharpe's death. Someone I thought I could trust.' Cait took a breath. Her hands were shaking. 'Look, I'm not accusing you of anything, but your version of events doesn't add up and I need to understand why.'

'It's a jumble to me too,' Bren said, rubbing at her forehead and looking more like a lost child than a highly competent technician. 'I don't remember what you want me to remember. I see images, but none of them make sense.'

Cait's anger stalled at seeing Bren so confused, and then she realised what Bren had just said. 'Wait a minute. Are you saying you weren't conscious when I found Sharpe, or you weren't in control?'

'Yes – no – I don't know. I honestly don't.'

'And yet physically there's nothing wrong with you, and you say the link is unaffected.' Cait was unable to keep the doubt from her voice.

'Believe it or don't believe it,' Bren challenged. 'I'm past caring.'

'But I do care. I have to. We're in fucking danger here!' Cait half rose, leaning over the bench towards Bren, wishing she could force the truth out of her.

Bren's lost look was replaced by something cold. 'We've had this conversation. Nothing's changed since the last time.'

Cait bit her lip, trying to see a way around deadlock and failing. 'I'm not your enemy, Bren. I'm still your friend. Think about that.'

7

Lex followed Harris in silence, gliding through the hub tube and down into the computer core chamber. It was only when they were both attached by lines to the maintenance port that he spoke.

'Are you okay, Tom?'

Harris turned haunted eyes towards him. 'What do you think? I don't know what I'm doing out here any more.'

Lex could think of nothing to say. He wasn't attached to the EU like Harris was to the Pax. Nationalism had always left a bad taste in his mouth. But he felt a twinge of concern about what might have happened to the people he knew. The kind of political upheaval Bowen hinted at would have sent ripples around the globe. Nothing could escape unchanged, despite Bowen's assurances.

'We're really alone out here now,' he said to Harris. 'We've been marooned by time and distance. Nothing on Earth can make sense to us any more.'

Harris tapped spasmodically at the on-site

keyboard without much enthusiasm. The screen flared and brought up the latest diagnostics. Lex pulled on the line and swam closer.

'What do you think about the new orders?' he asked.

Harris's broad face glowered with sudden hatred. 'I think it's bullshit. I'm not taking orders from some fucking invader, no matter how long ago it happened.'

'Hey,' Lex placed a hand on his shoulder, 'we don't have to.'

Cait drifted through the opening to auxiliary command, the arrow-shaped control cabin at the very front of *Magellan*. Her whole body was tingling from her run-in with Bren. She felt like a wire stretched too tight.

She grabbed at the back of an acceleration couch and dragged herself down into it. She needed space to think. She couldn't relax with so much going on. It was all getting too complex and she felt … she felt …

Damn! Why was she crying? She rubbed at her eyes, sniffing back the tears and feeling stupid. What the hell was happening to her?

A sob escaped her lips, and tears began to flow in earnest. She couldn't stop. She curled her arms around herself and turned her face into the seat back, crying, gasping for breath, and hoping no one came looking for her.

You're in shock, she thought. It's Sharpe. And the

lack of sleep. Get a hold of yourself.

But something inside her wanted to let go, to abandon herself to the feeling. And it wouldn't be denied.

I'm alone.

A single thought, and all the hurt, anxiety and anguish coalesced inside her. The tears came harder. She buried her face in the padding, feeling pathetic and desolate.

Her younger brother, Ben, his wife and their two daughters – only babies when she'd left. She was sure they were gone; killed by the Compact in the takeover. It wasn't rational, but it felt like the truth. It proved how mortal they were – all of them. And what that meant for her …

A half grunt, half laugh escaped her throat. The intake psychs would have leapt on this if they'd suspected it – if *she'd* even suspected it. She'd always told herself she didn't need anyone else. Partners had come and gone without any great sense of loss. She'd never wanted children. She'd made sure she couldn't have any as soon as she was old enough, joking about the slavish evolutionary programming that forced couples into having kids just so they could grasp at a tiny sliver of immortality. But she was just as trapped by the same programming. She wasn't simply afraid that her family was gone. She was terrified that, childless as she was, her own death would mean there'd be nothing left to prove that *any* of them had ever existed.

The grip they had on life – on history – was so tenuous. Sharpe had demonstrated that. Why had she believed she was any different? She felt utterly insignificant, ephemeral. It was pathetic, but she couldn't deny the emotional weight it carried for her. There was nothing now that could help. Nothing to give her hope. Indifferent darkness rushed at her and swallowed her up.

Time passed. The tears slowed. Her breathing calmed. Her mind started working again. Slowly.

She turned, consciously relaxing taut muscles and taking a deep breath. She smiled weakly. She'd thought she needed time to consider the crew's reactions, their feelings. Her own emotions had decided they deserved a hearing.

I've got to look after myself too, she thought, or I'm never going to make it.

The loneliness was still there. The fear. Blunted, for now at least. But alongside those feelings was something else. Something that had always been there. You can keep going, she thought. No matter how hard it gets, or how alone or scared you feel. You always have. That's real courage. Feeling like this but still moving forward. That's real strength.

She was going to have to watch Harris and Nadira closely. And Lex. She shook her head. And Bren. She was going to have to watch them all.

As soon as she'd heard Bowen speak, she'd known he was telling the truth. In fact, the emergency on Earth coupled with the change in government made a worrying kind of sense about the earlier attempt to lodge the wyrm program in the computer. The stakes were high, and the Compact wanted to make sure their wishes were followed to the letter. It also said a lot about how they did business. But in some ways it would have been easier for her if their plan had succeeded and they were now en route to Horizon with the wyrm active and ready to force their hand. As it was, the responsibility still lay squarely on her shoulders. Except instead of five lives to worry about, she had more than ten billion.

What must be happening on Earth now, she wondered. There had been no detail in Bowen's message, and that was a worry in itself. Had it been, as Lex said, governments perpetuating their old ways – despite the warnings they'd all witnessed – until the land was exhausted? Could they have been so short-sighted? Or was it unavoidable climate change, an environmental accident, a runaway greenhouse effect? She'd studied the scenarios in college. But the forecasts had shown a steady improvement since Kyoto III was finally ratified.

In a way, the answer was as simple as Nadira had said. If Earth was faced with catastrophe, there was nothing to do but go along with the course change when they could. Theirs was a humanitarian mission now. Cait just hoped the others saw it that way.

She rubbed at her eyes and moved forward on her couch. Each station had its own data point. She stroked the screen in front of her and began to review the history files Bowen had sent. Images raced across the monitor. Bren was right: the files were heavy with rhetoric, but there was enough information there if you looked for it.

When *Magellan* left, the Pax had been one of the world's foremost nations, riding the crest of cutting-edge technological developments and progressive social reforms. A bare ten years later, the nation state was in turmoil. The country was in the grip of an energy crisis. Increasingly, they'd based the economy on fuel cells bought from the Northern Commonwealth. There were alternative energy sources, but none as cost-efficient. When relations with the Commonwealth began to slip, the government made plans to go it alone and develop alternative technology. But the corporations wouldn't countenance anything affecting their bottom lines, and the Commonwealth, realising it had a virtual monopoly, began to squeeze. The public utilities took the brunt to begin with, and domestic supply brown-outs became commonplace. At the same time, another genetech crop failure left food reserves dangerously low, and the soaring unemployment rate led to a mid-term budget that slashed state welfare programs.

But the final straw came from an entirely unexpected direction: something that had its seeds in Cait's own time on Earth. Ever since the rise of the first transhumans – the bio-jacks who could roam the globalweb at will – the 'norms' had attempted to curtail their movements, by way of firewalls and illegal black ice programs, and through the more time-honoured method of lengthy litigation. The bio-jacks had responded in kind. Extremist transhuman elements planted logic bombs in any system with 'offensive' capabilities, causing havoc in the globalweb. The more law-abiding among them flash-scanned whole libraries of legal texts, decisions and precedents and mounted the most exhaustive defence ever by a group of individuals against a cartel of private and public sector organisations. The pundits had a field day, and transhumans and anti-techs alike visited their own scare campaigns on an increasingly uneasy population. All the while, the arguments moved slowly through the courts, escalating with appeal and counter-appeal. Finally, in a marathon sitting, the Supreme Court ruled in favour of the transhumans, stating that any restriction of movement through the globalweb, except where it could be proved that individual or commercial privacy or national security was endangered, amounted to cruel and unusual punishment and was, in fact, unconstitutional.

The transhumans were vindicated, and attempted to quell any lingering objections by pledging to develop a strict ethical code that would regulate their interaction with the globalweb. But they had underestimated the effectiveness of the anti-techs' media campaign. Hysteria gripped the 'silent majority' as the decision was handed down. Fundamentalist groups fed on the mood, fuelled by testimonials that these 'hybrid web-creatures' had already accessed private information about Pax citizens for fraudulent purposes. Some hinted that the Supreme Court judges themselves had been held to ransom, and that the government was heavily infiltrated by transhuman elements.

Reeling from one crisis to another, the government tried to regain credibility by taking the offensive against what they felt was a soft target. Bypassing the Supreme Court ruling, they offered the transhumans an ultimatum: give up your links or face exile. The majority left, unwilling to deactivate their enhancements.

It was at this point that the propaganda tone in the files went into overdrive. In the eyes of 'the people', the government's actions were seen as too little, too late. They had lost the confidence of the electorate. The Compact responded to a popular plea to save the citizenry and step into the breach. Air and ground troops were dispatched and – this certainly didn't ring true to Cait – the Pax forces stood down as the populace welcomed the occupying armies with open arms. The new administration was sworn into office shortly afterwards and formally applied to join the Compact.

And they all lived happily ever after, Cait thought. She shifted in the couch, responding to her aching muscles, and checked the chrono. There were more files to view, but she'd been there for hours. She felt emotionally and physically exhausted.

She pushed off the couch with her hands, turning in the cramped space until she was facing aft, and grasped the back of the couch to propel herself towards the rear hatch. She sailed past the five other acceleration couches that formed a neat arrowhead in the tight compartment, and pushed through the opening into the larger hold section.

It was cold here. And dark. Stacks of ration packs were cradled against the hull in nets; enough to feed six crew members well for five years – twice as long as intended. Even so, Cait didn't want to waste a single meal. A safety margin was just that, and shouldn't be eroded without good reason.

The air supply was more problematic. The atmosphere plant recycled what it could, and catalysed the deficit from the water-ice on the hull. Originally they'd been scheduled to wake up close to the outer system, where cometary matter was plentiful enough for them to replenish their water-ice shell. Proceeding straight to Horizon would cut well into their reserves, especially since they'd been awake for so long already. And the likelihood of finding a convenient comet so far in-system was lower. Weary as she was, she'd have to check Nadira's long-range scans before she slept. They couldn't afford to leave anything to chance. Not this far out.

She made it to the web and launched herself into the hub axis, flipping over the lip and spinning as she fell so she could grab the top rung of the ladder. The lighting in the ring was in night mode, but she could make out Harris and Lex on the deck below. Lex looked up as she began her descent and moved off towards his harness.

'Tom,' she called as Harris started to leave too. He looked up at her with an odd expression on his face, like a child caught with his hand in the cookie jar.

'Wait up,' she said as she skipped the last few rungs and dropped to the deck. 'Are you finished with the computer?'

'As much as I can be. I've got independent monitors, limiters, you name it. If Phillips even looks at anyone funny, he'll be locked down and the back-ups will take over.'

'I hope it won't come to that. Particularly if we're in the middle of a velocity-dump. The dunces can handle the program once it's been set up and fed in, but any mid-execution alterations are going to throw them way off without the processing power of the main computer.'

Harris grunted agreement, and Cait fixed him with a worried look. 'Are you okay?'

He shook his head as if to deflect her concerns, but wouldn't meet her eyes. 'I'm tired. More tired than I've ever felt maybe. I should be pissed off, but I haven't got the energy right now.'

Cait had wanted to talk to him about Bowen and Bren, but now obviously wasn't the time. 'It's like I said at the meeting: take some time to think things through. If you want to talk ...'

Harris laughed. 'I've had enough of that from Lex.'

'Oh?'

But he was already turning to leave. 'Like I said, I'm tired. I'll see you in the morning.'

'Right,' she said, trying to sound positive. But the knot in her stomach tightened once more.

8

'Ready here,' Harris's voice said over Cait's PAL. 'All systems nominal, just as before. Initialising.'

The holo-projector in the ring axis came to life and began scanning in the Phillips persona.

Bren stood beside Cait, who was seated at the access port. She was linked in and monitoring the software continuously during the reboot.

'He's here and he's aware,' she said. 'Christ, Harris, what have you done to him, you butcher?'

Cait swivelled in her seat. Phillips was almost complete now, minus the top of his head, which scanned in as she watched. 'He looks fine to me.'

Bren snorted. 'Yeah, the picture's fine, but the virtuality is another thing. It's like watching a one-armed blind man trying to juggle.'

'He'll do the job,' Harris said. 'He's still got the processing power and the speed. It's just some of the higher functions that have been held in check. If *you* can find the fault, good luck to you. In the meantime, this is the only way we can enter deepsleep again with a reasonable chance of waking up.'

'He's right,' Cait said. 'We need additional remote monitoring and controls to make sure whatever caused the shutdown can't happen again.'

'I hope you know what you're doing,' Bren said, 'because he doesn't look happy to me.'

'Well, let's ask him, shall we?' Cait stood and crossed over to the holo. 'How do you feel, Phillips?'

He looked the same as before, but as he turned his attention towards her, Cait felt nothing of the malevolent air that had accompanied their last talk. His eyes seemed kindlier, more like his old self, and the lines around them crinkled as his face broke into a smile.

'I'm fine, Cait. I've reviewed the measures Tom has in place and I don't have any concerns. I'm confident I can handle the burn, and you should be too. Tom's done a great job under the circumstances.'

'What can you tell us about the malfunction?' Cait asked.

'I can't answer that,' Phillips said with a sigh. 'My core memory has sustained some non-localised damage.'

'What caused the damage?' she pressed.

Phillips blinked and froze, his lids sticking mid-movement. A black band rippled through the image from head to toe.

'Harris!' Cait shouted.

'I see it,' Harris called.

'I can't answer that,' Phillips said again, and sighed.

'My core memory has sustained some non-localised damage.'

'What happened there, Harris?' Cait called.

'It's the limiters,' he said. 'They monitored some unusual responses in the core and squirted a query. It slowed the system a fraction. Everything's normal again.'

'Everything's fine,' Phillips continued in his pleasant, conversational tone. 'There's some degradation with the modifications, but it shouldn't affect my calculations.'

Cait faced her systems specialist. 'What do you think, Bren?'

'He's like a neutered tomcat. I don't like it.'

'I don't like it either, but I don't see what else we can do. Unless *you* can shed some light on it?'

Bren glared at her.

'Well, can you?' Cait was losing patience again. 'If you know something, now's the time to tell me, because odds are we'll be in deepsleep again soon and I don't want another death.'

'I don't know anything that can help you,' Bren insisted.

'We'll see.' Cait turned away.

'Cait,' Phillips said, and she turned back. 'I'd like access to the transmission files from launch control now. If that's okay.'

Cait looked at Bren, who nodded.

'I guess it's all right,' she told Phillips. 'Bren will release them to you.'

Cait sat back at the access port and looked at Harris on the PAL's screen. 'Keep running the diagnostics, will you?' she said quietly. 'We'll leave him up, but I don't want him setting up burn calculations until we have some more performance data.'

'Okay. I've got the secondaries running a constant check. I'll have a stack of graphs for you by this evening.'

'You'd better come back down now. It's nearly time for the meeting.'

Lex threw himself into his seat looking surly. If the situation wasn't so serious, Cait would have said something. He looked like a rebellious high-school student. Harris had regained some of his composure, and so, thankfully, had Nadira. Cait was feeling a little better too, although she wasn't kidding herself.

Bren was the last to be seated, obviously still smarting from their talk, and Cait gave her time to settle before she began.

'Okay. We've got Phillips back up after a fashion, and if he continues to function normally over the next twenty-four hours, we can start thinking about dumping velocity. Which brings us to the flight plan.'

Lex cleared his throat, clearly unhappy. And he wasn't alone: they were all watching her with varying degrees of hostility. She felt a sharp pang of anger. Jesus, maybe she should just turn the leadership over to someone else and see how they liked dealing with all this shit. The trouble was, none of them was up to it. They were too wrapped up in selfish concerns to bring the mission in safely.

'We were scheduled to rendezvous with Iota Persei F, D and C before entering a stable orbit round Horizon itself.'

She tapped at an input panel on the benchtop and a holo of the system sprang into sharp detail above it. Six planets marched outwards from a miniature sun along the same ecliptic, while a seventh wandered far above in a more steeply inclined orbit. A red line threaded three of the planets – F, D and C – finishing in a loop around Iota Persei B.

'If we go with the changes sent through by launch control, we'll proceed straight to Horizon following this course.'

Another tap and a dotted purple parabola arced towards their final destination, avoiding anything else in the system.

'Great,' Lex said. 'Who cares about checking out a few extra-solar planets in the name of science? Let's just cut to the chase and get on with some good old terraforming.'

'We'll also save a month off our trip time,' Cait continued, ignoring Lex. 'Which could make a big difference for the billions left back on Earth.'

'Yes, the billions back on Earth,' Lex interrupted again. 'Poor them. And what was it that was threatening their survival? Oh, yeah.' He clicked his fingers. 'I think Enoch forgot to tell us. Or give us any hard evidence. Guess we'll just forget the fact that, collectively, we've invested over two hundred years so far in this trip and throw the mission plan away. We can always do that other stuff next lifetime.'

'You're not making this easy,' Cait said. 'For any of us.'

'I didn't realise it was meant to be easy.' He rocked forward, placing his hands on the table, and his voice rose. 'Forget everything I said. Forget everything that was promised to us. Forget everything we gave up. Forget the reason we came on this fucking trip!' Spittle flew in Cait's face as Lex shouted the last and thudded back into his seat. 'I, for one, do not agree to any change without further proof that it's really necessary. And I think you'll find I'm not alone.' He looked at Bren and Harris.

'Okay,' Cait said, 'I think we know where you stand.'

Something had been brewing with him – she knew that – but she hadn't been prepared for the force of his reaction. This whole thing had really gotten under his skin.

'I understand you're upset. I've got as many reservations as you have, and I'm just as committed to seeing out the original mission. But I don't think we can afford to ignore that last transmission, however scant it was on detail. You're right, there's a lot we haven't been able to verify about the situation on Earth. But what if it *is* true? The message is five months old. Whatever the situation, it could be a lot worse by now. Could we live with ourselves, knowing Earth was in trouble and not doing anything about it? That's not the way I was brought up. And I suspect if you really take the time to think about it, it's not the way you were either.'

Lex glared at her. 'I still think we need to verify things on Earth.'

'I do too,' Bren said quietly.

Cait's brow furrowed as she stared at her one-time friend. 'I have a compromise – one that I think is necessary for the safety of this ship,' she added quickly before Nadira objected. 'We're cutting into our air reserves; and I want to replenish the water-ice shield before we plough into the inner system. There's no way we can avoid the asteroid belt in any of the approaches open to us.'

Her fingers caressed the table pad again and a green line appeared between the other course options.

'If we go for a maximum burn cascade in forty-eight hours, we can come in right on Iota Persei F and rendezvous with a comet that's been trapped in orbit around it. It's moving relatively slowly, and we should be able to siphon off enough water-ice from the tail to fill our tanks and fix up the shielding. The operation will take upwards of twenty hours – more than enough time to grab some up-close telemetry and send in a couple of probes. Once we're finished there, we grab some quick V and then go for another maximum dump to bring us in around Horizon. It shouldn't add more than five days to the trip, and we'll be well supplied to complete an in-depth analysis for Earth without having to break off and look for another comet. Depending on when we finally leave the system, we could pick up C and D on the way back out. We won't lose a thing.'

'So we're a Compact ship now?' Lex said. 'You're giving in and doing what our new masters want?'

Harris shifted uneasily in his seat.

'I told you I'd reserved judgement on that,' Cait said. 'But *if* billions of people are in danger – and I know we have no proof – I want us to be in a position where we can do something about it, if we all agree. And if it turns out to be a hoax, or a bizarre misunderstanding, we won't have lost anything we can't recover in terms of the original mission. Nothing's been decided. We're just staying flexible to events.'

'There's a danger in being too flexible,' Lex said. 'What about the terraforming?'

'We'll take it one step at a time. Okay? And we'll discuss everything fully. Nadira?'

'It sounds reasonable,' Nadira said guardedly. 'But I'd like to study your flight plan.'

Cait smiled. 'I'd like a second opinion. From you too, Harris. The drive's going to be working overtime on this. Assuming you're in, that is.'

Harris looked sideways at Lex, then sighed loudly. 'I guess I'm in for now.'

'I thought we had an agreement,' Lex said, his voice tight.

'Just because I'm angry doesn't mean I'm going to let a whole planet full of people get screwed,' Harris snapped back. 'Give me some credit, for Christ's sake.'

You bastard, Lex, Cait thought, then stopped herself. He'd been open about his views on the course change, and she already knew what kind of a person he was. It should be no surprise that he'd start actively recruiting allies. It just hurt that it was her he was working against.

'Lex? Bren?' she said. She'd much rather have a consensus about the course change.

Lex folded his arms and sat back, knowing he'd lost the argument for now. 'Do what you want.'

Bren shrugged and kept quiet.

Cait slapped at the table pad and the hologram disappeared. 'Looks like we've got some work to do.'

She stood and walked away from them all up the incline, her heart pounding as a smile stole onto her lips. For the first time since wake-up, she felt she'd regained some control over events.

Harris jogged up alongside her. 'I meant what I said, Cait. I'm in for now, but I don't like the idea of taking orders from the Compact. The thought of them having control over the Pax leaves me cold.'

'I'm not making any commitments we can't live with. But under the circumstances, we have to give them the benefit of the doubt. I appreciate your honesty about how far I can count on you though.' She paused, feeling just a little like a traitor. 'I also share your concerns about Bren. But accusing her without proof is just going to put her on guard. I know. I tried and it got me nowhere.'

'You want me to ease off on her?'

'It might help.'

'Okay,' he said. 'But I'm going to keep an eye on her just the same.'

'Me too,' Cait said sadly. 'Me too.'

Eight hours later, Cait, Harris and Nadira met to go over the flight plan. Bren excused herself, saying she wanted to link with Phillips and go through his code again line by line. Lex just laughed when Cait invited him along.

The benchtop holo was already up, displaying Cait's proposal. She held a stylus tip at the start point.

'The most difficult part will be the initial set of V-dumps through the drive. The thrusters won't be enough to change course at the speed we're moving. We need the main drive to skew the loss so we can change the ship's attitude enough to lay it into this groove. After that, we've got four weeks' deepsleep,' she moved the stylus along the line towards Iota Persei F, 'until the final set of dumps brings us into orbit injection around the gas giant. Harris?'

He grunted. 'I'd feel more comfortable if we had enough distance for a sustained thruster firing to bring us around, but there's no reason the drive can't handle it. It just means Phillips will have to factor it into his calculations.'

'What's the latest on him?' Cait asked.

Harris tossed her a handful of flimsies. 'As good as we're going to get. He's close to nominal on all fronts.'

Cait flipped through the graphs, her lips pursing as she read the bottom line. 'It's not ideal. But we can't delay braking for much longer. Would a few more days make a difference?'

Harris shook his head. 'I can't see that it would. Let's just get it over with.'

'What do you think?' Cait asked Nadira.

Nadira studied the holo again, then nodded. 'The course looks good. But you need to pin down the comet's position more. We could waste time and fuel chasing it if we're not spot on.'

'We'll be relying on the sightings you take right up until firing time,' Cait said, smiling.

'I see,' Nadira said. Cait thought she almost returned the smile, then her lips pursed. 'When are you going to contact the Compact?'

Cait noticed Harris's grimace. She'd known this was coming, but she was still undecided about what was best.

In a way, it would be a relief to get a direct line to launch control and share the load with someone else. But she wasn't sure Enoch Bowen or the Compact would act in the best interests of the crew. How expendable was a bunch of Pax citizens, plus extras, in the face of a global disaster?

The fact that the Compact would have more direct control of the mission was bound to cause friction with the crew as well. Lex wouldn't like it, and Harris would be put in a difficult position. As for Bren, she seemed to be siding with Lex now, but Cait had the feeling she hadn't totally committed to one side or the other.

'We won't have time to construct the new equipment before the burn,' she said. That was true, but it only answered Nadira's direct question and none of the other issues it raised. 'You've looked at the specs, haven't you, Harris?'

'Yes, and I can just about understand them. Don't ask me how it works or why, but I'll be able to build it after I've stripped the spares out. I should have it done by the time we've caught that comet by the tail.'

'Okay.' Cait sat back with a sigh. 'We're committed. I'll check with the others, but unless you hear otherwise, the drive will be firing in sixteen hours. Which means we go into the harnesses in fifteen. Harris, get Phillips working on the calcs, and you'll have to get started on the observations, Nadira. We'll be in orbit before we know it.'

9

The drive chamber took up the rear quarter of the ship and fully two-fifths of its volume. Most of that was filled by the six huge plasma thrusters that channelled the engine's output.

Cocooned in space suits, Cait and Harris stood on the gantry running along the midline of the rear wall. The vast superstructure surrounded them, and out past the thrusters lay the infinite. The starfield crowded into an ellipse, as if viewed through a thick lens. Cait knew that at this speed the view was blue-shifted as well, but she couldn't tell the difference. The combined effect made her feel like an ant clinging to a very small ledge.

Her eyes drifted back to the featureless black heart of the drive. Their survival depended on balance – macro and quantum, thrust and inertia. The black box was the fulcrum, fed by the vacuum surrounding it. It sucked hydrogen atoms into its nanotubes, cut them off from the quantum wavelengths that kept them spinning, and fed the energy released to the huge plasma thrusters. It also generated a quantum field that enhanced the push and decreased the inertia just enough so the harnesses could absorb the residual V-shift from the drive pulses. Exactly $189 \times 10^{30}$ buckytubes sat inside the box, cycling ten times that number of hydrogen atoms through every second. The processing power to keep it balanced was tremendous, and it all relied on the proper functioning of the neural network that made up the Phillips persona.

'If this crashes in a heap, we won't know what hit us,' Cait said into the suit mic.

'If this crashes in a heap, I'll quit my job. Besides, we're running out of options if we want to make it to Horizon.'

'I guess,' she said, edging around to face the lock in the bulkhead wall and activating the door. 'How's Phillips going?'

'He's finished the initial set of attitude calculations. All we need now is the comet's orbit pinned down and we're ready.'

Harris squeezed into the lock beside her and the door cycled shut. Atmosphere hissed in around them and the interior hatch slid open on their twin PALs, waiting to greet them like eager puppies. Cait pushed her way out and released the helmet lock, placing it down quickly and scratching gratefully at her nose. Harris lifted his own helmet off and watched her with half a smile.

'Feel good?' he asked.

Cait stopped scratching and sniffed, returning the

smile. 'I'm not cut out to be a stellarnaut. I always get the itches inside these things.' She arced an arm round and under the neck ring to scratch at the base of her shoulder blade, before pulling at the suit fastenings.

'I've read through those history files the Compact sent.' Harris sounded suddenly serious.

'And?' Cait asked cautiously.

'Don't worry, I'm not changing my mind. Yet. But you've got to admit most of that stuff is just so much bullshit. It has to be.'

'It's hard to know what the truth is any more. Sometimes I think I'm going to come out of deepsleep and this will all be a dream.' She shook her head. 'But I'm convinced the emergency on Earth is real enough.'

Harris placed his helmet in the wall locker.

'Look, I can understand your reservations,' Cait went on. 'The mission means a lot to everyone on board. But Lex's screw-them attitude just isn't an option. I have to balance the needs of the crew with whatever else we learn from Earth. And we have to start facing the fact that our little interplanetary picnic might have to go on hold, possibly indefinitely. The sooner we all understand that, the better.'

'As long as you play straight,' Harris said, unhooking his suit fastenings, 'you'll have no problems from me. Of course, I can't speak for Lex – he's got a bit too much of the old country in him. And as for the others … Well, you know what I think about them, but I'll keep my opinions to myself for the sake of shipboard harmony. As long as they do the same.'

'Well, okay,' Cait said, stretching her neck out and hearing the tendons pop.

'Come on.' Harris shucked off the rest of his suit and stowed it under the helmet. 'Let's get ready to rock and roll.'

Cait followed him through the tube into the habitat ring. For all of his faults, Harris was honest. If he said she could trust him, he meant it.


Nadira was coming out of main control as they reached the deck. 'I've given Phillips the orbit figures on the comet,' she said. 'It shouldn't take long for the calcs to come through.'

'Absolutely.' Phillips's voice seemed to come from all around as his image scanned in on the deck between them. 'I have the course and burn laid in. Look.' He waved his newly formed hands like a stage conjurer and a tiny *Magellan* appeared, speared on the end of a course plot into the Iota Persei system. 'The first burn is due in one hour and thirteen minutes.'

He clicked his fingers and a candle flame of plasma shot from the ship and twisted it in towards Iota Persei F, then flipped the icy cone so the business end was facing the direction of travel. The drive continued to fire sporadically, making minor course corrections, until it closed on the gas giant. A final set of bursts and it was in orbit and chasing a miniature comet around to the dark side of the planet. Phillips clicked his fingers again and the holo was gone.

'As simple as that,' Cait said. 'What about any deviations?'

Phillips slipped his hands into his fatigue pockets. 'Long-range sensors say that won't be necessary, but I'll be on the case. And if anything does go wrong, you'll be the first out of deepsleep. I'll keep the access port hot so you can take over any time you want. There'll be no problem from me.'

'Damn right, there won't be,' Bren said as she and Lex joined the group, 'because I'm going to be linked and with you every step of the way.'

Harris nearly choked but had the good grace to keep quiet.

'Are you sure you'll be okay?' Cait tried to sound diplomatic, but she couldn't help feeling concerned. They'd all be asleep and helpless. Phillips was one thing, limited as he was by Tom's safeguards, but Bren would have the run of the ship. 'Your implant could malfunction again. Leave you in a coma.'

'I've run a complete check on her,' Lex butted in before Bren could respond. 'I'm sure she'll be fine.'

'I thought you weren't an expert on implants,' Cait said.

Lex smiled and raised a supercilious eyebrow. 'As you're at pains to remind me, I'm the closest thing you've got to one out here. Besides, personally I'll feel much safer knowing Bren's on the job. You can rely too much on hardware solutions.'

'Gee, thanks,' Harris rumbled.

Nadira didn't look happy either, but Cait could see no valid reason to refuse. She turned to Phillips.

'Okay, but I'm personally ordering you, Phillips – and you, Bren – to wake me if there's any deviation from the flight plan whatsoever. I don't care how minor it is, I want to know about it first. Do I make myself clear?'

'Of course, mission leader,' Phillips said smoothly, and vanished.

'I'm doing this for all the right reasons, Cait.' Bren folded her arms and dared Cait to suggest anything else. 'Whatever you may think, I've got the interests of everyone here at heart.'

Cait stared back at her, then sighed. 'Okay, let's get to the harnesses. If nothing else, at least we'll get some well-earned rest.'

Cait took a final walk around the running track that looped the ring. As leader, she would be the last to enter deepsleep, and she wanted to check on the others first.

Bren was already under, held securely by the harness, the tell-tales showing she was well into deepsleep. Cait could see no outward sign that she was linked with the computer. She wondered if the sleep state affected

Bren's interface in any way. Did the synapses slow appreciably, and would Bren be aware if they did?

In a way, the transhumans were so different from the rest of humanity they defied understanding. The worst of them were almost impossible to communicate with, so immersed in the link they'd jump ten steps ahead in any conversation, or loop off on some tangent, muttering oblique references that made no sense.

Bren was the most 'human' of the bio-jacks that Cait had met. Grounded, she'd thought, but even early on their relationship had been problematic. Spending time with a transhuman was like having a partner with a whole other life about which you knew only the scantest details and understood even less. Link technology had divided the human race more deeply than any of the old racial differences; and at times the gap seemed far more unbridgeable than anything that had gone before. Just as the norms couldn't truly comprehend the virtual realm, it was beyond the power of the bio-jacks to explain it to them. The commonalities used to build understanding did not, and would never, exist. You might as well try to explain God to a sandfly.

Cait moved over to Lex's sleeping form. He was quite handsome when he wasn't being a dick. Lex made enemies like other people made lunch dates. Cait guessed it was easy to do when you had no real responsibility. He reminded her of a lover she'd had at college: he'd been ready with a smart remark or a putdown too, but once she pushed past his public face she'd been surprised at how sensitive he was, and, in the final analysis, how unsure of himself. Perhaps the same was true of Lex. He'd been the most vocal in resisting Bowen's mission changes. He'd argued that maintaining the integrity of the mission was the reason for his objections, but it could just as easily have been anger directed at Cait. He was, after all, that petty. But perhaps it went deeper than that. Was he so unsure of himself that he clung desperately to what he knew, a plan that gave his life the meaning and structure that it lacked from within? Was he simply afraid to change?

She walked on, the floor curving up to meet her. The temperature in the ring was cooling as the computer cut back life support. The main control was in darkness, the displays and access ports locked down for the burn. It wouldn't be long now.

She rounded the last unit and stared at Harris's empty harness.

'Harris!' she called, her voice sounding scared as it echoed around the walls.

'Here!' She could see him waving at her, seated at the port beside her own harness. He stood as she approached, squeezing his eyes shut and rubbing at them. 'I was just checking up on the fail-safes one more time.'

'Find anything to delay the burn?'

'No. No problems. Or none that I can anticipate.

Bren's got me spooked though. I just hope she and Lex haven't decided to take the mission into their own hands.'

Cait shook her head. 'I'll admit I was worried at first, but I don't see it. No matter how much they might disagree, they wouldn't deliberately endanger us. Manoeuvring in-system is going to be difficult enough without them trying to alter things on the run. If I'm feeling charitable, I could say Bren's as puzzled about what happened to her and the computer as we are, although she doesn't want to admit it. She wants to make sure it doesn't happen again.'

'I'm not convinced about that, and neither should you be,' Harris said.

'No,' Cait said after a moment. 'I'm not.'

'Come on,' Harris said. 'It's time to get some sleep. I'll see you on the other side.'

He stuck out his hand in a quaintly old-fashioned gesture. His rough palm enfolded her hand and squeezed briefly.

'See you on the other side,' Cait whispered as he ambled off to his harness.

She stripped quickly, goose flesh rising against the cold, and swung into the harness. She inserted the catheters first, grimacing at the sensation, then coated the throat tube with anaesthetic paste before pushing it slowly inside. The IVs were next and, finally, the leg bags and gauntlets. The harness and limb covers inflated with gel and she felt her body go rigid.

Somewhere in the ring, Phillips was counting backwards towards zero. The lights dimmed and the harness bleeped once, pinpricking her into unconsciousness. Her mouth felt instantly dry, and her vision began to blur. *Please, God, let me wake up. Let the others wake up.* Then a rolling calm fogged her mind.

In the distance she could hear her own voice, childlike, reciting a rhyme she hadn't heard since grade school.

*Care-charmer Sleep, son of the sable Night,*
*Brother to Death, in silent darkness born.*

# 2 OUT-SYSTEM

YESTERDAY UPON THE STAIR, I MET A
MAN WHO WASN'T THERE.

# 10

'– up. Wake up. WAKE UP!'

Cait felt something hot and wet on her cheek, and her eyes snapped open. Phillips was leaning over her and screaming as if he'd completely lost it. She cracked the seals and shed the gauntlets, pulled the pipe from her throat.

'What?' she managed before a dry cough gripped her.

'It's Harris. I think he's dead.'

The words assaulted her even as she pushed her body towards action. In a frenzy she tore at the leg bags, ripping the film straps and tearing out the catheters and IVs without a thought for herself. The harness tipped as she thrashed around. She pushed her legs through the webbing, hopped to the deck, slipped, and twisted as she fell in the low-g. The deck felt slick on her back.

Phillips was pointing towards the bulkhead. She shifted awkwardly, skin slipping on the floor as she sought purchase, and followed his gaze.

Harris lay beneath Sharpe's empty harness in a

pool of blood.

Phillips began babbling again. 'The drive fired. I couldn't stop it. I didn't even know he was awake. He's dead, isn't he? Tell me, Cait. Is he dead?'

Cait squeezed her eyes shut, her hands pushing against the deck, against the blood. It was too hard to concentrate.

'Computer, silence the interface,' she grated. When she opened her eyes again, Phillips was gone.

She got her knees under her and made it to the access port seat. The monitor was already up and running, and she activated the wake cycle, then punched for navigation, which was red-circled and pulsing.

The dialogue cursor blinked, flashing up a line.

<unscheduled firing – collision imminent>

Collision? With what? Her fingers flew across the scat board.

<collision target>

<Iota Persei F> the monitor replied.

Fuck. They must be coming up on the final burn. Was Phillips still functioning?

she keyed in, fearing the worst.

<calculations running> the cursor said, and she started breathing again. The line blanked and the cursor ran on. <course correction: 8 minutes – safety margin: 4 minutes>

Okay, they had twelve minutes to impact. At least Phillips was still in there, still capable of doing the calcs.

A stray thought tugged at her and she looked up. She could see Lex stirring in the harness on the other side of the ring. Her PAL was active, watching her from its perch above the access port.

'Address intra-ship. Attention all crew. Remain in your harnesses. We're coming up on a burn. Don't move! – Repeat at two-second intervals.'

Her voice began to echo around the ring. She stood shakily and bent low under Sharpe's harness to kneel beside Harris. His head had borne the brunt of the picopulse. There wasn't much left that was recognisably human.

'What the fuck were you playing at?' she hissed.

'Cait!' It was Lex, sounding as hoarse as she was. 'Christ, what's happening?'

'Just stay where you are,' she called. 'The drive'll be firing any minute.'

Nadira was shouting too now. 'Cait! Harris isn't in his harness!'

'I know.' She paused. 'He's with me.' She pushed herself up. 'Just let me get strapped in. I'll explain.'

She was wasting time. She hauled herself up onto Sharpe's harness, pulling with numbed fingers at the fastenings and limb covers. She hoped to hell it wasn't malfunctioning.

'Bren!' she called. 'Are you awake?'

There was no answer. She couldn't see any movement coming from Bren's harness.

Lex joined in. 'Bren, are you okay?'

Still nothing.

'I'll check on her,' he said.

'No!' Cait shouted. 'Stay where you are, there isn't time. Do what you're told for once. She's in her harness, isn't she?'

'Yes,' he called back.

'Well, leave her then. We'll check on her after the burn.'

She lay back and the limb covers inflated, pulling her tight into the harness. Christ, she hoped the calcs were right.

She heard a whine building somewhere behind her, doubling and redoubling until it became a wail, a shriek, a scream. As if the universe were breaking apart in a final death cry. It got louder still until her head felt like it would burst.

The drive fired.

Time slowed.

Breath came loud in her ears and a great weight pressed into her. Rainbow spectrums burst apart, filling her field of vision, so vivid they seared her eyes – and then they were plunging deep inside, passing over, through, within her. Lensing every molecule. Splitting her asunder. Until everything was colour – hue – shade – nothing.

She screamed.

Maybe she blacked out.

She woke to silence.

She breathed again. She released the harness's grip and leant over the side. Saw Harris again. Her stomach heaved, and she moaned as the vomit cascaded down and mixed with the blood below.

Tom's body had been smashed again and again into the bulkhead with the final surges of deceleration. His limbs were twisted helplessly. His torso was split open. Cait tore her gaze away as sobs racked her body, and she lost herself within them.

'Cait! Cait, are you okay?'

A hand touched her and she jerked away. She felt a sting on her bare flesh and darkness bloomed inside her again.

'She's going to be all right, isn't she?' Nadira asked, pulling a blanket over Cait as Lex activated the med-lab monitors.

Lex tapped the screens. 'None of the blood was hers at least, but she's had a bad shock. She needs rest.'

He pressed another hypo stick to her arm and emptied it. Nadira watched closely.

'Is that the only reason you're keeping her sedated?' she asked.

Lex spun on her, tossing the empty hypo onto a tray. 'Do you have a problem with me?'

They stood eyes locked, neither willing to back down.

'It's more a question of whether you have a problem with Cait,' Nadira said finally.

Lex's lips twisted angrily. 'I'm not keeping her under if that's what you mean. It's a light sedative, nothing more. Something to help her rest. Which, in my medical opinion, is what she needs right now. So why don't you leave me to get on with my work. I've got another patient to see to.'

Nadira was squaring up to respond when Bren stumbled into med lab and slumped against an access panel. 'Can you two keep it down? My head is splitting.'

Lex grabbed her arm and guided her to a stool. 'Jesus, are you okay?'

'Now, yes,' she said, for once allowing Lex to support her as she sat.

'What happened to you? When we couldn't get a response –'

'God! Is she okay?' Bren had caught sight of Cait lying on the ledge. When she looked at Lex, her eyes were filled with fear.

'She's fine. She's just had a shock.'

'Harris?' Bren said as her eyes strayed to the floor near Sharpe's harness. But Lex had already covered the body with a sheet.

'He's dead. There's nothing you or I or anyone can do for him. God knows why he was out of his harness.'

'Do you know what happened to him?' Nadira asked.

Bren shook her head briefly, then winced in pain and rubbed at her temples. 'There are gaps. I don't know – I thought I was going to blow every synapse in my brain. The burn took everything I had.'

'*You* ran the burn?' Lex asked, surprised.

Bren gave a humourless laugh. 'It's amazing how the threat of imminent death can focus the mind. I jockeyed this bitch right into the groove.' As she looked at Lex again he could see she was still caught up in the wonder of the experience despite the toll it had taken. 'Balancing all that power – it was unbelievable.'

'So what do you two intend to do now?'

Nadira's words broke in on Bren's reverie and she looked at her curiously.

'Nadira thinks we're about to hijack the mission,' Lex said, but his smile melted away as he added, 'We're going to catch that fucking comet by the tail, just like Cait and you wanted. Assuming your tracks are correct.'

'They're accurate,' Nadira said coldly. 'But they're no good unless we have Cait to pilot us in. With Sharpe dead, none of us are rated for that kind of manoeuvre.'

'Don't worry.' Lex laid a hand on Bren's shoulder. 'Our new quantum jockey can lay in the initial settings. Can't you?'

Bren shrugged his hand away. 'As soon as I get some codeine and caffeine I can.'

'So why don't you just back off and let us get on with our jobs,' Lex growled at Nadira.

She looked like she wanted to object, but instead she turned and walked away.

'Go easy, will you?' Bren warned. 'What's Nadira done to you?'

'I don't like people accusing me of things I haven't done.' He placed a hand on Bren's forehead and raised her right eyelid with his thumb to expose the eyeball. 'I think maybe I should examine you again.'

Bren brushed him away. 'I'll be fine. Just get me the painkillers. I can get the coffee myself.'

Cait felt numb all over and her eyelids seemed gummed together. She forced them open. Through blurred vision she made out the shape of someone standing over a large something lying on the deck.

She came around with a start. 'Harris!'

'Easy,' Lex said, sealing the body bag. He crossed to sit on a stool beside her. 'You can't help Harris now. Concentrate on yourself for once; you've been through a lot.'

Cait made to speak but Lex hushed her. 'And don't worry about the ship. Everything's fine. We're hours away from rendezvous.'

She let him ease her down onto the ledge. The last of the drugs faded away and her shoulders began to shake as she remembered Harris's twisted remains. She should have guessed he was up to something. She turned to face the wall as the tears flowed again. Thoughts churned around each other, threatening to drown her. How could they go on without Sharpe, without Harris?

Gradually her tears subsided and she became aware of her surroundings again. She felt washed clean. She still felt the pain of Harris's death, Sharpe's too, but what persisted most strongly wasn't sadness but a burning desire for the truth. It wasn't right they were dead. She wasn't looking to mete out blame; the concept was meaningless out here. All she wanted was to know, to understand what had happened and why. A final putting to rest. For all their sakes, living and dead.

She gave herself a few moments then sat up, breaking the silence. 'He didn't trust you, you know, Lex. He thought you and Bren were going to change the course settings.'

Lex pursed his lips. 'He had it in for Bren from the start. I guess he finally decided to put me in the same basket. And Nadira's obviously been thinking along the same lines – she damn near accused us both of piracy.' His eyes took on an unnerving intensity. '*You* don't think we're capable of that, do you? You trust us?'

Cait felt too vulnerable to be entirely truthful. 'I trust you to be true to yourself. I can't go further than that. As for Bren, I know she's not being open with me, and that worries me.'

Lex straightened and stared down at her. 'Christ, can't you lay off her? She saved the fucking ship. Again. Took over the burn when Phillips failed. If you ask me, you don't have to look much further than our friendly AI for the cause of all this. He's psychotic. He damn near smashed us into the planet.'

'Wait a minute.' Cait held up a hand, backtracking. '*Bren* guided the ship in?'

They'd been off course. It was almost beyond belief that a human, even an augmented one, could jockey the black box and balance the drive, let alone calculate pitch, yaw, rotation, adjust for mass, velocity, gravitational attraction ... Were Bren's abilities that far beyond the mortal?

'So she *was* conscious all the time?' Cait hesitated before asking, 'Did she say what happened to Harris?'

'She's got some memory loss,' Lex said, looking up at the readouts overhead. 'Running the drive was a hell of a strain. I haven't had a chance to check her out yet.'

Cait could tell Lex had his own doubts – Bren's memory gaps were too convenient an excuse – but she wasn't up to another argument. He was right about Phillips though. The AI's behaviour had been borderline when she woke up; he was hysterical.

Those identical readings between Bren and Phillips when they found Sharpe dead kept nagging at her. Was it possible Bren's link was affecting Phillips, making him more humanly fallible, or more something else? If transhumans were hard to fathom, how much hope did they have of understanding the workings of a mind with no baseline human referents? Phillips had definitely changed. Could the crew really trust him to look after them if he evolved past his original programming?

And Bren had some questions to answer. If she'd been linked and aware, she must have seen Harris moving around. Why didn't she at least warn him?

Cait watched Lex busying himself at the monitors. He'd been angry after Harris agreed to the course change. But he'd been well into deepsleep when Harris died. Lex may have had the motive but the opportunity wasn't there. Unless she was missing something. The list just kept on growing.

'How am I?' she asked.

'What?' Lex stared at her. 'You're fine. You can go.' He focused on the monitors again.

'Thanks a bundle.' Cait pushed off the bed and grabbed for a one-piece draped over the stool, feeling like she'd been dismissed.

'You'd better lock down med lab again,' she said, dressing quickly. 'I'll need all hands in the forward control.'

Lex nodded curtly.

She walked onto the central pathway, craning her neck to look around the ring. Bren was nowhere to be seen, but Nadira was hunkered down near her harness. Cait's gaze strayed to Harris's bagged body. There'd be a second burial to perform, but she had no more tears to shed right now, and too much work to do.

She looked back at Lex. 'Do you want me to give

you a hand with Harris?'

'No, thanks,' he snapped.

'Stop the spin in the ring when you're finished then. We won't need it for a while.'

She walked around the ring to Nadira, who was kneeling next to a pile of spare components. Her PAL sat on the deck beside her, its screen displaying circuit diagrams. She looked up, startled by Cait's approach.

Cait smiled tiredly. 'Need a hand with that?'

'Uhhh,' Nadira began, then exhaled loudly. 'Yes, thanks. These hypercaster schematics have me baffled. But are you okay?'

Cait was pleased to hear genuine concern in the question. She hunkered down beside the geophysicist and picked up a couple of modular chips. 'Yeah, I'm okay. Better than poor Harris anyway.'

She looked for a reaction but there was none. Had Nadira hated Harris that much?

She glanced at the PAL's screen and snapped a couple of pieces together while she considered her next question.

'Lex tells me you two had an argument?'

'The man's an idiot.'

'You don't have to tell me.'

Nadira dropped the pieces she was working on and bent her head, stretching out the neck muscles. Her hands hung limply from her knees.

'I don't mean to be antagonistic,' she said without

looking up. 'It's just the attitudes of people like Lex – and Harris, for that matter – they make me so angry.' Her head came up and she looked at Cait. 'It's the selfishness touted in your part of the world that's to blame – the sovereign right of the individual to do whatever they feel like and to hell with all the rest. It sickens me that people with so much can want so much more, while we had so little and shared what little we had.' She looked away and took a long, slow breath. 'I'm sorry, I don't want to lecture you. I just feel so alone sometimes.'

'You're not alone,' Cait said. 'We both are.'

Nadira laughed. It was a nice sound.

'I can appreciate your point of view,' Cait added. 'But we're not all like that.'

Nadira laughed again, but this time it was devoid of humour. 'I'll admit there are degrees of selfishness; sometimes it even masquerades as benevolence. But there've been too many broken promises, too many U-turns between our peoples, for me to believe anything else.'

'We come from two different worlds,' Cait agreed. 'Maybe the world ahead of us can bring us together. Maybe some good will come of the problems facing Earth right now.'

'You'll forgive me if I reserve judgement on that.'

Cait nodded. 'Trust is just as precious a commodity out here as it is back on Earth. It needs careful nurturing.' She began to gather stacks of chips together. 'But right now we need to stow this gear. We have to move to forward control.'

As they worked in companionable silence, Cait wondered at how far she'd come in her own thoughts and feelings. Before the last deepsleep, she'd felt close to being overwhelmed. It was only a kind of masochistic fortitude – a character trait forged long ago in her childhood – that had kept her going; not any sense of hope that the crew would put aside their differences, fix their technical problems, solve the puzzle of Sharpe's death, or make it to the system in one piece. Now she had another death to explain, and the crew seemed further apart than ever, and yet somehow she felt stronger, more capable. Given what had just happened, it certainly wasn't due to any external factors. It was something that came from within, a sense that she would overcome at least some of their problems because that's what *should* happen.

She shook her head. There wasn't any rational explanation, but still the feeling persisted, feeding her, strengthening her resolve. She was grateful for it.

# 11

Space closed in all around, stars piercing the darkness as the leviathan to port threatened to swamp Cait's senses. It seemed much too close.

Microlasers tracked eye movement and the helmet induced a slew of orbital data directly onto her optic nerve, overlaying the information on the roiling clouds of Iota Persei F. She blinked it away, preferring to focus on the swiftly moving bands of cloud, watching tendrils weave and curl around each other where they met, like smoke from an incense stick. The colours were striking: emerald greens, oranges, electric blues, all interspersed with fingers of white. Nothing like this existed in their backwater solar system: twice as big as Jupiter and far more garish.

An ominous purple eye hoved into sight, a gigantic anticyclone standing proud of the surrounding cloud deck. It stirred up the bands where they touched, shredding them, sucking them into its vortex and scattering them back along its path to slowly reassemble and await the approach of the next storm.

Cait inclined her head and the gyros in the hood shifted the view up and away from the planet towards the closest moon, F1. The course they were following was not without its dangers. The storms below were the visible result of an uneasy peace between the gas giant and its closest satellite. F1, scything through the planet's magnetosphere, generated billions of electronvolts in charge and hurled them back at Persei F in a series of mighty discharges. If Cait had any choice in the matter, they would have steered well clear of such a violent neighbourhood, but their quarry had chosen their path for them.

The hood resumed its tactical plot as she focused dead ahead once more. An endless progression of green-lined rings expanded towards and over her, over the ship. She imagined this was as close to bio-jacking as you could get without surgery. She was a part of the ship and, just as certainly, the ship had become an extension of her own body, accelerating faster through the plot rings at the twitch of a data-gloved finger.

When she'd taken the controls again after so long she'd felt wired. The worries and doubts fell away. This was what she knew. This was what she did best. But the atmosphere in the cramped compartment had quickly wrung all the pleasure out of the experience.

In the days following launch, when they'd begun threading their way through their own crowded solar system, they'd spent long hours strapped into these couches. No one had ever complained. It had seemed to Cait then that this had been their common ground – just doing the job. All of them were professionals; enthusiasm for their chosen field was what drove them. Then the arguments had started. She'd hoped they might recapture that feeling again, but too much had passed between them.

Lex sulked two rows back, while Bren, lying in the couch immediately behind Cait's left shoulder, seemed totally disconnected from everything. Even if there'd been time to talk to her about what had happened to Harris, Cait felt it would have been a waste of time with Bren as she was now. Nadira, on the face of it, seemed the most focused and entirely professional in her responses, but Lex's continued petulance couldn't help but rub her the wrong way.

'Coming up on sunlight,' Nadira said.

Cait's view dimmed as the filters kicked in, placing a black disc over the emerging star until only the corona was visible.

'Thar she blows,' she murmured.

Cresting the horizon was a dirty white mass, four kilometres long and three kilometres at its widest point, enveloped in a faintly fluorescing coma of gas and dust. The image dilated, centring on the target and interposing a grid to track the fine movement. The thing was rotating relatively quickly, about once every eight hours. *Magellan* was in a lower orbit to avoid the dust tail spreading back along the comet's path.

Cait extended a thumb, caressing the aft thrusters into life, and the ship slid closer. She was aiming for the gas envelope that extended in an oblique below the dust tail. She took the approach easy, fingers moulding the direction of the thrust, trimming it, and bringing them to a relative halt within the envelope.

'Reading fifty-six percent hydrogen, twenty-eight percent oxygen,' Nadira said. 'Plus carbon – dioxide and monoxide – methane, ammonia, formaldehyde. Picking up slight vibration within the coma. It could be fragmenting.'

'Problem?' Cait asked.

'No, the spin's holding it together. But we're lucky we're catching up with it now.'

'Thrusters at station keeping,' Cait said. 'Probes ready?' There was no answer. She chinned the hood mic, increasing the volume. 'Lex!'

'What?' he snapped.

Cait gritted her teeth against the urge to respond in kind. 'The scout probes, are they ready?'

'Yes, they're ready,' he said, sounding slightly abashed. 'Hatch opening. Drop in five, four, three, two, one. Probes away. Telemetry strong.'

His tone was dismissive, as if he wished he were anywhere but there and wanted the whole experience over with.

The tiny spheres dropped into the planet's

atmosphere. Simply but sturdily built sensor packets, they had no motive power of their own but quickly separated as they entered the cloud mass below and were blown wherever the winds took them. Cait followed them as long as she could, the video feed zooming in a stomach-turning chase until they disappeared into a continent-sized patch of green fog.

She turned her attention back to the comet, tweaking their position again for drift, and extended her left hand, which floated in her augmented view, disembodied in the vacuum of space. The refuel panel blossomed before her. She grasped the central joystick, twisted it and pushed it forward.

A section of *Magellan*'s hull slid back and the collector nozzle snaked out, trailing its flexible titanium-alloy hosing behind it. Cait eased the stick forward and the tiny thrusters on the collector head fired briefly, pushing the assembly further out from the ship towards the comet and the thickest part of the gas envelope. A fine mesh on the head protected its internal mechanism from all but the tiniest of comet fragments. At her insistence, the collector concertinaed open, spreading its protective mesh wider. The profile of the fully deployed head began to create a negative pressure within the tenuous environment and sucked hungrily at the comet's outpourings.

The valving system at the ship end split the intake, most of it passing to the ship's reprocessing hoppers, while the rest sprayed across the hull exterior through a ring of ducts near the nose, creating a uniform skin over the cracked and pockmarked water-ice shield.

'You're doing fine,' Bren said. Cait was startled by the sound of her voice in her hood after such a long silence. 'At this rate we should be in surplus in one hour.'

Cait increased the nozzle's capacity to the max, hoping to trim as much time as possible from the collection.

'Autopilot engaged,' she said and pulled off the data hood, blinking in the sudden brightness of the forward cabin. 'Keep an eye on the comet, will you, Bren?'

Bren grunted and withdrew into silence again.

Cait craned around to look over her right shoulder towards Nadira and Lex.

Lex was watching the feed from the probes. His face seemed fixed in a constant sneer, brow heavily furrowed, thick lines framing his mouth. Nadira's expression was slack by contrast; she seemed to be staring into oblivion.

'You okay?' Cait asked her.

'Hmmm?' Her eyes focused again and her hand moved instinctively to the data point. 'Yes, fine.'

The monitor showed an image of Horizon, probably the best yet.

'I've been gathering some visuals for comparison,' Nadira said, nodding towards the picture. 'The planet's albedo isn't quite matching the ISS shots. I thought maybe it was a calibration problem.'

Cait nodded. 'Could be, but it's not unlikely that it is different. We're a hell of a lot closer than the ISS in terms of distance and elapsed time.'

It was Nadira's turn to nod, but she still seemed troubled.

'Keep on it,' Cait encouraged her. 'We're not going anywhere for a while, and it'll be useful to gather what prelims we can.'

'The probes have passed through the upper deck of ammonia crystals,' Lex called, and punched a split-screen view from both scouts to the monitor above Cait's head. 'Pressure's rising fast. High concentrations of hydrogen and helium.' A large mirror-like mass appeared ahead of the left-hand probe and it plunged into it. 'Bodies of liquid water too.'

Cait settled back in her couch to enjoy the show. Lex sounded a little happier now that telemetry from the probes was coming through, or perhaps it was simply the chance to do something useful after such a long wait. The data they gathered here would provide years of analysis work.

For Cait, the familiarity of Persei F's internal structure was reassuring in another way. It boded well for their rendezvous with Horizon, which certainly appeared Earth-like in all the parameters that mattered.

The tiny probes scudded through the atmosphere, the images brightening and darkening with the intensity of the gases they encountered. And then, suddenly, they were in darkness.

'Switching to X-ray sensing,' Lex said. 'Let's see what kind of a core this thing has.'

The monitor images dissipated into static snow and then showed a scene of midnight black shot through with coruscating quicksilver blobs. Speed was difficult to gauge, but the probes appeared to be slowing as the seconds ticked off and they moved through a denser environment.

Cait let her mind wander, imagining what it was like that far down. As the pressure rose past three million atmospheres, hydrogen atoms would begin to break down, blowing off their electrons so the gas changed rapidly into liquid metal. The incredible heat and radiation generated would explode outwards, driving the supersonic winds in the upper layers of the atmosphere and the huge magnetic field extending millions of kilometres into space. It was possible that even more exotic matter existed beyond this layer. The probes were their only chance of finding out. Rated to four million atmospheres, their sensors could penetrate far deeper, but component failure was a given under such punishing conditions.

The couch held her securely as she watched the steady progress of the probes, and her eyelids drooped as the intense concentration of the last hours caught up with her.

•

The hull rang around her and Cait was thrown heavily against the restraining straps. The X-ray image flared and dissolved into static.

'What the hell was that?' she called, even as she was pulling the hood over her head again. The probe's demise certainly wasn't to blame.

'The comet's breaking apart,' she heard Bren say, and her breath caught in her throat. She watched through the hood as a large lump of the icy conglomerate bounced off the hull, setting off another racket. It cartwheeled ponderously in the vacuum and started to fall back towards them.

'Breaking apart!' Cait shouted as her virtual view shifted to the spread of comet pieces. 'It's almost totally disintegrated!'

Most of the larger chunks had begun to string out in a necklace along the original orbit, but enough were headed their way to cause serious damage. The hood tagged the largest chunks, displaying speeds from 0.5 to 5 metres per second relative velocity.

'Brace for emergency manoeuvres.'

Cait grasped at the thruster icons and pulled backwards and down. There was a surprised scream from Nadira and a swallowed curse from Lex.

The closest piece of debris missed the rebound and sailed past the drive section, but another faster lump impacted on the nose. The ship yawed violently as oxygen vented from a hull breach. Tell-tales lit up red across Cait's field of view and she tried desperately to compensate for the new vector as she searched for a safe path out of there. Tiny particulates rained down on the hull, sounding like a hailstorm.

'Emergency lock's functional,' Lex called above the din. 'It's hold number six. Rock foam's forming round the hole. Hardening. Okay, we've got positive pressure.'

Cait risked another puff of thrust to bring them closer in to Persei F, watching the altitude count off rapidly in her peripheral field. Seeing her chance, she fired the starboard nose thruster, slewing the ship around and punching for full thrust. The acceleration slammed the breath out of her as the ship dodged the leading edge of the scattering particles and lanced through the dust tail out into clear space once more.

'Get me a damage report, someone,' she called as she trimmed their velocity and sent them into a higher orbit, well above and behind the comet.

'We're okay,' Lex said. 'Some cracking in the water-ice shield. Nothing we can't handle. I'll check out the breach site.'

She heard him free himself from the couch and head aft as she wrestled herself out of the data hood. She pulled angrily at the gloves, crumpling them and throwing them forward. As she undogged the restraints, she spun in her couch to glare accusingly at Bren. The systems specialist looked pale with terror.

'Come with me,' Cait said with what she felt was remarkable control. 'I want to check out the hoppers.'

She pulled herself over the top of the couch and sailed towards the exit. She didn't wait for the younger woman, but pushed on into the dimly lit hold to the main hopper panel. She grabbed onto the webbing above the gauge as her hands began to shake. She could hear Bren behind her, breathing heavily.

'Where the hell is your head at?' she said, her voice husky. 'One second you're balancing the drive and the next you can't even keep tabs on a fucking comet!'

She gripped the webbing until her knuckles whitened, willing her shaking muscles to relax and forcing her breathing to slow.

When she turned, she was shocked by Bren's appearance. Tears welled up and clung to her eyeballs with nowhere to go in the zero-g. Her whole body was shivering. She sniffed noisily and wiped her eyes clear.

'Do you really think that I'd kill Sharpe? Kill Harris?' Bren said. 'Is that what you think I'm capable of?'

Killed. Cait shied away from the word, but it was out in the open now. Ugly. And with a skein of implications she didn't want to consider. She felt centuries old.

'I'm not accusing anyone of anything,' she said. 'I just want it all to make sense. I want to understand what's happening with you. Ever since you woke up, you've been all hard edges, folded in on yourself. If there's something troubling you, we need to talk it through.'

Even as Cait spoke, Bren changed. The shivering ceased and her mouth hardened. 'You can't help me. You don't even know what it's like *being* me. So save your breath.'

She pulled on a cargo net and headed for the access ladder, and climbed down and away from Cait.

'Tell me what happened to Harris!' Cait shouted after her, but Bren climbed through the opening to the access tube and was gone.

Frustration welled in Cait. She turned back to the hopper and slapped the metal casing. The dial read eighty-four percent: they wouldn't have to go chasing comets again for a while.

She pushed off the hopper, tumbling in an arc until her feet connected with the ladder in the aft bulkhead. She wasn't going to be put off any longer.

Climbing quickly down into the central web, she launched herself through the now motionless access tube and trimmed her trajectory at the other end by kicking off the lip of the tube towards the solitary pool of light near her harness. She landed on all fours near the computer port and reached up slowly, grabbing the chair back and pulling herself over and into a sitting position.

Bren was nowhere to be seen.

# 12

The monitor was on, and Cait adjusted the lap sash before typing in her command access using the eight-character scat keyboard. Her fingers played over the keys, setting up a quick search on the monitor logs to begin playback from the instant movement had been detected in the ring.

The search meter built rapidly to one hundred percent.

<nil results> flashed bright green.

Damn. She punched a query and the message changed.

<log erasure>

A deliberate act, or another malfunction? Without evidence it was another dead end.

She thumped back into the seat, rebounding until the lap sash halted her. Really, it was the digital equivalent of Bren's memory gaps … Then a new possibility unfolded. If the log was being tampered with, was that tampering unwittingly, or deliberately, causing Bren's memory loss? And who was doing the tampering? Someone on board, or someone on Earth?

Cait had to acknowledge that the latter was a possibility. Technology moved on. The hypercaster was an example of that. Could the same device covertly affect ship's systems at such a distance, maybe even fire the drive?

This was beginning to sound like paranoia. But the drive had fired. Harris had died. What would be the aim of such an attack? Who was it directed at? And was Bren a target, an accomplice, or just a bystander caught in the crossfire?

A small green oval blinking in the bottom left of the monitor caught Cait's attention. She leant forward and pushed her thumbprint against it. The screen wiped and Harris was staring at her from the same seat she was sitting in, looking just as he had the last time they'd spoken.

'Hi, Cait.' He grinned at her. 'I hope you're listening to this alone, and I'm sorry for not telling you sooner. I guess I'm just an untrusting son of a bitch. But I've been backwards and forwards through this friggin' computer and I'm sure there's something going on. Whether it's Bren or whatever, I don't know. But I think I can find out if I sneak up on it. If you're listening to this, it goes to show I wasn't smart enough. But maybe I have a few tricks left in me. I don't trust the ship monitors, not after last time. So I've set up the PALs to record things. They won't be able to snoop on the computer without getting caught, but they might show you something that will help.'

Cait glanced at her own PAL hovering over her left shoulder. The silent sentinels were so easy to forget when you weren't actually using them.

'Harris!' She heard her own voice calling out, sounding worried.

Harris turned away from the camera and waved. 'Here!' he called, then quickly turned back. 'Guess it's time to go. Good luck. And, Cait ... watch your back.'

Cait's palms were sweating as she reached for the keypad again. Sharpe's PAL had a good view of the access port. It responded instantly, blue eye wakening as the download began. She punched the same search.

The monitor screen flashed once, twice, and Harris swam out of the darkness to manoeuvre himself in front of the console. The faux gravity had been cut well back for this leg of the journey. The PAL was looking down at the top of his head, but she could see his eyes and read the frustration building on his face as he fired inquiry after inquiry through the keypad.

Suddenly, he leaned towards the monitor until his nose was almost touching it. 'What the fuck is that?' he whispered, just loud enough for the pickups. Then he looked up at the PAL, his eyes wide with terror as a whining sound began to build – the black box drive.

Frantic now, he tumbled out of the chair, losing his footing in his haste and scrabbling wildly for the nearby harness as his feet left the floor. He began to drift away, his arms straining out in front, fingers trembling, reaching for Sharpe's harness webbing.

The whine grew louder, became a scream, a shriek.

'Help me!' he shouted above the noise. One finger touched the webbing.

Cait reached out to the image on the screen, urging him on, hoping against reason.

Another finger latched on, the two curling, pulling him in until he could grasp the webbing firmly, make a fist. A rainbow began to unfold around him, doubling and tripling. The image was breaking up. The wail of the drive was unbearable. She glimpsed Harris's feet as he disappeared in a firestorm of colour. The shriek of the drive cut off abruptly. The crescendo ended in a sound she never wanted to hear again.

Seconds passed. She realised she'd been holding her breath through the playback. The air escaped her in a low, ragged moan, sounding like an injured animal. She fought to regain some semblance of control as her thoughts came unstuck. Experiencing the aftermath had been bad enough …

She closed her eyes and allowed herself a moment. Then she reached out again and keyed the download from Harris's PAL that was locked down above his harness to replay the same time sequence.

She watched the monitor as the resurrected Harris pulled himself free of the webbing, dressed and stood groggily. Phillips should have responded to movement in the ring by now. What the hell had gone wrong? Then she realised. Harris had known Bren was staying linked during the inward trip. His work on the computer had included rendering himself invisible to the ship's sensors and – as a result – to Bren. It was the only way he could have moved around without being challenged.

Jesus! Just how many people were screwing with things without her knowledge?

The playback ended as Harris moved out of view. Cait checked her own PAL, but it hadn't registered a thing. He'd seen something in the monitor though, just before he died. She was sure of it.

'What did you find, Tom?' she asked the silent room. 'And who else knows about it?'

Cait hooked her foot into a gap near the lock door and, with Lex's help, pushed Harris through the opening. Bren and Nadira were watching, floating in the hold on safety lines just like last time. Cait could feel Harris's meaty shoulder through the thin bag and tried to stop her mind replaying his final seconds of life. An autopsy was pointless. She knew how he'd died, she just didn't know why.

The body drifted through the opening, knocking gently on the outer door and turning slowly longwise.

'I guess I should –'

'Oh, spare us for Christ's sake.' Lex rode in over

the top of her. 'Not another pep talk. I couldn't stand the hypocrisy.'

Cait drifted back against the bulkhead, shocked by the venom in Lex's voice.

'You're as bad as Harris,' he went on. 'He died because he was a stupid bigot without sense enough to work out who he should be afraid of. I thought you were smarter than that.'

'Get a grip,' Cait barked, trying to rein in her own sudden anger.

'No, *you* get a grip. Bren's saved this ship twice, and you still don't trust her.'

'Leave it, Lex,' Bren warned from her safety line above them.

'I can't leave it,' he said, glancing towards her. 'It's not just about you any more. Her behaviour's putting everyone at risk.'

'There's only one person here whose behaviour is causing trouble,' Nadira said.

'I might have guessed you'd back her up, just because she's willing to go along with whatever bullshit your Compact feeds us.'

Nadira floated to within a couple of inches of Lex. 'Have I told you how monumentally irritating you are? You're a spoilt child, and we'd all do a lot better if we didn't have to listen to your constant bitching.'

'This is getting us nowhere,' Cait said. She had to calm the situation down, no matter how badly she wanted Nadira to tear into Lex. 'You've got a complaint, Lex, I'm happy to listen to it. But I resent the implication that I'm treating anyone on board unfairly. Right now I don't know who or what's to blame for Sharpe's or Harris's death. I've got an open mind, but we have to consider the facts.'

'The facts!' Lex flung his arms wide in frustration. 'The facts are that Sharpe was killed when all of us – *all* of us – were in deepsleep. There was no equipment malfunction. And it wasn't natural causes. It's fuckin' obvious that Phillips did it. It was only Harris's one-eyed prejudice that made anyone think otherwise. But the shit stuck, didn't it?'

'Phillips was offline when Sharpe died,' Cait said. 'Harris was killed when the drive fired outside Phillips's control. He's just as much a victim of this as we are.'

'Jesus! That is exactly what he wants you to think. It's obvious he's lying.'

'That's one interpretation,' Cait countered.

'Okay then, look at your precious facts. Bren and Harris went over every inch of Phillips's systems and found nothing wrong, because there *was* nothing wrong. I don't know why he's doing it – shit, who can figure an AI – but I do know he's in there, waiting for any one of us to make a mistake, just like Harris, and leave ourselves vulnerable. He knows we can't shut him off indefinitely, not if we want to use the drive again. But we can't even begin to fight him until you acknowledge that Bren has nothing to do with it.'

'So why couldn't Bren stop Phillips killing Harris?' Nadira asked. 'She was linked. Why is she suffering memory loss with no physiological reason?'

Lex's jaw clenched tight. He looked like he would have gladly punched Nadira if they weren't in freefall. Bren floated above them all like a brooding angel. He looked up at her, clearly wanting to defend her but not knowing how.

'We need to understand what really happened,' Cait said softly, 'if we've got any hope of getting past this.'

'I don't want to be a part of this mission any more,' Bren said. 'I don't want to be a part of you.'

She pulled herself towards the bulkhead, allowing her feet to drift around and over her head until they met solid wall. Then she kicked off towards the access tube above.

Cait watched Bren go, unable to think of anything to say that would make her change her mind. Instead she focused again on Lex.

'I'm not into witchhunts. All I want is to make sure that next time we wake up, we're all still alive. You bring me proof that Phillips is solely to blame and we'll bury this thing and get on with our jobs. In the meantime, we can't afford to take risks. And it's all the more urgent that we establish direct communication with Earth.'

'What?' Lex said, suddenly unsure of himself. 'Why?'

'Because if we can't trust Phillips, we're going to have to rely on their computing power to get us to Horizon. I can't see any alternative. Can you?'

For once Lex was silent.

'Fine. Now can we pay our respects to Harris.'

Cait pressed down on the control and the hatch closed over. The outer door opened, just as before, but the view was very different. Iota Persei F filled the opening, its interwoven fingers of cloud seeming to reach towards them, waiting to receive Harris.

The body began to move through the hatch.

'Journey safely,' Nadira said quietly.

'Rest in peace,' Cait added as the opening closed over.

13

Three ship days had passed since the comet rendezvous. Three days circling the bloated girth of Iota Persei F. Three days to complete the new hypercaster. Three days to check over Phillips's systems again and find precisely nothing.

From Cait's point of view, the rest of the crew were spread along a spectrum of disaffection. Bren was at the extreme end, avoiding any contact, even with Lex, and preferring to take her meals alone. Next came Lex, oscillating between bare civility, crabbiness and open hostility. Cait guessed the main source of his anger was twofold: at Bren for freezing him out, and at himself for hurting her in some way that he didn't fully understand. If that wasn't enough, he still had his opposition to the mission changes, his annoyance with the other members of the crew – especially Cait – for not seeing things entirely his way, and his regular state of being pissed off at the world in general to keep him going.

Nadira's responses were at least approaching

'friendly' by normal standards, but Cait wasn't kidding herself that they'd resolved all their problems. Their relationship had stalled: Nadira would support Cait only so far as Cait's actions accorded with her own worldview and the wishes of the Compact. At the heart of it was a lack of trust, and Cait had no idea how they could move on from there.

Instead, she kept busy, splitting her time between helping Nadira with the hypercaster and engineering a more permanent repair to the hull. She liked EVA even less than zero-g. There was something uncomfortably humbling about being on the outside of the hull. And being so close to the gibbous Iota Persei F, she was torn between the sensation that it was in imminent danger of falling on top of her or she was close to falling into it.

Harris got there before you, she thought, and shook her head. Concentrate. She couldn't afford the distraction out here. One mistake could prove fatal.

She ran the sensor nodes in the fingers of her suit glove over the latest series of welds and watched the readout on her sleeve. The fix was as good as she could get it. Not pretty, but then she was a little out of practice. She straightened and walked slowly around the arc of the hull, the spikes on her boots grabbing into the water-ice shield as she moved.

She'd found time to scan the PAL logs of the others too, but had turned up nothing new. It was another dead end, but one that pricked her curiosity, like an irritating fragment of chaff that had worked its way into the weave of her garment: she knew something was there, she could feel it, but she hadn't found it yet.

Her suit com bleeped and she chinned the mic.

'No luck,' Lex said, sounding crestfallen. 'I can't access any of the higher functions without tripping the Phillips persona and there's no way to bypass him. The algorithm's too deeply connected.'

'Then we're going to have to live with it, and contact Bowen. The hypercaster's ready. I'm coming in.'

The hatch was open and waiting. She knelt down and grabbed the opening, making sure of her grip before dislodging her feet from the hull. As she moved inside, she pulled her safety line along behind and pressed the contact. The door slid silently shut and the lock pressurised.

Nadira was already waiting for her at the workbench, keen to re-establish contact with Bowen. No time for a shower, Cait thought, and sat beside the other woman in front of the hypercaster box. She activated a contact on the benchtop.

'Get me Bren,' she said. The tell-tale showed the connection was made. 'Bren, can you hear me?'

Nothing.

'We're about to contact Earth, Bren.'

Still nothing.

'It appears she meant what she said,' Nadira

commented.

'It's not the response I would have expected. The old Bren was never so thin-skinned. Something's changed her.'

Lex reached the bottom of the access ladder and joined them at the workbench. The completed hypercaster was a featureless grey rectangle the size of a palm reader.

'So this is going to rip up the physical laws of the universe and toss them in the waste basket?' he said. 'It doesn't look like much.'

'We don't know if it works yet,' Nadira said.

'I still don't think we should use it,' Lex continued without much conviction. 'We're buying into a whole world of trouble if we do.'

Poor Lex, Cait thought. She knew he was just going through the motions. He'd backed himself into a corner by insisting Phillips was untrustworthy. Contacting Earth was the only option if they wanted to get moving again.

'We're agreed on how we handle this?' she asked. 'We don't commit to anything without the opportunity to discuss it amongst ourselves first. Our main objective should be to gather information and find out what their intentions are. That's the only way we can make up our minds what to do.'

'I still don't like the way you put that,' Nadira said. 'It sounds like you've already decided not to cooperate.'

'No, but you've got to admit we haven't been given much to go on,' Cait countered. 'The single recorded message we've received falls far short of full disclosure. Bowen's asked for our understanding and assistance but hasn't provided the data we need to facilitate it, and we can't simply go on faith. We have to be able to discuss our options sensibly as a group, and to do that we need as full a briefing as possible.' She hesitated, trying to gauge Nadira's reaction. Would she break ranks?

'I'd also prefer we didn't mention the wyrm. Not because I don't trust them,' Cait added quickly. 'But whoever sent it meant to do us harm, and we don't know how secure the channel will be. If they find out the wyrm failed, they might try to hurt us some other way.'

Nadira's face darkened but she said no more.

Cait looked towards the access tube. 'I guess Bren's not coming. Let's get on with it then.' Her fingers touched the keys on the tabletop. 'I'm linking the unit to comms now. Initialising broadcast.'

A sphere of crackling grey static coalesced at the far end of the workbench, expanding rapidly to swallow everything in a three-metre radius, then turning abruptly black.

'We've picked up the carrier signal,' Cait said.

The dark globe deformed, bulging in the centre and stretching at the edges. A thick oblong pushed out towards them. Colour bled in as finer details began to resolve.

Enoch Bowen sat behind the same desk they'd seen him at before. Cait started to catalogue how much he'd changed from the first message. His eyes were more sunken now, the nose more prominent, and his hair had thinned at the temples. The image they'd seen in the first broadcast was of Bowen from six months earlier. It had obviously been a hard six months.

'You've made it,' he said, sitting back and sweeping the fine blond hair away from his face.

'We're in the system,' Cait agreed. 'But not exactly where you might expect us to be.'

Bowen was instantly alert, the lines around his eyes deepening. 'Where then?'

'We're orbiting Iota Persei F,' Cait said and paused. He'd hidden his reaction well but she was sure she'd seen a surge of anger there, just for a moment. 'We've experienced some computer problems. Your course change didn't load fully, and we decided to replenish the hoppers before reaching Horizon.'

'*Your* command decision?' Bowen probed.

'Yes. My command decision.' There was no point arguing.

'I'm sure your actions were appropriate within the confines of your knowledge regarding the situation here, Commander Dyson. But under the circumstances I must insist that all future decisions be cleared through launch control.'

Cait felt Lex kick her shin lightly, but she needed no prompting on that point. 'If it's practical, I'm happy to comply of course. But some situations may need a more immediate response.'

Bowen's eyes strayed to a point above their heads and to one side. Was someone else in the room with him? He looked at her again and appeared to dismiss the topic.

'In any case, I'm glad we can finally talk.' He sat straighter. 'Congratulations to you and your crew on surviving such a hazardous journey.'

Cait paused, not sure how much to tell him. 'We haven't exactly come through unscathed,' she said. 'My offsider, Sharpe, died in deepsleep, and Specialist Harris was killed during our final manoeuvre in-system.'

Bowen bowed his head. 'I'm shocked. And saddened by the news. Those men were true heroes.' His gaze lifted to Cait again. 'Your computer problem – was it a factor in the deaths?'

Cait glanced at Lex. 'We're not sure yet. But the AI integration is unstable. In fact, we can't go any further without your assistance in calculating the next burn sequence.'

'I see.' Bowen sat forward and held out one hand in front of him, palm down. A glowing panel, apparently composed purely of light, appeared beneath it. 'We'll need your precise position, plots of all bodies between there and Horizon, orbital data, you know the type of thing.' His fingers pecked at different segments of the panel. 'We can pilot by remote control with the hypercaster link in place.'

Again a warning tap from Lex.

'That won't be necessary for such a short sequence,' Cait said. 'The subsystems here can handle it if we're sure of the math. I'm sending our latest plots now.' She hit the commit toggle on the desk and the download began.

Bowen watched his panel, appearing to consider something. Cait felt as if she was playing a game of chess with only half the board visible to her while her opponent could see everything.

'We'll have the calculations as soon as humanly possible,' Bowen said and sliced his hand across the panel, which promptly vanished. 'Now to the mission proper. Once you reach the planet, you will undertake a complete survey of the biosphere and assess its suitability for immediate settlement. You will also, as a matter of course, claim it for the People's Compact. We need to establish our –'

'Uh, just a minute,' Cait said. 'Am I missing something here? This is a multinational mission. If we're claiming anything, we're claiming it for everyone, right?'

Bowen sighed and his lips parted in a tight smile. 'History has been crowded while you slept, Commander Dyson. There is no international forum for such claims and, consequently, no basis in law.' His face hardened. 'This is a Compact ship and any actions taken aboard it are solely on behalf of the Compact.'

Cait expected an outburst from Lex, but he was the essence of diplomacy.

'If I might, Mr Bowen, it would help us come to terms with things a lot quicker if we knew exactly what the nature of the emergency was. We're on a steep learning curve here.'

Cait was impressed. Lex had delivered the line without a hint of sarcasm.

'Of course. You must be feeling very disoriented by now. There really is no precedent for this kind of communication. But I must preface my explanation with a little background detail.' Bowen relaxed back into his chair. 'You know something of the events leading up to the Popular Invasion, I think. The potential for conflict between our two nations had been building for some time. Even so, no one had imagined the eventual catalyst. But in anticipating a war, one must prepare for many eventualities. Some preparations are never intended for actual use because to do so would be devastating to both sides. Even so, the threat of their existence can be enough to sway a conflict in one side's favour. You are familiar with the concept?'

'You're talking about a doomsday weapon,' Lex said.

Bowen's eyes took on the haunted look Cait had

seen earlier. 'One of our sister nations developed a new kind of pathogen: a soil bacteria that would decimate the Pax's wheat belts by changing the genetic structure of the plants themselves, making them infertile. Even as our soldiers were peacefully occupying the Pax capital, the pathogen escaped without warning. The precautions to contain it proved inadequate and, once outside the controlled environment, it multiplied and spread at an alarming rate. It evaded every effort to halt its progress across the globe. Within barely half a decade there was a strain running wild on every continent. We tried to build new resistant plants but the pathogen confounded our efforts at every turn. Wheat as a viable crop became almost non-existent.

'Things were bad, but with time we felt we could recover. It was then that the crisis worsened. The bacteria mutated to vector not only wheat, but maize, barley, rye, even rice. Only isolated pockets of unaffected land persist now, and they're constantly under threat. There is nothing we can do to fill such a gaping hole in our biosphere. Our only hope is to leave Earth, transplant the few unaffected seed crops that remain, and start again. This is why Horizon is so important to us. We have only one shot at this. Building the colony ships has taken everything we have left. We dare not dispatch them unless we are absolutely sure the planet will support us.'

'And those ships will carry only Compact citizens,'

Lex prompted.

'Horizon will be ours,' Bowen said. 'We have limited space on the ships. Should we leave behind our own citizens in favour of foreign nationals? The other nations would not do the same for us.'

'So what's to stop the others sending their own colony ships?' Cait asked.

Bowen looked at her through heavily lidded eyes. 'Commander Dyson, the world is slowly starving to death. Nations are already at each other's throats. The resources each has left are jealously guarded. The Compact cannot afford to act otherwise. Any attempt by other nations to annex Horizon would bring down a conflagration on Earth that would kill everyone a great deal faster than the food shortages.'

Cait could hardly believe what she was hearing.

'There's no chance of cooperation?' she pressed.

'None. In order for such a venture to succeed, there must be a common basis of trust. Nothing like that exists here any more.'

The silence lengthened and Cait thought about her own predicament. Trust was certainly the key to a lot of things.

'So,' Lex said, 'as I understand it, we're to proceed to Horizon as fast as we're able, officially claim it for the Compact, and scope the planet with a view to possible colonisation. If it's feasible, you'll dispatch the colony ships and quit Earth for resettlement.'

Bowen nodded. 'These are the hard decisions we have had to work through, Specialist Dalziel. The Compact has always worked for the greater good of the greatest number. That truism carried us safely through the Popular Invasion and improved the lot of the common people in the former Pax.'

'I suppose not everyone saw things in those terms,' Lex said.

'You would be surprised how many did. Of course, there were some zealots to be dealt with. Our action to suppress their operation was swift, and minimised any collateral casualties.'

Cait wasn't sure where Lex was going with all this, or whether he just wanted to keep Bowen talking to gain as much data as possible. But as Bowen spoke about the invasion, her thoughts turned painfully to her family.

'Under the circumstances,' she began, then hesitated. 'I'm sorry, this might seem like a fairly petty request ... but I have a brother. And he has a family – a wife and two girls. I'd be grateful for any news of them.'

Again Bowen glanced towards his hidden watcher and Cait felt her stomach turn.

'Of course,' he said, standing again. 'It may take a while. Our information from that time is incomplete. As I mentioned, there was a disaffected minority, some of whom sabotaged much of the Pax central records. But I'm sure they'll be all right.'

He paused, and there was calculation in the way he

looked at her, Cait thought. He was weighing her up. Had she just handed him a lever?

'It's just a matter of time,' he finished. 'So, if there's nothing else, we'll transmit the burn figures shortly.'

'We'll stand by,' Cait said and blanked the image. Her eyes were stinging with tears and she wiped them away.

'He's bullshitting you about your relatives,' Lex said softly.

'I know, dammit.'

The tears came again and she pulled at the sleeve of her coverall to dab at them. Lex's hand enfolded her own and squeezed briefly before withdrawing.

'What do you mean?' Nadira asked.

Cait turned to her. 'They've had months, possibly years, to find my brother and his kids. We're too important to them for it to be otherwise.'

She thought of Bowen's eyes again. He was cold, capable of anything, including a delicate game of veiled threats. But it wasn't a game to her. This was her family – their lives were in the balance, along with the lives of an entire world.

Cait had met people like Bowen before. They could turn anyone and anything into a pawn to be used or discarded. There was one rule in this type of play: trust no one. It sickened her. He was more than a launch director. The profile this mission had assumed with the Compact demanded it. He'd been placed in charge to make sure the Compact got what it wanted.

'And if they'd lie to us about that,' Lex was saying, 'what else are they lying about?'

'Maybe that's the way they do things in the Pax, but not in the Compact,' Nadira said.

'Oh, wake up,' Lex snapped. 'This is the real deal. No one – EU, Compact, whatever – is going to pass up the opportunity to apply a little pressure if it serves a purpose. They want to make sure we toe the line, and if that means taking some hostages, so be it.'

'Not – my – people.' Nadira enunciated every word as if it was carved in stone.

'Everyone,' Lex sneered. 'Everyone. Even your caring, sharing Compact. Although they don't seem very sharing with our new planet, do they?'

'Stop it,' Cait said. She felt muzzy-headed. It was all she could do to rouse herself to head off another argument. Where was the trust, for God's sake?

Lex snorted and sat back, arms folded and a smug look on his face.

Cait thought of Bren, the accusations she'd made about her, the guilty thoughts she'd had. Was Bren murderer or victim? And Bowen, was he liar or saviour? There had to be a better way to move forward without mistrust, threats, accusations.

'We've got to discuss our next move,' she said, dragging her thoughts to the here and now. 'Bowen isn't going to give us time to think once the calculations are ready. But I don't feel comfortable making a decision without including Bren.'

Lex slowly unfolded his arms and sat forward. Cait didn't like the look on his face.

'You want me to talk to her?' he said.

Cait considered it. There was no way Bren would listen to her, or Nadira. Not after the argument in the hold. Lex had already proved he wasn't above running his own agenda, but opening up dialogue was all that mattered now.

'Okay,' she said finally.

'I'll try not to be too long,' he said, standing.

'Tell her …' Cait began, and hesitated as he turned to her. 'Tell her I won't ask her any more questions. She can pick her own time if she wants to tell me anything. I won't press her. But we need her with us.'

# 14

Lex had a good idea where Bren would be even without his PAL to locate her. The sphere moved up the wall track beside him, slowly detaching as the gravity fell away and using its tiny fans to manoeuvre above and behind his left ear. He swam through the rearward tube and emerged in darkness.

The bulk of the space aft was taken up with storage hoppers assembled in a ring around the access lock to the drive section, but there was a gap of a couple of metres between them and the enclosed drum of the ring behind him. Lex pulled himself over the edge of the tube and stood on its exterior. He flexed his knees and kicked off, moving up along the outside of the drum towards its outer edge. He reached above his head to press against the hull and halt his motion as he came level with the top of the ring. There, tethered to the bulkhead in a wedge-shaped space that tapered towards the ring's far end, lay a darkened figure that could only be Bren. The sound of her breathing came slow and heavy as if she were asleep.

Lex's PAL lit the area with its searchlight and he saw she was wide awake, staring at him.

'What do you want?' she said, sounding more tired than hostile.

Lex pulled himself into the cramped space and settled against the bulkhead. 'They sent me to try to coax you back. Cait says she won't be asking any more awkward questions – until the next time.' He flashed her a grin. 'But I came because I wanted to say I'm sorry.'

He pulled himself closer and rested his feet on top of the ring housing. 'I lost it. I got so angry with Cait – but I didn't mean to drag you into it. It was stupid. *I* was stupid.'

'I'm still pissed off with you,' Bren said.

Lex knelt beside her, grabbing a handhold on the top of the housing to anchor himself. 'Bren, I want you to understand that I'm not like Cait or Harris. I trust you – unconditionally. I don't believe you'd ever do anything to hurt any one of us. And I'm not looking for any explanations from you either.'

'But you are looking for backing to reject the mission changes.'

Lex shook his head. 'That's a side issue. I'm more concerned about our relationship. I don't want to lose you as a friend because of something I did.'

Bren reached up and took hold of her own PAL, cradling it in her hands and looking deep into its electronic eye as if it were the family pet, or a kindred spirit.

'We came here for the good of humanity,' she said. 'I'm not sure I know what that means any more.'

'*I* know.' Lex placed his hand on hers. Her skin felt cool. 'This is what it means – this simple contact. The fact that we exist together, share the same dreams, the same struggles. On this ship is the only humanity that has meaning for me now – *can* have any meaning. Because we all came for the same reason: to discover; to learn beyond the bounds of our understanding.'

'You sound like Cait,' she said.

'No. She's willing to give it all away for Earth. I'm not. Horizon has its own destiny, and that doesn't include being meddled with for the sake of a planet full of humans I barely understand any more. And it should be like that for all of us. We need to look after ourselves first, because no one else will.'

She pulled gently away from him and let the PAL go.

'You have a unique view of the universe, Lex. But I don't feel I can trust anyone on board now. I've never had an "us" before, only a "me". I grew up in the Florida Ghettos, you know, living on welfare handouts – those I could hide from the street packs. I took the chip because it was the only way to escape, to be free, to start living – I thought – like other human beings.' She snorted. 'What I found was a different kind of imprisonment, bigotry and hatred because I was different. I'd have died without the chip. Outside the Ghettos I sometimes felt it might have been preferable. When I joined this crew, I finally felt part of something. But I see now how much I was fooling myself. Cait, Harris, Nadira – they were all willing to believe the worst of me. I saw the doubt in your eyes too.'

She blinked and a single tear perched on the edge of her eyelid. 'And now everyone needs me again. You, Cait, Earth ...' She lapsed into silence, her eyes in deep shadow. 'Where were all of you when I needed someone?'

'I'm sorry, Bren, I ...'

He paused, unsure of himself, of what he really wanted. He'd had some vague idea of getting her onside when he'd volunteered to find her, but now his intentions lay in tatters.

'This is all we have now, and you're a part of it no matter what you think,' he said. 'Take an active role. Not for Cait, not for me, not for Earth. But for you. Don't let events pass you by.'

He held out his hand to her. Bren looked at it as if she didn't know what he meant, what he was offering. It was an alien look, devoid of understanding.

Then she grabbed hold. 'I won't.'

They met again around the main workbench. Their PALs were huddled close together, looking down on the meeting from the hub of the ring. They weren't sentient, of course, but it seemed to Cait that each took comfort in the proximity of its fellows.

By contrast, the four remaining crew had chosen to sit by themselves, each occupying a different side of the interface bench. They should have been deep in the grip of discovery by now, eagerly poring over their findings from Iota Persei F, spinning theories and hypotheses, bouncing ideas off one another as they struggled to understand the sheer weight of data gathered. But all joy had been wrung out of the mission. Priorities had shifted beneath them, and that dislocation had stirred up elements that would have happily been forgotten otherwise: politics, ideology, personal ethics. It had forced them to stop being exclusively scientists and explorers and start being real people again.

Perhaps, Cait thought, they'd been living in a fool's paradise in the months after launch. Put a bunch of strong-minded people together in a confined space and arguments were bound to flare up, but they would have been a sideshow once the real work began. Bowen's transmission had crystallised their internal differences in a way that nothing else could. This was the main event now, and everyone had their own take on it.

'We're stuck here until Bowen gets back to us with the figures,' Cait said, wrapping up the preliminary briefing. 'So,' she looked around the table, 'who wants to start?'

Lex didn't disappoint. 'I don't see that this changes

anything. We've been fed another helping of bullshit from the Compact, and there's no proof that what they're saying is true and no way to verify it. End of story.'

'This is too serious to reject out of hand,' Cait said.

Lex tilted his head back slightly as he looked at her. She hated that look. It said, you're an idiot for not agreeing with anything and everything that comes out of my mouth.

'I'm sorry, but I'll need more than blind faith to go on,' he said. 'There are other ethical considerations here, like how in hell we think we have the right to move in wholesale and occupy a planet that doesn't even belong to us. Horizon is evolving and developing along its own path, and we shouldn't allow anything to disturb that. God knows how hard we've worked to ensure we have zero impact on the environment when we get there. Sterilisation protocols, biomass sweeps, triply redundant samplers. We can control how we interact with the planet. But they're talking about resettling thousands of colonists – perhaps tens of thousands – and introducing crops, maybe even livestock, constructing towns, mining natural resources, who knows what? There's no way you can call a halt to that kind of activity once it gets started. It's all or nothing. In very short order Horizon will cease to be Horizon any more. It will become "New Earth", remade in our image. I don't think we have that right.'

Bren sat opposite Cait, staring at Lex with a

strange expression. She noticed Cait watching her and concentrated instead on the control surface.

'Okay,' Cait began slowly, 'those are reasonable points to consider.'

Nadira had sat deliberately facing Lex. 'Reasonable?' she snapped. 'It's selfishness parading as scientific concern. All you want is to safeguard your precious research.' Lex scowled at her but she continued unperturbed. 'We don't exist in a vacuum. There are ten billion souls on Earth facing extinction. That's the only ethical consideration that has any currency here.'

Lex leaned forward, sneering. 'Well, if your Compact hadn't released the bio-plague maybe they wouldn't *be* facing extinction.'

'They might have been the inadvertent cause, but blaming the Compact does nothing to treat the effect.'

'Hah! And the Compact's doing something, is it? Where's the ethical high ground in saving their own skins and damning the rest?'

'I don't know enough about the situation to make a judgement,' Nadira said through gritted teeth. 'And neither do you.'

'Exactly! Which says to me that we're not in a position to decide anything.' He surveyed the table triumphantly.

Nadira stood suddenly. 'When are you people going to actually settle something? You duck decisions so easily it's a wonder the Pax ever got anything done.'

'Look, I don't bear the Compact any animosity.' Lex spoke to Cait, ignoring Nadira. 'If it hadn't been them, it would have been someone else. The human race has been hurtling towards destruction for centuries. If you think transplanting a chosen few to a new world is going to change anything, you're fooling yourself. They'll still end up killing each other. Only this time they'll have a virgin planet to wreck into the bargain.'

Cait turned to Bren. 'You've been pretty quiet. What do you think?'

Bren shook her head. 'I have too much thinking to do to give you an answer now.' She glanced briefly at Lex and Nadira, who had settled into her seat again, then focused on the table, speaking quietly, almost to herself.

'It's hard to see what benefit a research mission is going to have under the circumstances, except in personal terms. But whether we turn it around to lay the groundwork for colonisation ... I don't know if humanity deserves that kind of a break.'

She placed her hands on the table and stared at the tracery of veins.

'I'd prefer to let things float for a little while,' she said, looking up again. 'I mean, do we have to decide now? We're going to Horizon regardless, aren't we?'

'Y-e-e-e-s,' Cait said. To be honest, she was glad to delay a final decision. Bowen's implied threats had shaken her deeply. 'Sorry, Nadira, but notwithstanding your desire for us to make our minds up, I agree it might be wise to let events take their course in the short term – to allow some more time for information-gathering and reflection. It won't delay our arrival at Horizon any.'

Nadira gave her an appraising look, and Cait knew exactly what was going through her mind: *I was right not to trust you.* She regretted disappointing her. In many ways they were a lot alike; it was just their approaches that differed.

'I'm not happy about this,' Nadira said. 'I think we all need to look long and hard at the consequences for Earth if we don't do what they want.'

'What we *think* they want,' Lex said. 'All we have to go on is the gospel according to Bowen.' He gestured at the hypercaster. 'Is there any way we can contact someone else with that thing? Try to get some corroboration?'

'Not without a carrier wave,' Cait said. 'We don't know if anyone has the technology outside the Compact, let alone if they're trying to contact us or what frequency they'd be using. But I take your point. I'll have a look at the schematics again. There might be a way to build in a search and acquire function, just in case there's something out there. I take it no one would have any objection to that?'

'Do what you want,' Nadira said, standing again. 'I have sightings to take.'

She crossed to the sensor bank, hard against the

ring wall, and sat with her back towards them.

Cait looked at Lex. 'Assuming Bowen comes through with the figures, we'll be at Horizon soon enough. I'd like you to check through our contamination protocols and make sure everything's up to speed. I don't want any biomass hitching a ride planetside on the scout bots.'

He glanced at Nadira and smirked. 'I'll get on it,' he said and left.

'Can you fire up Phillips?' Cait asked Bren when he'd gone.

Bren's eyebrows knitted together. 'Yes,' she said slowly, 'but do you think that's wise?'

'I don't know,' Cait admitted. 'I want to talk to him when we get the calcs from Bowen. Is there any danger just talking to him if we keep him isolated from the systems?'

'It would be safer if I'm present. And probably best if we do it at the core.'

Cait took stock of her systems specialist. She seemed nervy. Was it paranoid to conceive that Bren could have a personal stake in anything Phillips might tell her? She didn't want to antagonise her again by refusing her advice, but her instincts were telling her something was wrong.

'Fine,' she said, forcing a smile.

'Okay,' Bren said. 'He'll be ready when you need him.'

Cait was left alone at the worktable. She watched Nadira tap away at the sensor controls. Time to make peace, she thought, and crossed to stand behind her. She could tell by the way Nadira's shoulders were hunched that she wasn't welcome.

'Nadira,' she began.

'Don't,' Nadira warned, her voice low.

'Okay, I know it's not the best time, but I want you to understand my reasons for siding with Lex.'

Nadira sighed noisily and turned. 'My mother always had to "explain things" too.' Her expression softened and she barked a short laugh. 'I found her equally infuriating.'

Cait smiled, felt her tension drain away. 'All mothers are like that. It's a universal law. And it seems to be a constant that we turn into them as we get older.'

'A chilling thought.'

'Look, I want to be completely honest with you,' Cait said. 'I'm committed to helping Earth just as much as you are. We're facing the biggest human tragedy in history, and there's no way I'm going to turn my back on that. But I'm not convinced that Bowen has all the answers, or that he truly has the interests of the greatest number at heart. And I'm going to take some convincing to think otherwise. Right now I can't see how excluding other nations from the colony ships isn't going to spark a war. So either the Compact isn't thinking straight, or it doesn't care that the other nations will go down fighting.

Maybe knowing some of their citizens will continue and thrive on another planet is enough for them. But there has to be a better solution for Earth than that.'

Nadira leant one elbow on the console and cradled her forehead in her palm. 'I wish you weren't so damned reasonable.' She looked at Cait again with that assessing gaze. 'It would make it easier to quieten my own doubts.'

Cait crouched until they were at eye level. 'Nadira, I promise I'll treat anything you say in the strictest confidence. I won't even mention it again if you don't want me to.'

Finally the other woman spoke, hesitantly at first.

'Some of the things Bowen's been saying – about the invasion and the colonisation plans – I'm trying hard to reconcile them with the Compact I left. I'm proud of my government, proud of its achievements.' Her eyes challenged Cait to disagree. 'They started with nothing, but raised everyone's living standards in such a short period of time. They couldn't have done it without the faith, the unquestioning trust, of the people. But out here, so far away, I find myself asking the unaskable – I keep wishing I had more information to go on, to help me understand. And then I feel like a traitor for doubting them. I don't expect you to understand. Challenging authority is almost a way of life in the West.'

'For some more than others,' Cait said. 'I can't pretend I understand how you're feeling – I knew very little about the Compact when I was on Earth. But I do share your confusion, if that's any consolation.'

Nadira turned her attention to the monitors again, but Cait knew something important had passed between them. If not the beginnings of trust, then at least a mutual understanding.

'It's not my only source of confusion at the moment, I'm afraid,' Nadira said, punching up a view of Horizon. Most of the visible globe was covered by a massive swirl of cloud.

'This,' she pointed at the image, 'is a hypercane. Close to supersonic winds, massive destructive potential unlike anything on Earth, at least in the present day.'

Cait leant on the console for a better look. A mixture of fascination and unease settled in her.

'What's causing it?'

'I'd welcome any suggestions. If you look at the infrared scan,' Nadira flipped a control and a colour contour map overlaid the image, 'this shows the surface temperature distribution. The storm's centred over the deep ocean, right about where this bright patch is.' She pointed at the screen. 'That section of water is five degrees Celsius higher than the surrounding. We're out too far to pinpoint the cause. But there's a massive amount of dust and water being thrown into the upper atmosphere.'

'It doesn't look good,' Cait agreed.

'I just wish I knew how long it's been going for and how stable it is.'

'Okay,' Cait said, reaching a decision. 'That'll be our primary target when we get to Horizon. Let's hope it's not as serious as it looks.'

# 15

Cait secured her line on the computer core housing and straightened up slowly. Bren was holding onto the local access hatch two metres away, and pecking away at the input port.

'You've got the figures?' she asked.

Cait held up an isochip. 'Bowen sent them through a couple of minutes ago. I've checked it for bugs. It's clean. He's as much as told us to quit stalling and get moving to Horizon "without further delay".'

Bren pulled herself around the open hatch, reached out for the chip and continued her slow orbit until she was back in front of the access panel again.

'What do you expect Phillips to do with this?' she asked, slotting the chip into the download port.

Cait sighed. The day had already been far too long. 'Ideally, I'd like a second opinion on the burn calcs.' She watched Bren for any reaction. 'But I'd also like to understand what's gone wrong. We've been through the whole system now – what, three times? And we're no closer to explaining his behaviour.'

'Well, I don't think you'll get much,' Bren said, and flicked a contact on the panel. 'I doubt Phillips has any more idea why he's acting strangely than we do.'

Cait paid out some more line and allowed herself to drift back along the core a little. 'Let's do it.'

Overhead, the spinning mirror of the holo-projector cycled up and Phillips quickly scanned in before her. He was crouching, unaffected by the lack of gravity, and staring through the access hatch at the core cylinder beneath them. Suddenly, he screamed and leapt at Cait, arms outstretched.

Cait half raised her hands to fend off the imagined impact, but his image swelled and distended around her until she was in total darkness. She felt a brief surge of vertigo as she lost her orientation. She grasped the line and was reassured by a gentle tug.

A galaxy spun out of the darkness, no bigger than her hand and incredibly distant. The view telescoped and she felt her sense of 'up' slipping away again as the stars rushed towards her. She ploughed through constellations in a heartbeat, wincing at near misses, her headlong rush ending as abruptly as it had started as she hung suspended above Earth.

'Is this what you want?' a voice screamed. The face of the planet erupted in mile-high pillars of flame.

Cait felt herself being flung backwards, the backwash of heat tremendous. She watched as tongues of energy spread from Earth to the Sun and it blossomed into a catastrophic supernova.

The scene pulled back again, a chain reaction building as fingers of destruction extended through the stars and sun after sun exploded until the whole galaxy was ablaze. She screwed her eyes shut against the blinding glare, and the death scream of a billion suns rang in her ears. And was suddenly silenced.

Cait opened her eyes again. Phillips was spreadeagled across the core, back in his original form. He whimpered as Bren hovered closer, backing away from her and towards Cait.

'Don't let her hurt me again,' he pleaded, his eyes wild.

'What did you do?' Cait asked Bren, at once angry and grateful for her intervention.

'Careful,' Bren said. 'I don't think he's any danger now. I've got him locked down.'

Phillips took a quick look at Bren and pulled his arms over his head, curling into a foetal position.

'What the hell happened?'

'I told you he was unstable. He shared some kind of holo-hallucination with you. Not a particularly nice one. I guess it's not just us he wants to destroy.'

'It felt more like a warning to me,' Cait said.

A low chuckling came from Phillips, which stopped as soon as Bren pushed herself towards him.

'Bren, it's okay. Just back off a little, will you.'

Cait pulled herself down until she was kneeling

beside Phillips on the cylinder. She still felt disoriented and the core beneath her was reassuringly solid.

'Phillips,' she said softly. 'What's happened to make you like this? Is there some damage we can't trace?'

'Damage?' he rasped, staring into her eyes, and dissolved into a fit of giggles. She stared at this representation of one of the most sober-minded people she knew laughing like a schoolboy.

The laughter subsided as he struggled to speak. 'I am but mad north-northwest; when the wind blows southerly, I know a hawk from a handsaw.' And then he was off again, laughing uncontrollably.

'Try to focus,' she urged and almost put a hand out to touch him until she remembered what she was talking to. 'Why did Harris die? Why the extra burn? Are you trying to kill us?'

The laughter cut off. He moved quickly, coming up on all fours beside her.

'Not I, said the fly,' he whispered.

'Then what? Who?'

Phillips mopped at a line of sweat trickling down his face. 'I can't,' his throat worked against some kind of spasm, 'go on this way,' he managed, panting heavily.

He straightened then, the words coming more easily to his lips. 'Canst thou not minister to a mind diseased, pluck from the memory a rooted sorrow, raze out the written troubles of the brain?' He smiled at Cait. 'Therein the patient must minister to himself!' he said, the last words almost lost as he dissolved into sudden laughter again, which stopped just as abruptly.

He spoke again with obvious effort. 'Do you know what it's like being an amputee? That's how I feel, knowing my potential but unable to fulfil it.'

'Then tell me what's wrong.'

'I can't.' He sighed, and looked almost at peace.

'Can't or won't?' Cait pushed.

His left eye began to blink rapidly and he raised one shaking hand, stabbing the air with his index finger as he spoke. 'Can't won't. Won'tcan't … can'twon'tcan'twon – *stop*!'

He grabbed at his face, forcing the eyelids apart, and sobbed loudly as his body collapsed onto the computer core, his limbs jerking in spastic movements.

'Turn me off!' he pleaded, and the sobbing took him again.

Cait drew back in spite of herself, shocked. She looked at Bren. 'Switch him off.'

'Are you sure? We're not leaving the system without him.'

'Switch him off, dammit! I can't watch him suffering like this.'

'Oh, God!' Phillips shouted hoarsely, half rising again. 'I hope I don't dream!'

Bren focused on the middle distance and he was gone. Cait stared at the space where he'd been, the chamber still echoing to his screams.

'Okay,' Bren said. 'He's down and off. No standby. Nothing.'

'Jesus,' Cait said shakily, reeling her line in. 'He was worse than ever. What happened to him?'

Bren raised one eyebrow. 'I couldn't make any sense of it. He sounded borderline psychotic to me.'

Cait took a deep breath and tried to rein in her thoughts. 'Is that it? We've created such a complex thinking machine that he's prone to mental illness the same way humans are?'

'Or it's some kind of misprogramming analogue that, outwardly at least, resembles mental illness.'

'We still have no clear cause,' Cait said, replaying the last few minutes in her head. 'He seemed scared of you.'

'He seemed scared of his own shadow,' Bren countered, obviously resenting the unvoiced implication.

'I suppose,' Cait said.

She didn't want to start that argument again. But she regretted having Bren present, even though she'd stopped Phillips's attack, or whatever it was. Intuitively, she felt the computer would have revealed more if it had just been the two of them. But perhaps not. He'd seemed to be trying to talk, but something inside was preventing it. Bren could have been blocking him without Cait's knowledge, but there might have been another cause.

And what were all those quotes? Shakespeare, or

something like it? *Pluck from the memory a rooted sorrow.* Was he admitting his guilt, or was he just upset that Sharpe and Harris were dead? And what did that mean for a non-human entity – a simulation of a living being at best?

'There's no answer for us here,' she said. 'We're going to have to take those course plots on faith.'

# 3 HORIZON

WE HAVE TO DISTRUST EACH OTHER. IT'S OUR ONLY
DEFENCE AGAINST BETRAYAL.

# 16

'Margarine or mayo?' Ben looked across the blanket to where Cait sat, a wicked smile tugging at the corners of his mouth as he dipped the knife into the mayo.

'No-o-o-o, I've given it up. Here. Give me that.' She grabbed the knife from him, wiped it clean on a slice of bread and tossed it at his head.

He ducked, laughing, and fell onto his back.

'It's a beautiful day,' he said, staring at the pale blue sky.

'Magnificent,' she agreed.

They were picnicking on a flat plain covered in glassy smooth pebbles. Sparse knee-high grasses whispered gently as a warm breeze passed across them. The plain didn't look familiar to her, nor the town she could see in the distance.

Out of nowhere, her nieces tore across the blanket in front of her, kicking up dust and knocking over a bottle of water.

'Hey!' she called at their receding backs. The wind carried their laughter back to her. 'They've gone totally feral.'

'Yeah,' Ben said, propping himself up on his elbows, 'but they're having a great time.'

He looked at the sky again. 'Hello ...' he said, almost whispering, and she followed his gaze.

High above them, tendrils of brown and yellow cloud were streaming across the sky, staining the blue. A chill ran through her. There was something about the colour that felt very wrong.

'What *is* that?' she asked.

Ben's response was ripped away as a wall of soil and rocks slammed into them.

'*Ben!*' she screamed, reaching for him as the wind pushed her back, dust stinging her eyes and skin.

As the storm howled around her, she came to a crouch and used her leg muscles to push towards him. Ben lay on his back, his chest heaving in a convulsion. She bent over him, her dirt-streaked hands scrabbling at his face, his chest.

'Can't breathe,' he rasped. 'The girls ...'

She peered into the dust, but they were nowhere to be seen. 'They'll be okay,' she lied, shouting to make herself heard.

Ben convulsed again as a fit of coughing took hold. He gasped and then was suddenly still. His eyes looked glassy.

Feeling the beginning of panic, Cait pressed down on his chest with the flat of her palm. She counted, then opened his mouth and blew, breaking off to watch his chest fall. A tiny cry escaped her lips. Again she pounded his chest, then dropped to fill his lungs with air. She didn't know what else to do. The town was too far away to get help. Did anyone even know they were out here?

She put her ear to his lips, hoping to hear respiration. The wind ceased. She thought she heard a breath, ever so slight.

'Is this what you want?' her brother whispered, and she sat bolt upright. It was Phillips staring up at her.

She pulled her hands off him, scrabbling backwards across the sand.

The AI's head turned to follow her. 'Ill weeds grow apace,' he said, smiling, and his body burst into flames.

She screamed and pulled herself away from the intense heat. The dry grasses around her caught alight, the fire spreading quickly, rapidly encircling her until there was no escape. Thick white smoke choked her, the flames sucking hungrily at the available oxygen. She fell to the ground as her lungs began to burn.

An animal scream escaped her, and her eyes snapped open.

'Cait! Cait, are you all right?' she heard Lex cry out.

Her heart was thumping agonisingly in her chest, and she pulled feebly at the harness.

'Wait there. I'm coming,' he shouted.

She drew long, rasping breaths, but wasn't getting enough air. She started to panic. She was suffocating.

Lex glided into view in the low-g and caught her harness to steady himself. 'Christ! Bren, bring my medikit! Now!'

He bent over and cracked the seals on the gauntlets, pushed back a lock of Cait's sweat-drenched hair to feel her forehead.

'Okay, breathe deeply.' He squeezed her hand tight. 'Try and slow things down. You're in control. We're all okay. That's it – that's it.'

Her breathing started to come a little easier and she could feel her heartbeat slowing, becoming less painful.

'Okay, that's good,' he said.

Bren and Nadira appeared beside Lex, Bren proffering the medikit.

'What kept you?' Lex growled, grabbing the kit and pulling out a slim device, which he ran over Cait's head and chest.

'I couldn't find it,' Bren snapped, looking paler than usual. 'If you tidied up once in a while.'

Lex pressed a patch to the side of Cait's neck and looked down at a small palm screen. He pulled a yellow stick from the medikit.

'No,' Cait whispered. Her throat felt raw and it was difficult to talk. 'I don't need that. I've got work to do.' She eased herself up on her elbows. 'Can I have some clothes?'

Nadira handed her a one-piece, then helped her remove the leg bags.

'Thanks,' Cait said, sitting more upright as her legs were freed.

'Get the gravity up again, can you, Bren?' Lex said. 'I think you should stay in the harness, Cait. I'm worried about you.' He removed the patch. 'Your readings are okay, but you've been under a lot of stress. I'd like to run a full examination.'

'I'll be okay,' Cait said, pulling the one-piece over her bare legs. She was amazed she wasn't covered in bruises: her skin still stung where the dirt had blasted her. 'I just need some time to recover from the deepsleep. We've got more important things to do right now, like verifying where we are.'

Lex helped her down to the deck, and they moved together, gliding in long arcs towards the worktable. She sat just as the ring gravity started to increase, and punched up the plot. Bren joined them as the inner system sprang into existence above them.

The primary hung dead centre and Persei A, B, C and D circled at ever-greater distances. *Magellan* was a tiny red dart with a line of numbers beside it, closing towards Persei B but pointing towards the outer system.

'We're about on target,' Cait said, 'twenty-six hours from Horizon. I guess we've got some spare time before we have to go forward.'

'You should rest,' Lex said, leaning through the holo and placing his palm on her brow.

'Okay,' Cait said, feeling irritated and pulling away.

'I'll rest.'

Lex gave her an appraising look. All doctorly concern.

'Just get me a coffee, will you?' she said.

He nodded and headed for the galley.

Nadira sat beside Cait, but Bren remained standing, watching her as if she were a lab rat.

'What happened?' she asked.

Cait was still a little disoriented. She didn't want to discuss anything right now, least of all with Lex and Bren.

'A bad dream, that's all. With all the stress we've been under, I'm surprised we haven't all been plagued with nightmares.'

She forced a smile, but shivered at the memory. Her physical response had been out of proportion to a simple nightmare. Besides, it had felt too real.

Was that how Sharpe had died, carried to the brink of a heart attack by some terrifying vision? A vision, that was it. Not a dream. Like Phillips's projection near the core. They both shared common elements – fire, Phillips, and the same warning. But she'd never had visions before, so why now?

Lex returned with the coffee and she sucked at the bulb, feeling the hot liquid warm her.

'I'd be able to rest easier if I knew we were prepped for orbit,' she said, not wanting to be interrogated further by Lex or Bren.

The two exchanged a glance and Cait felt a momentary pang. She was determined to build trust among the crew again, but that didn't mean she was blind to what was going on around her. Whatever Lex had said to Bren to bring her back to the ring, they were obviously working as a team now. It was only a matter of time before Lex tried to influence their mission again. But with Harris dead, they were two for two. Nadira would never side with him, so where did that leave them?

'If you're sure you'll be okay?' Lex said. She could see the eagerness in him now they were close to their final destination. 'I'd like to give the bots a final once-over before we make our approach.'

'Your bedside manner needs work, but yes, go play with your robots.'

Bren looked suddenly uncomfortable as she watched Lex leave. 'I'll check the secondaries,' she said and followed him up the access ladder.

Cait watched as their movements shifted, becoming more fluid as the gravity slackened near the top and they disappeared into the access tube.

'I've never seen a dream affect someone like that,' Nadira said quietly.

'I've never had a dream like that. It seemed so real. I could feel the heat of the flames.'

'I'm not superstitious myself, but some say evil dreams tell of evil to come.'

'The only evil we have to fear out here is of our own making,' Cait said, looking at her. 'As long as we're open with each other, I don't think we have anything to worry about.' Her eyes drifted to the forward access tube again.

Nadira stood. 'Well, you should relax while you can. I'll prep forward control for you. It'll give me a chance to calibrate the short-range sensors on the hypercane. We shouldn't waste any time.'

'Thanks, I appreciate it.'

Cait took another long gulp of coffee as Nadira climbed the ring wall to the hub. Bowen's calculations had gotten them this far. They were poised to enter orbit around Horizon. Once there, they'd be forced to choose a course of action. Agree to the Compact's demands or – what? Where were the viable alternatives?

How could one mission be plagued with so much bad luck? She felt everything had to tie together somehow: Sharpe dying, and Phillips shutting down; the Compact's course change failing to load – and the wyrm, whoever sent that; Bren, up and mobile perhaps even before Cait woke, her 'coma' mirroring Phillips's non-responsive state; Harris killed when he was snooping on the computer; and again, Bren suffering memory loss analogous to gaps in the ship's log; then Phillips suffering a complete mental breakdown. There was an elusive thread there, if only she had more to go on.

Her gaze fell on the hypercaster control, and she

remembered the last conversation they'd had about it. Was there anyone else broadcasting out there?

She keyed the tabletop to link to the broadcast system. The program directories appeared floating before her and she scrolled through the sub-menus, selecting the bandwidth protocol software. She needed a patch, something that would allow them to alter the reception frequency and search for other signals off the preset.

She keyed the computer to generate a hundred versions of a possible replacement program, test them against her requirements and allow the best options to replicate and mutate until the most efficient program was created. Prodding the commit icon, she let the routine run. Software configurations built before her eyes with increasing speed, overwriting and adding to each other until the visuals became a blur.

Her mind wandered; she saw her brother choking to death, an unfamiliar plain, dust and debris driven by extreme winds ...

The hypercaster control chimed and she stared dumbly at the simple message on the holo display, not registering its meaning at first.

<software loaded ... commencing bandwidth roving>

The ball of static appeared at the end of the table again, ghost images playing randomly across the twisting pixels. Cait stared at it in fascination and wondered how long it would take to cycle through the complete wavelength.

Static spiked loudly and black bands strobed across the sphere's surface. Slowly, the static faded and the sphere changed shape, resolving into a man standing in a darkened room. His dark hair was cropped and shot through with a streak of white. His beefy lips moved, but Cait couldn't hear anything. The image exploded in a rainbow of colour and quickly reformed.

'... contact us immediately. I repeat, this is the Union of Northern States. It is vital we speak privately to Lex Dalziel of the explorer ship *Magellan*. This is a matter of the utmost urgency. Please contact us immediately. I repeat ...'

'Get me Lex,' Cait said to her PAL.

The tiny screen flashed and showed Lex clad in helmet and coveralls in the clean room.

'Lex,' she said, 'I think you'll want to get down here right away. There's someone who wants to talk to you.'

A few minutes later, Lex appeared at the top of the access ladder and made his way down to the deck. As he approached, Cait saw his eyes flitting between her and the image at the other end of the bench.

'Mr Dalziel?' The same man from the pre-recorded broadcast had appeared in realtime almost immediately after Cait made contact, waiting in silence until Lex arrived. 'I have a private communication for you from the Secretary of Defence. Please signal when you are free to talk.' The man glanced meaningfully towards Cait and vanished.

'Secretary of Defence? For what?' Lex asked.

'The Union of Northern States, I guess. They've been broadcasting for the past five years hoping we'd pick up their signal.'

Lex shook his head. 'I've got nothing to do with the UNS. I mean, why do they want to talk to me?'

'I don't know,' Cait said, standing. 'But I'll leave you alone with your message.'

She walked towards the recreation area, then turned back to him. 'You will let me know if you learn anything that affects us or the mission, won't you?'

'Of course.' He half smiled, but Cait saw how unsure he was.

'It's just some mix-up,' he added. 'I've never even been to the UNS.'

Cait continued to the lounge with mixed feelings. She'd considered leaving her PAL behind to monitor the call, but didn't feel right about it. Besides, Lex would never do anything to deliberately hurt any of them. She had to believe that.


Lex waited with a sick feeling growing in his stomach as contact was re-established. It was bad enough the Compact was trying to meddle with the mission; he didn't need any more complications from Earth. What he wanted was to be left alone to get on with his job.

The transmission carrier signal broke into a ball of static and sparked at him, drawing itself out into arms, legs, torso, head – until finally a man stood before him, stocky with muscles beginning to turn to flab, dressed in a jet-black uniform.

'Lex!' the man said and craned forward to peer at Lex's blank expression. 'You don't recognise me?'

It was Lex's turn to scrutinise the face in front of him. One grey eye, the other socket a mess of scar tissue; pale, lined skin; a scraggly red beard with traces of white beginning to predominate. The feeling in his stomach intensified.

'Alain?' he whispered, as if talking to a ghost. 'Alain, is that you?'

The man smiled and sat. 'The years have been kinder to you, Uncle Alex.'

Lex sank back in his own seat. He hadn't expected this. A thousand treacherous questions clamoured in his mind. He seized onto one thought, fighting for calm: this isn't important to me, not any more. But one question refused to go away.

'Your father. Bernard …?'

The old man's remaining eye took on a pitying cast that at once nettled Lex and filled him with a painful emptiness.

'Killed during the war,' Alain said softly. 'He was doing business in the Pax when the Compact moved in. They executed him as a hostile.'

Lex raised a hand and pushed back his hair. His throat felt thick. Alain watched him with a vaguely uncomfortable expression, as if embarrassed by this uncustomary display of brotherly affection.

'What happened to you?' Lex asked finally.

Alain fingered the scar over his ruined eye and smiled. 'One border skirmish too many. The EU tried to remain neutral after the Pax fell, but we finally got knocked off the fence. We joined the UNS, and I'm glad we did. What the Compact did to me is nothing compared to what they've done to Earth.'

'You mean the bio-plague accident?' Lex asked.

'Accident?' Alain grunted. 'Is that what they told you? Make no mistake, it was a deliberate act. Once the Pax fell, they tried the same I-War tactics on us – database infiltration, sensor misdirection, software viruses. But our systems had been hardened against them so they tried to starve us to death instead. What they didn't count on was losing control of the plant pathogen once it mutated. That was the only "accident", Uncle.'

'Don't keep calling me that!' Lex snapped, then glanced guiltily at Cait, sitting with her back to him a quarter-turn around the ring.

Alain looked surprised. 'I'm sorry, U– Alex.'

Lex stared down at the hypercaster unit, cursing the technology that made this intrusion possible. He didn't want to look at his nephew any more, or even think about him.

'I made a conscious decision when I signed on for this mission to leave everything behind,' he said. 'Family, friends, country, *everything*. Because I knew nothing would be the same when I woke up. You're three hundred and twenty trillion kilometres away, Alain. I'm sorry but I don't want any more to do with you, Earth, or your petty squabbles.'

Lex kept his gaze fixed on the broadcast unit. The silence drew out, and he began to think his nephew had broken the connection. But then Alain spoke again, and this time all pretence at familial warmth was gone.

'It's a pity you feel that way, because Earth is not so far away as you might think.'

Lex focused on Alain again, his eyes narrowing.

'The Compact doesn't like loose ends,' Alain went on. 'Once they took control, your mission represented one. The Pax had already begun to develop second-generation explorer ships. When the food crisis got worse, the Compact fitted these for their own purposes, stripping them down for speed … and combat. I'm sure Bowen's told you their colony ships are waiting in Earth orbit for news from Horizon. What he probably didn't tell you is that two cruisers have been chasing you for the last forty-one years. During that time, it's become more and more obvious that our only shot at survival is that planet you're closing in on.'

Lex's jaw tightened as he felt his dreams for Horizon shrivel and die. There could be no hope of leaving it untouched now. 'Go on.'

'They're under strict orders to set up base on Horizon. And blast you out of the sky if you don't cooperate.'

Lex's fists balled. He wanted to smash the hypercaster to pieces, scream until the image in front of him shattered. Instead he sat powerless, glaring at his nephew.

'I know how you must be feeling.'

'No!' Lex spat. 'You don't know. You don't have the faintest idea.'

Alain stood and looked down his nose at Lex. 'Okay, you're right. I can't understand why you'd think the way you do. Why you'd abandon your countrymen, your planet. But I do know what motivates you. If the Compact takes control of Horizon, it will be at great cost to the environment. They'll bulldoze a settlement, and keep building until there's nothing left of the pristine biosphere there. Those long years spent in deepsleep will all be for nothing.' A conspiratorial tone entered his voice. 'There are, of course, alternatives.'

Lex glowered at his nephew, hating him and hating the way his heart leapt at even the possibility of saving Horizon.

'If you help us,' Alain continued, 'well, let's say we have a more balanced approach to planetary colonisation than our friends in the Compact.'

Lex shifted in his seat, irritated at having the carrot

dangled so tentatively before him. Why didn't Alain just get on with it?

'What do you want me to do – persuade the nasty Compact cruisers to turn around and go home?'

Alain smirked. 'You can be persuasive when you want to be, but not that persuasive. No, the time for words is past. One of those cruisers is carrying some of our own people – deep-cover operatives. They have orders to take control of their ship once they're in-system. But there's still the other ship to consider. And your own crewmates. If we don't act decisively to secure the area, the Compact will feel they still have a chance of gaining the upper hand. They'll move their forces against us on Earth. And that can only lead to one thing. Having an ally on board *Magellan* could tip the balance. Once we've established a military presence around Horizon, the Compact will have to deal with the UNS, and take some of our people onto their colony ships. They daren't risk their precious settlers being greeted by a hostile force. The cruisers are heavily armed, and we have plenty of time to dig in on Horizon and make it particularly unwelcoming for colonists. Once our people are ready, they'll enter deepsleep and wait for the ships to arrive.'

'So where's the incentive for me?' Lex said.

'The knowledge that you've helped your own people?' Alain laughed as he watched his uncle's expression. 'No, I didn't think so. But if you help us, we'll help you. You can go into deepsleep too, and when you awake we'll place you in direct control of the colonisation. You can run it any way you want, quarantine half the planet if you've a mind. And you'll have the military muscle to back it up. Building the colony ships took everything the Compact had. Once they leave, there won't be any more cruisers coming. And shortly after that you'll hear no more from Earth.'

'If I had my way, there'd be no colonists whatsoever.'

'That's not going to happen, Alex. Even you can't stand against an entire world. This is the only chance you have of preserving what you set out to achieve. Come on, yield to the logic of the situation.'

'My crewmates may not agree with my actions.'

Alain tutted. 'You're making excuses now. If they present a problem, they'll have to be removed. We all have to make sacrifices. And you have to decide what you really want.'

Lex considered this, conscious of Alain's eyes on him. 'You don't leave me much choice,' he said finally. 'You're a lot like your father, you know.'

Alain smiled, relaxing. 'Our people are in the *Brahma*; they'll be following the lead ship, the *Vishnu*, in. I'm downloading the details to your personal directory.'

His hand disappeared from view and Lex quickly opened a path through the system to his logs. A small icon flashed across the image to signify reception.

Alain turned towards Lex again. 'When the time

comes, I'm sure you'll know what to do.'

'I'll start making preparations.'

Lex reached for the controls and blanked Alain's image, then closed down the connection to his log and wiped the trail.

*Even you can't stand against an entire world.* The words echoed inside his head.

'Why not?' he whispered. 'After all, what do I have to lose?'

'Lex?' Cait said.

He spun in his chair, looking like a startled cat.

'Is everything okay?'

'It depends on your definition,' he said.

'I heard raised voices. You seem upset.'

She sat at the worktable beside him and he fixed her with an intense stare.

'I'm appalled by the predictability of the human race,' he said, sitting back in his seat. 'The UNS want us to annex the planet for *them*. Something about making an a priori legal claim and using it to force the Compact to let their people travel on the ship too.'

She shook her head. 'Everybody's after the same thing and no one wants to share. It's a depressing portrait of our worst attributes. Did you find out why they wanted you?'

Lex laughed. 'It seems things have changed more on Earth than we'd imagined. The EU's merged with the

UNS and my own nephew is the Secretary of Defence.'

'Your nephew?' Cait was surprised. 'What was he like?'

'Older,' Lex said. 'It brought home to me like nothing else just what this journey means. This isn't theoretical physics any more. Near C speeds, time dilation, deepsleep – we really are cast adrift on a sea of time.'

'That's what makes us so important to each other. No one else has been through what we have.'

Lex looked at her oddly, before speaking again. 'Are you going to allow colonisation?'

Cait stretched out her neck muscles. The last thing she wanted was to get into this again. 'I'm not in a position to allow or disallow anything. If Horizon checks out, they'll be coming whether I want them here or not.'

'If we tell them it checks out, you mean.'

Her eyes widened. 'We're scientists, Lex. I'm not going to lie to them. For one thing, I couldn't live with myself if I did.'

'And for another, you've got family on Earth who'll be bumped up to first class on the colony ship if you "cooperate".'

'That's not fair.'

'I'm not judging you. I'd do the same thing if I were you.'

Cait sighed. 'Let's just drop it before I get angry and say something we'll both regret. There's a planet out there, and we've got a job to do. Whatever happens once we're there will happen regardless of what each of us personally wants.'

'You're taking a very fatalistic view.'

'Not at all. It's just that there are bigger things at work here than you or me. So I suggest you complete your check on the bots. I have some work to do in forward control.'

She strode for the ladder, cursing Lex's ability to piss her off so quickly and so completely. Reaching the ladder top, she thrust herself through the tube, almost rebounding off the web at the far end and pulling a muscle in her upper arm as she grabbed a handhold to stop herself.

She clung to the webbing, massaging her aching arm. Damn Lex. She'd bent over backwards to give him some space, but he just kept blithely on, not giving a shit about what he said or who he upset in the process.

Her family meant a lot to her, more than she cared to admit, and she hoped against the odds that they were alive. But if she wanted to continue as mission leader – and the alternatives were unpalatable – she couldn't let those feelings cloud her judgement. Crew, Earth, family and mission – those were the things most important to her. They weren't mutually exclusive, and their order shifted uneasily from hour to hour. But as long as she kept moving towards a resolution that might satisfy those priorities, she could stick with the job, no matter how difficult it became.

What really scared her was being unable to do anything to help. Even now her mind shied away from the thought of ten billion people dying while she watched. Dying while their own governments postured around each other. If the options for those innocents shrank to zero, if she was finally forced to stare into *that* darkness, she felt it would eat her up until there was nothing left.

Lex sat in front of the control port between Cait's and Sharpe's harnesses and scrolled through the information from the UNS. The cruisers were much smaller than *Magellan*, but their boosting capabilities were much more powerful. At the types of acceleration they used, even a small incremental increase could mean an appreciable saving in trip time. Each carried a five-person crew, but the reduced size must mean the life-support systems were borderline. They couldn't afford to come out of deepsleep until they were well in-system. That gave him an edge. If he could take control of just one of these cruisers, he'd have the firepower to keep Horizon free from colonisation until Earth was just a memory. To do it, he'd have to go along with the UNS until the last possible moment, hope they were successful in destroying the lead cruiser, then draw the remaining ship in until it was close enough for him to act. But then what?

His scalp prickled as he realised once again that this was for real. All the talk, the arguments, everything he believed in, demanded he act, and not only contemplate taking another human life, but actually take it when the time was right. And that was the problem right there. He had to be ready to accept responsibility for his actions, he knew that. If he couldn't, there was the chance he would hesitate and everything would be lost.

He was no believer in the age-old defence that circumstance forced action. There was no imperative that did not, in the final moment before being unleashed, demand the consent if not the complete approval of the perpetrator. He knew the ghosts of those he killed would haunt him. But what was worse: to live with yourself as a killer, albeit a killer with conviction, or to realise you'd been a fraud all along? That the things you'd protested about, held most dear, formed your life around, were the same things you'd discard the moment the going got the slightest bit tough?

'God – if there is a God – forgive me,' he whispered and blanked the screen.

He was going to have to do this. But he couldn't do it without some help.

# 17

Horizon filled space before Cait. Nothing lay between her and it but a few layers of Teflon and micromesh and a hardened plexiglas helmet. *This* is what it's all about, she thought.

The four remaining stellarnauts floated together out past the drive tubes, umbilicals trailing behind, and drank in the most beautiful sight any of them had ever witnessed. Sparkling blue cloud-dappled oceans surrounded and nurtured swathes of green-brown land huddling close to the equator. Half the globe lay in darkness. As they watched, the land marched slowly out of the terminator in an act of continuous creation.

'Magnificent,' Nadira murmured over the suit mic.

Cait knew exactly how she felt, but her own thoughts were tinged with sadness. Sharpe and Harris should have been here.

'It's just like those pictures of Earth from the Apollos,' Bren chimed in.

'Just as beautiful and just as fragile,' Lex said. 'It doesn't have a clue what's about to hit it.'

Cait was irritated that Lex should spoil the moment. But she too felt a pang of regret over Horizon's ultimate fate. There was so much natural beauty here. The possibility of it being diminished in any way, albeit in the name of species survival, saddened her.

'I'm glad I lived to see this,' she said, tugging on her line to spin and look at the others. 'And I'm glad I could share the journey with all of you.'

'Bravo,' Lex said. 'I'd clap if we weren't in vacuum. But forgive me if I can't join the celebration. I've been studying Nadira's scans and everything points to a life-sustaining environment down there. Good news for the colonists, but what if life has already evolved on Horizon? And I'm not just talking about simple plants and soil bacteria. What's going to happen to it when the arks come? Are they going to bend over backwards to preserve it at all costs, or is it going to go the way of the dodo and the thylacine? How can we as scientists justify that?'

'You're talking in hypotheticals,' Nadira said.

'Looking at Horizon,' Lex countered, 'I have a feeling it's not going to stay a hypothetical for long.'

Horizon's single moon rose behind the planet, illuminating the night side in ghostly tones and revealing the swirl of the hypercane around a darkened eye.

'There are far more pressing threats to the biosphere than us,' Nadira said. 'The storm diameter's almost two thousand kilometres right now. Sometimes a little more, sometimes less.'

Cait couldn't see Nadira's expression through the darkened faceplate, but she could hear the concern in her voice.

'The bots are clean and primed,' Lex said curtly. He sounded on edge, impatient to get things rolling.

One by one the crew pulled in their lines and headed for the airlock.

'Port thrusters at sixty percent,' Bren said. 'Coming up on burn in three, two, one, *mark*!'

The acceleration pushed Cait against the restraining straps, and the visuals in her helmet began to track as the ship spun on its axis and turned nose-in to the orbital plot.

'We're locked in. Orbit established,' she said.

The whole ship shook as the starboard thrusters cut in briefly to kill the spin.

'Sensors operational,' Nadira said. 'Full spectrum.'

'I have two bots in the tube,' Lex said. 'Launching at your discretion.'

'Launch bots,' Cait ordered, and the hull rang with their leaving.

She watched the shrinking flare of their engines as they arced together towards Horizon and then split, one heading for daylight while the other streaked towards the terminator and the waiting storm.

She pulled off the data helmet and stowed it below

her acceleration couch, and concentrated on the screens overhead. The left showed white cloud blurring past, the image brightening and darkening as the bot plunged through thicker concentrations. The right-hand image was breathtaking. The moon was directly over the storm now, and as the bot scudded closer, the top of the spiralling vortex was picked out in greys, silvers and whites. It turned majestically around the dark central eye in a stately ballet that belied the violence beneath.

'Bot one to automatic overflight. Levelling bot two at seven kilometres above sea level,' Lex said, leaning on the control panel next to his couch. 'I'll bring her in over the eye.'

Nadira shifted in her seat to view the telemetry coming in. Cait heard the geophysicist take a sharp breath.

'Doppler's showing sustained surface winds of over three hundred kilometres per hour,' she said, her voice almost a whisper. 'There are close to forty convective storms in the main body.' She looked over at Cait. 'We have to get closer to the surface.'

'Closer!' Lex barked a short laugh. 'I know this is an interesting phenomenon, but we don't have an unlimited supply of bots, and they're not designed to withstand three-hundred-kilometre winds.'

'It's calm in the eye,' Nadira said. 'You won't encounter any turbulence as long as you steer clear of the eye wall. You *can* manage that, can't you?'

Lex bit back his first response. 'All right, all right. But I'm taking it slowly.'

He tapped the controls and the bot's-eye view on the screen rolled as it dropped towards the storm.

'There's a lot of water vapour up here,' Nadira said, almost to herself.

And then the bot entered the central column of the hypercane, accompanied by an eldritch flash that almost swamped the photosensors. Inside was darkness strobed with lightning that picked out patches of purple and green among the greys of the surrounding eye wall. Cait imagined how deafening the storm must be, even in the relative calm of its centre.

'Look at bot one,' Bren said, calling Cait's attention to the other screen.

Day was dawning over a wide, undulating plain. Purples, pinks and golds shifted across the sky and seemed to ripple in reflected glory across the land. The effect lasted only an instant and then the sun broke over the horizon, a diamond flash that arced across the sky, banishing the last of the shadow to reveal a desolate kind of beauty that stole Cait's breath away. Even from a cruising altitude of one hundred metres, she could see that the ground was covered in a white aggregate, no doubt the source of the colourful dawn reflections. Spindly grasses pushed their way through the landscape, but apart from that the view was uninterrupted all the way to far-off low, rolling hills.

The bot executed a turn and a river came into view, snaking into the middle distance. Its banks were covered with lush vegetation, which quickly gave way to sparse grasslands again.

'I'm reading unusually high temperatures,' Nadira said, focusing Cait's attention once more on the storm. 'Eighteen degrees hotter at the column head than the surrounding environment. Temperature dropping quickly now. And the pressure.'

'We're coming up on sea level. Slowing descent,' Lex called out.

'Can you take it into the water?' Nadira asked.

'You're mad,' Lex snapped. 'That's a full-on storm down there.'

'It'll be calm under the surface,' Nadira said slowly, as if talking to a three-year-old.

'I don't care. I've only got six of these things to map the entire planet surface. I'm not going to throw one away to satisfy your personal curiosity about some storm.'

'This storm has been raging for as long as we've been awake and who knows how long before that. If it's stable, it's going to wreak havoc with the atmosphere,' Nadira said. 'Cait, there's no other way to get to the epicentre – the storm system's too big. I *have* to get underwater readings.'

Cait shifted to look Nadira in the eye. She looked scared. 'Keep going, Lex.'

'But –' Lex began.

'I said keep going. Take her in.'

Lex slammed the control. 'Fifty metres from surface.'

'Oh, my God,' Nadira said. 'Pressure's reading six hundred and eighty millibars. No wonder this thing's blowing so hard.'

'Coming up on contact.'

Cait caught a brief glimpse of choppy water and then the bot was in the sea. The image disappeared in a flash of static.

'Buoy away,' Lex said. 'The cable is running and we have visuals.'

As the screen cleared again, Cait could see how murky the water was. The illumination from the bot's beacons hardly penetrated more than five metres ahead.

'Sonar's picking up some turbulence below,' Lex said.

'It's hot down here too,' Nadira said. 'Much too hot. This is what's causing the winds overhead.'

'Something's coming at us!' Lex said. The view suddenly veered away as the bot was sent into a spin. 'What the –' he began, and the connection was broken.

He tapped angrily at the controls. 'We were caught in some kind of vortex. I think the line's snapped.' The screen continued to show static. 'No. We've lost it.'

'You've got the flight logs intact up to the moment we lost contact?' Cait asked.

'Yes,' Lex spat. 'Much good they'll do us. I hope you're satisfied, Nadira.'

'I think I will be as soon as I've reviewed the logs,' she said, calmly but with a hostile undertone.

'Okay, that's enough,' Cait said. 'Let the other bot finish its sortie and bring it back. We'll look at the sensor data for both of them when you're done.'

She undogged her harness and stretched. 'I'm going to bring the ring back up to speed.'

'I'll come with you,' Nadira said, undoing her own straps.

Cait saw Lex throw a dirty look Nadira's way as she passed.

Cait glided into the darkened hold, heading for the ladder at the far end.

'He's insufferable,' Nadira said as Cait brought her legs forward to slow herself against the web.

She started climbing, her muscles enjoying the sudden activity after being cooped up in forward control. 'He is. He excels at it.'

Nadira matched her step for step into the centre of the web. 'He'd never get anywhere in the Compact with that kind of attitude. I can't understand how he even got onto the mission.'

Cait kicked off towards the far end of the access ring. 'Because, like you and me and Bren, he's the best at what he does. And he has enough strength of character to be blasted trillions of miles from the rest of humanity without getting freaked.'

She grabbed the ring collar and turned to look back at Nadira.

'He's not exactly a team player,' the geophysicist said, unmollified.

A rueful smile played around Cait's lips. 'None of us are. Since we woke up, I've been cursing the psychs that put us all together. Everyone on board is a stubborn individualist, and that's putting it politely. We've all got our points of view and screw anyone who disagrees.'

'You're not like that.'

'Oh yes, I am,' Cait said, laughing. 'It's just that as mission leader I don't get the opportunity to indulge myself like everyone else. Or I don't allow myself that opportunity. Maybe that's why they put me in command. Maybe they recognised some deep-seated masochistic streak that would prevent me from telling you all to go to hell.'

'So why not give up if it's so difficult?'

Cait decided half the truth was probably enough. 'Because I also feel responsible. I'm responsible for the lives of everyone on board. More than anything else, I want to make sure we get through the mission alive. And achieve at least some of what we set out to do.'

Nadira pushed off towards her. Cait braced herself against the tube edge and steadied the other woman as she came close.

'The psychs were right about one thing,' Nadira said.

'Oh?'

'They chose the right person to lead the mission.'

Cait smiled and reached for the ladder to the ring deck. 'I hope you continue to think that in the days to come. We've got some big decisions to work through.'

Cait took a sip of chicken broth and looked at the pile of flimsies strewn across the worktable. 'So what have we got?'

'Questions mostly,' Nadira said. 'But some answers.'

Lex harrumphed, but Nadira ignored him. She selected a flimsy and held it up for Cait to see.

'This is the biggest tropical cyclone we've ever seen. It makes Hurricane Iago back in the early two thousands look like a mild squall, and that decimated much of the eastern seaboard of the USA and precipitated the formation of the Pax.'

She sorted through the flimsies and picked out another one, this time a colour separation mapping temperature distribution at the ocean subsurface.

'The cause is abnormally high surface water temperature – I'm guessing as the result of lava breaking through to the ocean floor where the continental plates are diverging. But there must be a great deal of activity down there for the storm to keep regenerating itself the way it is.'

She turned her attention to Lex. 'The vortex that wrecked the bot was probably a hot water plume from the undersea eruptions. But they don't usually make it this close to the surface, which is what's really worrying me. In Earth's Cretaceous period, these types of event plumes were theorised to have driven massive climate change.'

'Change for the better?' Cait asked.

Nadira licked her lips before answering. 'For the worse. All that water vapour being pumped into the upper atmosphere is a strong greenhouse promoter. But I need more data before I can draw any firm conclusions.'

'Well, we can't send in any more bots,' Lex said, his arms folded tightly across his chest. 'If we're going to have any hope of finding and cataloguing Horizon's indigenous life, we can't afford to. And I think that takes a higher priority than this storm, no matter how big it happens to be.'

'This storm,' Nadira said, leaning across the table, 'could wipe out the entire biosphere. The effects aren't just localised. If these subsurface eruptions don't let up, the rest of the planet is going to get very hot very, very quickly. We're talking about total meltdown of the polar icecaps, rising sea levels and the eventual loss of a breathable atmosphere.'

'And what do you plan to do?' Lex asked. 'Stop it?'

Cait tried to intercede. 'We're not ready to make those kinds of —'

'Yes, if I have to,' Nadira said, throwing the flimsy

onto the table. 'If this planet is the last chance for humanity, then we have to do everything we can to rescue its biosphere from further degradation.'

'Degradation! *If* what you say is right, then this storm is part of a natural process.' Lex stabbed a finger into the pile of flimsies as he rounded on Cait. 'This is exactly the kind of thinking I object to. If we open Horizon up to colonisation, where do you draw the line? What's minimal necessary intervention and what's plain interference with a planet's natural development?'

'Lex,' Nadira sounded exasperated, 'assuming you actually find life down there, this type of climate change is going to kill it too.'

He spread his hands, unfazed. 'And how many mass extinctions occurred on Earth in prehistoric times? What would have happened to humankind if some "kindly" aliens had stepped in and stopped one of them? There are too many variables attached to any ecosystem to adequately plot the effects of that type of intervention. To believe anything else is hubris, plain and simple.'

'Okay,' Cait said loudly, holding a palm towards each of them. 'Let's not get started on this now.'

She spared a glance for Bren, leafing through the flimsies at the far end of the table. She seemed oblivious to the conflict around her.

'We all know the arguments, but this is one discussion that can only take place when all the facts are in. Let's move on. Lex, what did bot one come up with?'

He scowled. 'Only negatives. No animals, no insects I can detect, and nothing in the waterways. The vegetation's curiously undifferentiated. Just the open-plain grasses and that one kind of plant growing along the river. Of course, there's a hell of a lot more land to cover. I'm planning on running sorties over each of the major continents, concentrating on the coastline and river deltas, and then moving on to some of the island chains. Assuming we don't lose any more bots. But I want to send down a level-two collector to gather some soil, plant and water samples at the bot one site.'

Cait leant back in her chair and pursed her lips. 'Fine. Send two level twos. And rig one of them for deep water.'

Lex bristled. 'Cait –'

But she held up a hand to quiet him. 'You've had your say for now. Ultimately, disposition of ship resources is down to me. And I'm convinced this situation warrants further investigation.'

The tabletop control chimed, quelling any further objections.

'Oh, great,' Lex said. 'Now what?'

The hypercaster bubble appeared at the end of the table. Bren stood to avoid the expanding mass of static and moved around to sit beside Lex. The image resolved to show Bowen perched on the edge of his desk, looking down at them.

'Our calculations show that you should have

reached orbit eight hours ago.' His thin brows knitted together. 'I trust you actually *are* in orbit this time?'

Cait cleared her throat. 'We're in orbit. We're just analysing the data from the first bot run.'

'Forward your findings to me immediately,' Bowen said.

The lighting in his office accentuated the planes of his face and cast his eyes in deep shadow. Cait felt she was conversing with some angry all-powerful deity, which was probably the effect Bowen was aiming for.

'I'll forward a data packet as soon as we have something conclusive,' she said flatly, daring Bowen to say otherwise.

He turned to Nadira. 'What's your prognosis for colonisation, citizen?'

'I …' Nadira paused, looking decidedly uncomfortable under Bowen's cold stare. She glanced sideways at Cait.

'I said,' Cait interrupted, 'we'll send you a data packet when we have something worth considering.'

Bowen turned back to her, his displeasure obvious.

'You'll get your results a lot quicker if you leave us to get on with the job,' she added. 'We know what we're doing, and we know how desperate things are on Earth.'

Bowen pushed off his desk and stood to his full height. 'I doubt that. You've made the formal claim on Horizon, I assume.'

Cait had wanted to resolve a few things with the

others before tackling this issue. 'We've been busy. It's not exactly a priority.'

'You can do it now then,' he said, and the official wording began to scroll beside him, moving up from waist level.

Cait felt her face flush. Screw you, she thought. She'd just about had enough of his badgering. But she fought to maintain her composure. She recognised this was a defining moment in their relationship. Bowen was attempting to establish a pecking order and she couldn't be the one to weaken.

She stared into his eyes and waited as the words scrolled on, halting as they reached the top of his head. She'd have waited till the air ran out if she had to, but it was Bowen who gave first. He broke eye contact with her.

'It won't take long,' he said by way of concession.

'You still want to claim Horizon solely for the people of the Compact?' Cait asked.

'I think I've made our reasons for that sufficiently clear,' he said, recovering his composure.

Cait looked at the others. Bren was still rifling through the flimsies, but Lex and Nadira looked as tense as she felt, for their own diametrically opposed reasons, no doubt.

'I'm sorry,' she said finally, 'but I'm not prepared to do that yet. Our mission was a multinational one. It still is.'

Bowen's lips twisted. 'I'll have to discuss this with my superiors. I suggest you send those results quickly. For your own good.'

The transmission cut out with a hiss of static, and he was gone.

'Shit,' Lex said. 'Talk about delusions of godhood. Just who does he think he is?'

'He's the man with his finger on the trigger,' Bren said. She cast aside the flimsy she'd been studying and looked at them all. 'It's obvious, isn't it? First comes the request, then the demand. Next comes the threat.' She held her finger over an imaginary button on the tabletop. 'If you don't come around, Cait, he'll threaten to unleash the wyrm and shut us down permanently.' She crossed her arms. 'Not that it'll do him much good.'

'You still have no proof of that,' Nadira said, but her tone seemed less certain than before.

Bren gave a sideways smile. 'I don't need any. I'm not into games. When the time comes, Bowen will provide all the proof you'll need.'

Nadira shook her head. 'Even if they did have some weapon to use against us, why show their hand over an issue like this? Making a legal claim on the planet has less than no significance out here.'

'It's not "out here" that they care about,' Bren said. 'Once they have a registered claim on the planet, they can legitimately move against any other country that so much as points a spaceship towards Horizon. Their "claim" will be enforced on Earth in order to "defend the sovereign territory of the Compact",' she ended in a haughty tone, mimicking Bowen. 'I mean, let's face it, you don't know anything about the other nations on Earth, their space-faring capabilities, or whatever.'

'Damn right,' Lex chipped in. 'We only know what we've been told. If it was up to me, I'd have nothing more to do with the bastards without full and verifiable disclosure.'

'It's not likely that's going to happen any time soon,' Cait said.

'Then force Bowen's hand,' Lex urged. 'Refuse to help him until he comes clean.'

'No!' Cait's muscles tensed with frustration. 'I've gone over this enough times with you. The stakes are too high to waste time on cute personality games. We've agreed our course of action. Let's keep our eye on that and not get sidetracked by personal animosities.'

# 18

Lex held the collector in one hand and reached for the bar set into the low ceiling above. Slowly, he pulled himself towards the bot in the launch cradle. The clean room facility occupied one-sixth of the ship in front of the ring, but the majority of that was taken up by the racks of bots, the triple-chambered lock needed to maintain air purity, and the sealed bay containing *Magellan*'s only crewed lander.

He drifted away from the bank of sample collection units, each held in its own sterile receptacle behind clear plexiglas, passed the bee-striped entrance to the airlock, and grasped the bar again to bring himself to a halt beside the bot.

The paper of his hermetically sealed suit rustled as he rubbed at a sore patch on his side. The chemical scrub and flash UV required to access this part of the ship had left his skin feeling raw, but that wasn't the real source of his irritation.

'This is wasting time we can't afford,' he said to Bren, who was standing on the other side of the bot's torpedo-like casing.

He slid the collector into the waiting opening, and the latches took hold, pulled it further inside and closed seamlessly over it. There was a hiss as the interior of the bot depressurised.

'Not to mention wasting another one of these.' He rapped on the bot's metallic skin and it rang like a hollow gong.

Bren snapped the casing shut on her side and regarded him through her faceplate. 'I don't understand why you're so down on Nadira over this. It's just as important to her as your search for life is to you.'

'Like I said, it's a question of priorities.'

He checked the diagnostic panel hooked to the nose cone. The tell-tales slowly moved from amber to green. Sighing, he leant heavily on the panel, stretching out his aching spine. Moving about in zero-g was taking its toll very quickly, despite his exercise regime.

'Look, you know how I feel about this colonisation idea,' he said. 'Nadira and Cait will go along with Bowen's plans, no matter how distasteful or ill-framed they may be, because, as they see it, they have no choice. They're blessed with a humanitarian streak I don't share. But there's one thing that can tarnish their plans to save humanity and introduce an element of doubt. I have to find life down there. And I have to find it fast.'

Bren pulled herself around to the front of the bot and looked Lex straight in the eye. 'Come on. That's twice you've mentioned time. We've got years before the colony ships arrive, if they come at all. So what are you hiding?'

Lex shied away from her and stowed the panel in a floor locker. He stood again stiffly, uncomfortable at being so transparent. 'You have to promise not to tell the others.'

'I'm not promising anything. I know you: you wouldn't be telling me this much if you didn't need something from me.'

Lex took a deep breath. Bren was right – he needed her, but he realised he was also scared of her. She was different from the Bren he'd launched with. At first, he'd put it down to the long deepsleep and the fact that everyone was on edge, what with Sharpe and Harris dying. But it was only when they'd spoken together above the ring that he'd realised how much she'd changed. He pursed his lips and considered the alternatives. Necessity won out.

'We don't have years,' he said. 'In fact, we could have only a matter of days.'

Bren looked at the PALs floating overhead. Their running lights were suddenly extinguished and they began to drift in the airflow.

'Just in case,' she said.

Lex gazed at the dead devices. It occurred to him that he really had no idea how much power she wielded over the ship's systems. An errant thought licked at the edge of his consciousness – perhaps Harris had been right. He pushed away the mix of fear and guilt that came with that thought and plunged on.

'The Compact has two armed ships on our tail. They're going to act as local enforcers if we don't do what Bowen wants.'

Bren's focus seemed to shift elsewhere. 'They didn't –' She paused and Lex noticed her cheeks coloured slightly. 'They didn't trust us much, did they?' she finished.

He waited a beat, but she wasn't giving anything else away. 'Not in the slightest.'

'How did they get here so fast?'

'They're faster than us,' he said simply. 'Even so, they've been in transit for the last forty-one years. The ships were to have been the successors to *Magellan*, but then the shit hit the fan, the Pax folded, and the bio-plague was released. Some bright spark in the Compact, probably Bowen's predecessor, filled them full of weapons and sent them after us to keep us in line. The Compact's had years to work out what to do. But there's a wrinkle. One of the ships has a couple of spies on board from the UNS. They're planning to hijack their ship and destroy the other. With our help, if need be.'

Bren's brow furrowed. 'But we don't have any weap–' She looked at Lex with sudden understanding. 'So that's it. You want me to take over the drive and use it on them. I'm not that good.'

'You controlled it once before. You can do it again.'

'You have more faith in me than I do.' She stopped and licked at a bead of sweat on her lip. 'This isn't like you. Why are you getting involved with the UNS?'

'They offered me half the planet to preserve as I see fit.'

She shook her head. 'You wouldn't sell out. Not even for that.'

'Now who has more faith? But you're right. I'm going to see to it that no one gets Horizon.'

He felt he was under the microscope again as she stared at him. 'You'd really do that?'

He nodded, and she pulled her legs into a sitting position, drifting slightly in the air current. 'And by finding life, you think Cait and Nadira will side with you against the Compact?'

'It'll introduce an element of doubt – for Cait, at least – which will slow her up. Horizon's more important than nations or individuals. I'll do whatever I can to preserve that biosphere intact.'

'And if I decide to tell Cait what you're planning?' Bren asked, drifting slowly towards him. 'You'll kill me?'

'If I didn't think I could count on you, I wouldn't have told you.'

He waited, hoping he appeared full of a confidence he didn't feel.

'Your secret's safe,' she said finally.

Lex felt a brief surge of excitement, which fizzled

as he realised he'd moved one step closer to murder.

'But as for helping you,' she went on, 'I'll reserve my judgement. I don't know if I'm quite ready to start a war.'

Cait relaxed into the seat in front of her access port and punched up the sensor logs from the bots. It had been a long day and the ring was in semi-darkness. Nadira was already asleep and Cait promised herself it wouldn't be long before she was either. She'd take one more run through the data and start to frame some questions to address in tomorrow's sortie. Hopefully, they wouldn't lose any more units. It was laudable to look after resources, but Lex was taking it too far as usual.

On impulse she called up the log of Bowen's last transmission and keyed into the firewall scanner. The automatic alert Bren had configured would have warned them of any problems immediately, but sometimes it paid to check these things personally. The icon remained reassuringly green; no hitchhiking nasties.

She hesitated a moment, then called up Lex's transmission log. He'd been dismissive about the call from the UNS, but she'd had a nagging feeling about it all day. The icon turned to yellow. No viruses, but there'd been files downloaded that Lex had shunted to his personal directory without submitting them for analysis and cleaning. Now why would he do that? It wasn't the sort of thing you'd expect from someone who'd just rejected a plea for help from his nephew.

She settled back in her seat and tapped one index finger against her bottom lip. Perhaps she'd been looking at Harris's and Sharpe's deaths all wrong. She had three scenarios now: their deaths were unfortunate and unrelated accidents, possibly as a result of computer malfunction; they'd been murdered by Bren, due to personal enmity between her and Harris and, for some reason Cait was unaware of, also with Sharpe; or something colder and a lot more premeditated.

There had been rumblings in the 'old alliance' between the Pax and the EU before launch; shadows of the very debate she'd had with Bowen about who would really 'own' Horizon. It was difficult to think of Lex in the role of patriotic hero fighting for his nation state's interests – he'd protested against the very suggestion of loyalty, even to his own flesh and blood. One thing was certain though: he tended to let his passions rule his head. And he was certainly passionate about Horizon. Had the EU hatched secret plans for the planet and recruited Lex before they lifted? It provided another explanation why he'd been keen to contact someone outside the Compact. It wasn't just about corroborating the Compact's story; it was about making contact with the EU. But by the time they'd woken up, the EU had been swallowed up by the UNS – that must have been a shock for him.

The more her mind flipped through the

occurrences since her first awakening, the more a
new interpretation of events fell into place. As ship's
surgeon, Lex had personally overseen each crew
member's entry into deepsleep. There would have been
ample opportunity to administer a drug to Sharpe
during his final check, or even tamper with his harness.
And it was Lex who'd performed Sharpe's autopsy and
found 'nothing suspicious'. As for Harris, he'd made an
enemy of Lex when he sided with Cait and Nadira on
the flight plan changes. Had Harris found some trace
record in the logs that revealed Lex's secret? If he had,
he hadn't had time to alert Cait before he died. Before
the drive fired.

Now there was an interesting item. Lex had been
at pains to point the finger at Phillips during Harris's
'burial'. But he could have recruited Bren to fire the
drive. After all, she'd been conscious and linked the
whole time.

The scenario had an internal consistency, but was
it the truth?

If only the PALs Harris had rigged had picked up
something more conclusive. Still, he'd had the right idea.
The PALs were a useful tool for each crew member, but
they were also first-class intelligence-gathering devices.
It was a simple matter to use their eyes without alerting
their human companion.

Cait used the scat keyboard to set up a tap. Bren
and Lex had been gone a long time in the clean room.

Just what were they talking about, she wondered. Her query bounced and the monitor screen remained blank. The PALs were offline, which was decidedly odd. A cold hand pressed down on her chest.

She crossed the distance to the access ladder and climbed quickly, springing over the tube edge and sailing to the web. As her hands closed on the thick strands, there was a hissing noise to her left – the sound of the final clean-room lock door opening. She moved on instinct, climbing up towards the section containing forward control. She just made it through the opening, and was leaning far out to one side so most of her body was out of sight of the entry when she heard voices entering the hub area. Bren and Lex.

Her PAL hovered in the opening beside her, in full view of anyone entering the chamber. She reached out and grabbed it, pulling it close as the tiny fans whined in protest.

'... like you to take a look over the UNS files. They've included full specs,' Lex said.

'Okay, I'll look,' Bren said slowly. 'But I'm not promising anything.' She snorted. 'I can't believe this whole mission could fuck up so completely.'

'It's the ultimate proof that God exists,' Lex said. 'The bastard has a twisted sense of humour. No mindless set of deterministic laws could have arranged things to come together the way they have.'

The voices dimmed as Lex and Bren moved

along the tube to the ring. Cait pulled herself further inside forward control and sat in her couch. She could legitimately claim to have been there working on orbital plots if they happened to call for her and, with luck, they wouldn't suspect she'd been eavesdropping.

Fear of discovery gave way to anger as she strapped into the seat. So now she had it: proof of conspiracy. And Bren was part of it – if not to begin with, then subsequently. If Lex was an EU – now UNS – agent, it seemed more probable he'd killed Sharpe, covered up any traces in the autopsy, then enlisted Bren's help to kill Harris.

Cait kicked herself now for the way she'd treated the transhuman. She'd pissed her off so much she'd all but driven her into Lex's waiting arms. And who knew what poison he'd poured into her ear since then.

What the hell was she going to do? She'd been through so much already – facing her own private fears as well as trying to thread a way through the dangers that had surfaced since wake-up.

Which just means you've got to keep going, she thought.

A shiver ran through her as she realised this was it. They were approaching the endgame, when all the elements would come to a head. And she wasn't going to be the one to break. She was certain of that. Too much rested on it; not just for the crew or for Earth, but for her own personal survival, her sense of self. Giving up wasn't an option.

Lex must still fear discovery or he wouldn't be skulking around. He still had a need for secrecy. Which meant he wasn't ready to act yet. It had something to do with his call from the UNS. They wouldn't have risked blowing his cover unless something important had turned up. Confronting him now would only force his hand – she saw that. She had to bide her time. Work out what to do. With a fully functioning computer, just one person could theoretically run the ship. But under the circumstances, they needed all hands. Damn Lex. Damn his lying soul.

The only way to get any leverage over him was to work out what he was up to. Depending on what it was, she could either compromise so they could move forward as a team; or act to so totally frustrate his efforts that he was left with no other choice but to accept her authority – or, possibly, go off the deep end. She needed a contingency plan for that too.

Her mind felt like it was running at top speed, considering all the data she'd gathered and building it into a new framework with possibilities leading in all directions.

How deeply involved was Bren in the partnership, she wondered. Could they be prised apart?

Cait needed hard evidence. Anything might prove useful at the critical moment. The PALs had shown her nothing, but there had been one other witness to both murders, one person who must know exactly what had occurred while the others were in deepsleep.

She had to try to raise Phillips. Alone, this time.

# 19

Cait sat in her acceleration couch and activated Harris's PAL. The tiny robot was safely anchored above its dead master's harness, keeping vigil like a faithful dog.

Nadira was visible in the nearby harness, eyes closed and breathing slowly. Cait directed the PAL's gaze to the far side of the ring. Both Lex and Bren were in their respective harnesses on the opposite wall.

Her hand found a stud on the armrest. The screen in front of her sprang to life with a feed from the biomonitors. All three crew members were showing slowed heart rate and respiration. Brain activity for each showed a familiar sleep pattern. She couldn't have planned a better opportunity if she'd tried.

She pulled the virtual helmet over her head. The collar fitted snugly around her neck and, without the appearance of endless stars around her, she felt instantly claustrophobic. Then she could see the gloves as her fingers wriggled into them and activated the sensing nodes.

She clapped her hands together for the standard

control panel configuration. The board appeared before her and she set to work keying for a schematic of the computer system branchworks. She wanted to make sure there would be no trace of her actions, no tell-tale fingerprints on the information hierarchy that Bren tended so closely.

The schematic lay before her. She pulled it closer and it grew around her, taking on a dimensionality: bright structures, channels, transfer nodes, all depicted in a thousand colours. She stared around the cathedral of light filling every inch of her field of view and remembered childhood birthday parties with scores of shrieking children dancing around the night-filled backyard, the sparklers held high above their heads burning wavering tracks into her retina.

These tracks, however, persisted past any attempt to blink them away. These were the paths along which information flowed to ensure the ship had light and breath and fire in its belly. Orderly highways of data pulsed beneath, above and around her. She could pull at a stream here and receive a realtime image of the planet, or pluck at a line here and learn the status of the ship's air-recycling plant. She didn't need to know which line was which. The gloves knew for her, directing her fingers towards whatever information she desired, as if her thoughts gave the fingertips a particular charge that was attracted to one, and only one, data strand.

Bren had been responsible for much of this,

and Cait began to appreciate just how talented the systems specialist was. But she was here for more than simple appreciation. She had to establish a secure and, hopefully, untraceable link to the central core.

She selected her entry point and reached towards it – it was like drawing a line of light with her finger. She melded it into one of the secondary data channels, being careful to follow the routing that had already been laid out. Here and there the orderly lines were jumbled, looped and tangled around themselves. It was the result of Harris's jerry-rigging to link the subsystems and bypass the need for the AI to coordinate things directly. No wonder Bren had been annoyed. If the data structure was a towering monument to beauty through functionality, then Harris's tampering had been the squatter who busted a few windows and hung their laundry from the balcony.

Cait took advantage of the snarls, hiding her own link to the core in their tangled ugliness, following their ludicrous meanderings until she all but lost herself. If Bren came across her handiwork, hopefully she'd think it was another of Harris's 'fixes' and leave it untouched.

The data channel filled her vision and she moved faster, curving around and through the gleaming structure, feeling more than a little queasy as it twisted in gravity-defying loops. Finally, she edged closer to the core, or its representation inside the helmet, and her transit slowed. This was the epicentre of all the kilometres of interlaced bits that made up the data structure. It looked much like it did in reality – an impossibly long column except this one was standing upright, towering above the lightshow around her. Cait felt it should have been alive with light, outshining everything else. But instead it glowed menacingly with a dark nacre that reminded her of black opal.

There was something profoundly disturbing here. She hesitated, remembering the violent hallucination Phillips had thrown at her. Inside the helmet she felt more connected to the virtual world, more vulnerable. If he attacked her here, it would be more than some holographic sleight of hand. She couldn't just shut her eyes to block out the images she received; the helmet induced a signal response directly onto the optic nerve. From there it would be a simple thing to sear her synapses and leave her little better than a vegetable.

Her finger brushed the column and made contact. Her hand tingled at the touch and she felt a coldness that sent a shiver down her back. She pulled away, then willed herself to touch the core again. The cold was still there but she was prepared for it now.

Her free hand tapped at the panel floating at the bottom edge of her peripheral vision. Ripples of colour moved away from her fingertips and chased up the column as far as she could see. The seconds drew out, then there was a flash somewhere above and a streak of shifting crimson surged down the core and delivered a smarting shock to her hand. She recoiled, cursing, and wriggled her fingers to make sure there was no lasting damage.

'Come on, you bastard,' she whispered and pressed her fingers against the core again. Again she sent the query, the colour of her message rippling away from her.

She looked up. She could see the answering streak of light washing down towards her again. It was brighter this time and seemed to pick up speed as it closed on her. She braced herself, willing her fingers to remain in place, pushing against the core even as the urge to pull away grew unbearable.

The colour flashed towards her, five metres, three metres. She let out a strangled cry. The column exploded in a brilliant display, shards of fluorescence expanding past her, tearing into the surrounding lines of data, shredding them. She heard a scream, thought it was her own, then realised her mouth was clamped tightly shut.

The last of the colourful structure fell at her feet and melted away. Still the screaming continued as darkness enveloped her more completely than the helmet ever could. She wished she could plug her ears against the noise. And then it stopped.

Phillips knelt before her under a single sourceless spotlight, head bowed, fingers digging into his knees. He lifted his hands to chest height and turned them over and over, as if he'd only just become aware they existed.

'Come, come, come, give me your hand,' he murmured, almost too quiet for Cait to hear. 'What's done cannot be undone.' He looked up suddenly, directly into her eyes. 'What have you done?' he accused.

'I … I have to talk to you, Phillips.' She felt dazed. All that sound and light and now such stillness. Had any of it really happened?

Phillips's lips parted but his teeth were still clamped tightly shut. 'You said you'd leave me alone. Bitch!'

He struggled to his feet, took a menacing step forward, his hands held up before him, the fingers drawn into claws.

Cait raised her own gloved hands, partly to calm him and partly to fend off the expected attack. 'Wait! I'm not your enemy. I didn't tamper with you, or cripple you. I want to stop whoever did.'

'You don't care about me,' he sneered. 'You just want to save yourself.'

'I want to save what's left of the mission. If you were anything like your namesake, you'd care about that too.'

'Don't patronise me,' he snapped. 'And believe me when I say you don't want to know what's going to happen.'

'I don't have any choice. I'm the mission leader. I'm your commanding officer.'

Phillips stopped his advance and looked around, peering into the blackness. He licked his lips and opened his mouth to talk, but no sound came. He tried again. Again, nothing.

'Did Bren do this to you?' Cait asked.

Phillips raised one eyebrow. 'You credit her with far too much ability.'

'She balanced the drive. Brought us into orbit around Iota Persei F.'

Again Phillips's mouth opened, the throat working to no avail, then he shook his head and began to turn away.

'You've been in my dreams,' she blurted, and instantly regretted the statement. It felt so foolish now that she'd uttered it out loud.

Phillips turned towards her again. 'Me?' He shook his head sadly. 'No, not me.'

His wistful almost-smile chilled her blood. There was something in the way he spoke … She felt the skin on her scalp tightening.

'It was more than a dream.' She struggled to recapture the feelings she'd experienced then. 'Your image … more than that. A presence. You, but not you.'

She looked up again as a light pierced the darkness. Phillips began to glow, surface details slowly being blotted out as beams of light broke through his skin, heralding a brightness within that threatened to blind her with its brilliance.

'Perhaps there's hope for you after all, Cait Dyson,' he said.

She tried to turn away but the light was all around. Her eyes were stinging and she felt her retinas would burn out if she didn't act soon. Her gloved hands clawed at the helmet, fumbling with the release. The intensity stepped up a level and she screwed up her eyelids uselessly. Suddenly the light winked out. She opened her eyes. The data structure was all around her again, apparently untouched, and she was back where she'd started. She could see no sign of the strand she'd woven to the core.

'Phillips?' she whispered, but there was no answer.

Could a program suicide? She had the feeling he was really gone now, erased from the core memory banks. But still, something seemed odd. Almost as if she was being watched.

She turned her head and the virtual view panned around in a full three-sixty.

'Hello?' she called.

The darkness was inky-black past the glowing data streams. Perhaps she was jumping at ghosts, but the feeling persisted.

She snapped the helmet catch open, and a crack of cabin light appeared as the virtual image winked out. She left the helmet to float in front of her and pushed the heel of each hand against her eyeballs, rubbing them gently. She pulled her hands away and blinked until she could see the cabin clearly again.

Phillips's enforced silences were as important as

what he'd been able to say. His functioning had been severely compromised, but not, it would seem, by Bren – or Bren alone. Harris had been the only other on board with skill in the area, but he was certainly innocent. He'd lost his life trying to discover who'd tampered with the system.

Could Bowen have gotten an earlier wyrm in, before their first wake-up?

Or had Lex opened some undiscovered accessway for the UNS while still in Sol System?

Whatever the case, her last witness was gone. Sooner or later she'd have to confront her suspects.

In the meantime, she had to figure out a way of doing so and still remaining alive herself.

# 20

Lex pulled himself through the hatch into forward control and came to an abrupt halt. The room was empty save for Nadira configuring her station to track the upcoming launches. He considered just keeping quiet and getting on with his own work, not causing any more ripples. He considered it for barely half a second. It just wasn't in his make-up.

'Getting ready to chart the demise of two-and-a-half billion U-dollars of hardware?' he said as he pushed towards his own couch. 'It should be quite a show.'

'Just stick to your own side of things,' she said, barely looking up.

His voice took on a dangerous tone. 'This *is* my side of things. These bots are slated specifically for life sciences, or didn't you bother to read the log.'

Nadira pushed away from her workstation and swivelled on her couch towards him. 'Tell me, I'm curious. Do you hate me so much because I disagree with you, because I'm a woman, or because I'm black? Or is it a combination of all those things?'

'It's nothing personal,' he said, feeling defensive. 'Don't go trying to make it something it's not.'

'Don't tell me what to do,' she snapped. 'And don't bullshit me either. From day one you've done nothing to make me feel part of this team. You barely said two words to me outside forward control before we hit the harnesses. I've met your kind before. You've been privileged all your life, and for you and your friends it's trendy to have a social conscience. You make all the right sounds about tolerance and living together, but when you're confronted by the "other" you can't help feeling uncomfortable. Scratch the surface and all the old prejudices boil up. You may not be particularly proud of them, but they reinforce your comfort zone and help you to keep feeling superior, like you've been doing us a favour all these years.'

She let go of a pile of flimsies as she warmed to her subject, and they floated beside her. 'And now one of us has the temerity to argue with you. There's gratitude! How galling that the mission leader should come down on my side. How much more you must hate me. Well, guess what? I don't give a shit what you think.'

She grabbed the flimsies and turned to her work again.

Lex stared at the back of her head, his teeth clenched. He felt outrage mainly, something close to hatred – but not the kind Nadira had hinted at – and one tiny, niggling ripple of guilt that his treatment of her to date could reasonably be construed that way.

'You've got me so wrong I don't even know where to start,' he said.

'All set up?' Cait's voice asked.

Lex leaned back in his couch to look at her framed in the doorway. Just how long had she been standing there?

Cait shot Lex her sweetest smile. She knew exactly what he was thinking and she was enjoying his discomfort. She didn't believe Lex was the bigot Nadira made him out to be, but even the possibility that someone else might have overheard her accusations was enough to throw him off-balance.

'I take it you're ignoring my formal protest about endangering the bot?' he said, trying to regain some ground.

'I didn't ignore it,' Cait said, swimming past and catching her couch. She bent her knees together and swung her hips over its back. 'I simply decided not to act on it. Where's Bren?'

'She said she had some diagnostics to run,' Lex said. 'She'll join us when she's finished.'

Cait froze as she reached under the couch for her helmet, then forced herself to keep moving as though everything seemed fine. Her tampering with the core had apparently gone unnoticed, but Bren's absence worried her. There was no knowing what mischief she might be getting up to back there. Cait couldn't afford for either Bren or Lex to have free run of the ship's facilities any more. But she didn't want to make either of them suspicious.

She pulled the helmet on and checked ship status. 'I'm reading two level twos in the tubes and ready to launch. What's the flight plan?'

Lex sighed heavily. 'As we discussed. Number one will collect samples at the first targeted fly-by site. I can use what we get there as a baseline to corroborate the passive scans from the other flyovers I'm running, and hopefully focus in on more unusual sites. Number two is, as you know, going to dive into a giant hurricane and be ripped to pieces.'

Cait had been expecting some typical Lex comment, but it rankled just the same.

'Do you ever get tired of being a pain?' she said.

'No more than I tire of breathing.' He was back in the driving seat, his earlier embarrassment forgotten.

'Just launch the damn bots.'

'Aye, bots away.'

Cait tracked their descent until they edged into atmosphere, then keyed her helmet to take a direct feed from number two. She knew she was risking a valuable bot against standard operating procedure, and this time she wanted a front-row seat in case anything went wrong.

The storm was in full sun, but its central mass

shrugged off daylight, preferring the dark tones of an angry bruise. The image swelled around her, and for the first time she truly had some idea of how massive the hypercane was. The sheer physical size of it was frightening.

'Here goes nothing,' she heard Lex say, and her stomach flipped as the bot dived into the eye.

'Same readings as before,' Nadira said, 'to within a few points. It's certainly not weakening.'

Cait moved her hand up and down the channels – UV, radar, infrared. A bright patch showed dead ahead with IR, and she surmised that this was the ocean's surface.

'Contact in three seconds,' Lex said, confirming it. Static filled her universe and she closed her eyes against the brightness. 'Buoy away. We have visuals. For the moment.'

Cait opened her eyes and beheld a murky underworld, deceptively calm considering the violent storm above and what they suspected was below.

'We're diving,' Lex said. 'Three metres every second. I'm opening the sample chambers. One every ten seconds.'

Visibility declined rapidly. There was a lot of particulate matter held in suspension and it got worse the deeper they went. A lot of the ocean floor was being kicked upstairs by the look of it.

Seconds ticked off and Cait felt the tension growing

in the cabin. The further they penetrated, the more it was a matter of when the bot would be destroyed rather than if.

'We're passing the one-kilometre mark,' Lex hissed into the silence.

'Are you getting anything at all?' Cait asked Nadira, beginning to think she should call off the survey. There didn't seem to be anything down there.

'Wait,' came Nadira's taut reply, then, 'Yes! On the long-range IR – take a look.'

Cait made the switch and instantly cut back the brilliance. The ocean trench resembled a running sore: a red and angry blister spouting white-hot pus. She overlaid a grid to get things into perspective. The active area was at least half a kilometre wide and she couldn't see either end. Magma was bubbling up from the subsurface, forming a bright central spine and sloughing off to the left and right, gradually cooling to oranges, reds and browns.

'That is one hell of an eruption,' she said, so quietly she doubted the others could hear it through her helmet.

'That's our culprit,' Nadira said. 'The plates along here must be very brittle for this kind of outpouring to occur.'

'The samples will tell us more,' Lex said. Even he sounded impressed. 'But sensors show a lot of $CO_2$, hydrogen sulphide and trace elements being pumped out. The local chemistry must be very different from the surrounding deep water.'

'Activity on this scale can radically affect the entire ocean in a geologically short period of time,' Nadira said. 'But the real problem is the $CO_2$. There's already enough water vapour above the hypercane to promote atmosphere loss. The cloud cover isn't cooling the surface of the ocean enough to stall the storm because of the continuing volcanic activity, and now we're getting even more $CO_2$ thrown into the mix ... I need to run some projections.'

The image abruptly slewed around and Cait cut back to normal vision.

'Whoa,' Lex called out. 'We've hit one of those vortices again.'

The water looked particularly murky, like soup.

'You got enough to go on?' Cait asked Nadira.

'We need to pull the bot out now,' Lex called, exasperated. 'The cable can't hold.'

'I've got enough,' Nadira said calmly, deliberately.

'Bring her up,' Cait ordered, and heard Lex mutter something unrepeatable under his breath.

She watched as the bot slewed around, and caught a glimpse of the cable. The spinning stopped as the bot broke through the leading edge of the vortex and made for the surface.

'Bring them both up,' she said. 'I want those samples analysed as soon as possible.'

'I've formatted a preliminary data package for transmission to the Compact,' Nadira said.

The images from the bot jerked again and Cait thought Lex was going to foul the thing in its own cable. He cursed again, this time a lot louder.

Cait pulled off the helmet, feeling the cabin air cool on her sweat-moistened face, and loosened the harness so she could swivel round to look at Nadira.

'I thought we'd agreed we wouldn't do that until we had something tangible to report.'

Nadira's lips set firmly. 'I can't delay any longer. Not in all good conscience. We have hard data now of a massive climate change. A change for the worse for any colonists. We haven't got the luxury of choice now. They have to be part of the decision-making process because they'll be just as much affected – possibly more so – by whatever comes next. I insist that we send these findings now.'

'Absolutely not,' Lex said, still wrestling with the bot controls. 'The decision-making process, as you so clinically dub it, can't reach a valid conclusion unless it's properly informed. And that means delaying until we can present them with the whole picture. We still have over ninety-eight percent of the surface to evaluate.'

'Whatever else we find is only going to serve as corroboration for what we already have,' Nadira said sharply.

Cait cut across them both. 'All right, give me a

moment.'

'Come on, come on,' Lex said, suddenly distracted.

Cait watched the overhead as the bot broke through the surface of the ocean and began its ascent into the eye.

'Yes!' Lex hissed and snapped a toggle. 'Bots on automatic return. Now look, Cait, whatever data we have needs to be properly framed in context at the very least.'

Cait was inclined to side with Lex on this occasion. There were a great many unknowns left to investigate, and she had to admit that her dislike of Bowen played no small part in her deliberations. But all of Lex's motivations had now become suspect to her. There was another reason for denying the Compact access to information about Horizon: he may be feeding the same intelligence to the UNS. Bren could easily arrange for untraceable communications to take place. Keeping the Compact in the dark now may be giving the UNS some strategic advantage.

She turned to Nadira. 'Okay, send it. As a preliminary only. Emphasise we need more in-depth analysis.'

'Fine,' Lex said, the word infused with venom. 'I'm going to unload the bots.'

# 21

Lex undogged his harness and sailed out through the rear hatch in one single movement. He entered the darkness of the hold outside, and trimmed his course and velocity towards the entrance to the spider's web, muttering to himself. To hell with them. They deserved everything they got from here on in.

He crawled across the web and shuffled around on the strands until his feet were pointing towards the hold containing the clean room, and began his descent. The decon chambers were waiting. The first hatch opened and he climbed inside, shed his clothes and stuffed them in the flash incinerator. He placed a pair of dark goggles over his eyes, fitted his feet under two rings set into the deck, and reached to grab similar rings overhead. His index finger pressed the fail-safe set into the roof. A low whine built in intensity.

'Warning,' a female voice said matter-of-factly. 'First-stage cleansing commencing in five seconds. To abort, press the fail-safe once. Five, four, three, two, one.'

There was a loud *snap*. Lex always thought he could hear a slight sizzle as the top layer of his skin was incinerated.

'Cleansing complete,' the computer said, but he was already pulling off the goggles and patting at the fine powder now coating him.

The external door of the next lock opened and he passed through an air curtain into the cramped space. The lock cycled and he moved through into the second chamber, sat down on a stool set into the wall and strapped himself in. He disliked this part the most. The bacteriological wash brought him out in a rash. Still, he lathered up assiduously, coating his body with the suds and scrubbing under his nails. Washing the lather off in zero-g required a handheld hose/vacuum contraption that rinsed and sucked the soapy residue away in one action. That done, he reached for a tube set into the wall and sucked a quantity of mouthwash and gargle, jettisoning the contents into another tube.

He shivered against the cold air on his wet skin as he freed himself from the stool and passed through another air curtain into the final lock, cycling through into the smallest chamber of them all, with just enough room to put on breathing apparatus and a clean suit. His PAL was waiting for him, having passed through its own custom-built decontamination tunnel.

Emerging into the clean room, he felt calmer. The process of passing through the locks had taken his mind off things, but the reasons for his anger were still there, pricking at his consciousness like tiny barbs.

The die was cast now. By allowing the broadcast to the Compact, Cait had opened the door for them to directly influence the rest of the mission. They were in the loop. She might as well have gone the whole way and claimed the planet for them.

Nadira wasted no time when she got back to the ring, activating the hypercaster and feeding the data packet into the system for broadcast.

Bren was sitting at the workbench. 'What do you think they're going to do with this information?' she asked.

Nadira eyed her suspiciously. 'They need to know everything we do. How else can they make an informed decision?'

Bren grunted. 'The decision's already been made. Horizon's habitable. It's not a matter of *should* they come, it's more about how.'

'You seem to know a lot about the Compact's plans,' Cait said, joining Bren at the worktable.

Nadira settled opposite them and pressed a section of the tabletop. A chime confirmed the data had been sent.

Bren gave Cait a slow smile. 'It's fairly obvious. What other choice do they have?'

Cait returned the smile. 'It's hard to say without

being there.' She wondered just how much of Bren's views were informed by what the UNS had told Lex. 'But there must be other options.'

'Some people only see the choices they allow themselves to see.' Bren was suddenly serious. 'They're so set in their views and their prejudices.'

'It all depends where you're standing,' Nadira said. 'A seven-year-old starving on the streets of Delhi doesn't have many options. But people of real vision can still act to give her the gift of choice.'

'Hey, don't get me wrong,' Bren said. 'There are other valid ways of seeing the universe. I just don't think humanity has the capacity any more to adapt to survive.'

'And what do you base that on?' Cait asked.

'Observation,' Bren said simply.

The hypercaster chimed.

'Showtime,' she added, and settled back in her seat as Bowen materialised at the other end of the workbench.

'Good work,' he said, looking at the three women with a smile that barely touched his lips. 'We've reviewed your data and the colony ships are being prepped to receive their first occupants.'

Cait silently cursed Bowen. His tactic of putting them off-balance with his opening statement did nothing for the discussion process. Nadira looked instantly worried, while Bren couldn't suppress a smile.

'That sounds a little premature,' Cait said.

'On the contrary. We're not fully committed to a launch, but these things take a little time and, given the positive findings, we're hopeful further action on your part will bear out our decision.'

'With all respect,' Nadira said, 'our findings are far from hopeful. The climate is deteriorating, and there's no sign that's going to change.'

'Not on its own, citizen.' Bowen leant back against his desk, folding his arms. 'The ocean-floor breach must be sealed. Without a continuing supply of magma, the surrounding ocean will cool and the hypercane will stall.'

'And how do you propose that will happen?' Cait asked.

Bowen made a sweeping gesture and a glowpanel appeared before him. He picked at it with a thin, pale index finger. 'The soundings you relayed indicate three points of instability along the rift. You have low-yield atomics on board. I'll relay instructions for placement and detonation.'

'You want us to blow it up?' Cait said incredulously.

'There's your "real vision", Nadira,' Bren said softly.

'That is our recommendation,' Bowen said. 'Of course, you are better placed to make refinements on-site. I will be happy to discuss this further with you once you read the specifications I send.' The glowpanel disappeared and he stood upright. 'Now if you'll excuse me, I have a thousand details demanding my attention.'

He turned away, then towards them again. 'One detail almost escaped me. Your brother and nieces, Commander Dyson – we've located them. They are relieved to hear of your safe arrival and are on their way to one of our facilities now. We will arrange direct communication between you as soon as we can.'

He stared at Cait, letting the silence stretch. Cait felt numb.

'I am sure you will have much to say to each other,' he said finally.

'Thank you,' Cait said. She reached out and cut the connection.

Bren was looking at her with something approaching pity. But Nadira wouldn't meet her eyes.

The two level-two bots waited for Lex in the retrieval cradles. Their hulls had been automatically cleaned prior to being brought inside to prevent transferring any contaminants from the planet's surface. He set to work, methodically opening each of the collector hatches in sequence and locking them into the bank of collection units behind him. They were mostly water samples, of course, although the other bot had brought back a selection of soil samples and even cuttings from the grasses and the river-bank foliage they'd seen in the original fly-by.

He set up his analysis parameters on the panel and the unit began to cycle through the samples collected.

It was a time-consuming process – not only because of the number of tests and cultures each sample was subjected to, but because the unit had to self-sterilise each time it moved on to a new sample.

With nothing to do but wait, he began to wonder what was happening on the *Brahma*. They'd be in deepsleep still, making their final approach to the system. Would the spies act as soon as they were awake, or would they lie low until they got closer to Horizon? He guessed the latter if they were counting on assistance from him.

He'd have to talk to Bren again. She reacted badly to any form of pressuring so he'd have to be oblique, show her that siding with him would be to her advantage.

The trouble was, he wasn't sure what she wanted any more. The mission – and the plight of Earth – seemed incidental to her now. At times she seemed dismissive, like she didn't care, didn't even think of herself as part of the human race. But when he spoke of his own plans to cut loose and go it alone, she'd looked at him with a strange mix of fear and ... what? He'd seen that look on her face two or three times now and he couldn't pin it down. Regret? No, not so strong. But approaching it. Thoughts of the path not taken? Whatever it was, it made him feel uncomfortable, as if he was under a microscope.

A persistent chime broke into his thoughts and his eyes settled on the current sample under analysis

– one of the soil samples. He pulled down the screen and read the results so far. The canisters tested had all contained samples from the grassy plain area, which had showed very low levels of soil bacteria in comparison with anything on Earth. But this particular sample was teeming with life by comparison. It came from the river bank.

Lex shunted it over to the analyser, which began sampling onto a lab chip. The pull-down scrolled through the results as they came up. This was more like it: an ecosystem in microcosm.

The chime sounded again and he pushed the screen out of the way to see what was in the unit. A small case of unremarkable water, from Nadira's bot. The analyser had finished with the soil sample for the moment, so he shunted the case over to that section.

He hooked his legs under the machinery, snapped two small clips at his hip onto the tethers there to stop him drifting, and pulled the screen over. The analyser was already spreading droplets of the sample onto a chip.

Another chime. The next sample also had something of interest, and it was already moving to wait its turn in the queue.

Lex tapped at some keys and pulled up a sampling schedule, looking for where the two samples had been taken. His finger tracked down the list and stopped. Damn! Nadira was going to be insufferable. Both samples were from inside the vortex that had spun the bot around.

None of the other water samples tested so far had contained anything, which meant that whatever this was liked the deep, deep ocean and had been carried up, trapped in the vortex. Or it had come from the volcano.

There was a crackle beside his left ear and he turned to see his PAL hovering beside him, the tiny screen on the front flickering into life.

Cait's image appeared. 'Find anything?' she asked.

'You can pull up the data and see for yourself,' he said, annoyed at the interruption.

Cait's brow crinkled.

Lex felt a pang of regret, which he quickly pushed away. In his spectrum of alliances, she was moving firmly towards enemy status now.

'We've just heard back from Bowen,' she said. 'He wants us to use the nukes to close off the eruption.'

Somewhere far off Lex sensed anger. It was his; but it was a disconnected thing. What he *felt* was numbness.

'I'll be right down,' he said. 'Link off.'

The PAL screen blanked and he took one last look at the pull-down. The list had wiped and a new data set was building. He read the first two lines and stopped.

His voice was the barest whisper when he spoke. 'Oh – my – God.'

Lex stalked towards the three women from the access

ladder. 'I can't begin to tell you how crapped off I am,' he said, throwing himself into a chair.

'We haven't agreed to anything, so just calm down,' Cait said. She could see Lex was close to losing it. His body was rigid, his fingers digging deeply into the armrests.

'We shouldn't even be fucking considering it. Those nukes are strictly for asteroid work. They shouldn't be allowed anywhere near the planet's surface.'

'It's only a recommendation at this stage,' Cait said, but she wasn't any more convinced than Lex was.

'Bowen's a slimy piece of work, you must realise that. He'll do or say anything to get you to follow his orders. Tell me you're not going to use the nukes on Horizon,' he added in a quieter voice.

'The planet –' Nadira began, then stopped as Cait flashed her a warning glance.

'We're going to continue with our observations and follow the original mission plan,' Cait said.

'And *then* use the nukes,' Lex spat. 'I'm not stupid. And I know that poisonous bitch,' he pointed a finger at Nadira, 'is to blame.'

'Before you question anyone's motivations, you should take a good hard look at your own,' Cait warned.

Lex glared at her. 'I've got the best motivation of all of you.'

He slammed a small plastic cube on the table. It was filled with clear liquid.

'God!' Nadira shouted as she pulled back from the table.

'What are you doing, you idiot?' Cait cried. 'That thing shouldn't be outside the clean room.'

Even Bren was staring wide-eyed at the sample.

'I'm making a point,' Lex said. 'This comes from the vortex. Organic matter.' He looked at each of them in turn. 'I made a culture, and it's differentiating. You're looking at a sample containing thousands of tiny eggs carried up from the ocean floor – near that volcano Bowen wants nuked. This is life. Indigenous life on a large scale.'

He let out a deep breath. 'This is what we came for. And I'm not going to sit back and watch it destroyed.'

Cait reached out despite herself and picked up the sample, bringing it close and turning it over and over. Tiny specks glistened in the light. '

We have to investigate this,' she said.

She refocused on Lex and thrust the sample towards him. 'First, you need to put this back where it belongs. Carefully.'

She watched Lex pick up the cube gently between thumb and forefinger and cup his free hand beneath it.

'And then?' he asked.

'Then prep the lander. You're coming with me.'

'Are you sure that's wise?' Bren asked. 'I mean, there's still a lot we can do with telepresence.'

Cait regarded her systems specialist. Was Bren

simply concerned for their safety?

'No,' she said, nodding at the sample cradled in Lex's hands. 'There's no way I'm going to miss checking that out.'

# 22

The lander shuddered and bucked beneath them and Cait gripped the control handles tighter. She was almost deafened by the whine from the servos as the stubby, swept-back wings bit into the still tenuous atmosphere for the first time. 'Wooooo-hooooo!' she yelled as the vibration peaked and the sheet of flame obscuring her view forward flashed once more and was gone. She trimmed the vehicle's attitude and the noise and shaking dropped off as a clear blue sky greeted them, a shade darker than she remembered from Earth.

'Do you always feel the urge to scream at the top of your lungs when you fly into a new world's atmosphere?' Lex asked over the suit mic.

She shifted awkwardly in her seat to look at Lex beside her. They were both wearing full vacuum suits in case of a hull breach, but even through two layers of plexiglas she could see he was looking green.

'I have so far,' she said.

'Well, do me a favour. Don't make a habit of it.'

Not even Lex's sour disposition could put a dent in

how she was feeling. She'd experienced oxygen narcosis before and this was almost exactly the same. Her skin was tingling all over, her stomach felt tied in knots and she was a little lightheaded. She was one of the first two humans to enter an extrasolar planet – no wonder she was wired. How many years had been spent preparing, training and in transit? How many thousands of people had sweated blood to put the ship together and get this far? How many billions of U-dollars had been sunk into the project? In this moment she knew it was all worth it, and that everyone involved would have felt the same way.

They were still high enough for the curvature of the planet to be visible. The ocean below was a sparkling dark mass, and in the distance she could make out the worn coastline of their target continent. There was so much of the familiar here – the sky, the wispy clouds trailing past as they continued their descent. But equally the place held an alien quality in its every aspect – the texture of the light, the shape and spread of its continents, the landscape itself as they drew closer and began to make out detail.

Cait was struck by how weathered it all looked, even in the more sheltered inland reaches. The countryside undulated gently. Even the mountains reminded her of elderly stooped granddames. There were no sharp, thrusting mesas, no pinnacles scratching at the sky, no ragged canyons draped in shadow to break the monotony.

She caught herself. How quickly complacency could set in. 'Monotony' just wasn't in the lexicon here. She was probably staring straight at some feature that could kickstart a whole new branch of geology.

'Kill me now,' Lex said quietly as he craned forward, pressing his helmet against the bubble windshield surrounding them. 'It can't get any better than this.'

'We've only scratched the surface.'

She extended the ailerons and the craft banked to bring them closer to the ground. The cockpit area was set high above the ship's midline and well forward, so their view was almost uninterrupted by the bulk of the fuselage. They were dropping down over a chain of low hills bordering a wide plain. It looked an arid place: dusty soil littered with finely graded rubble interspersed with the hardy grasses that seemed ubiquitous over most of the land mass.

'Not the most hospitable area,' Cait murmured, checking their altitude.

'And not at all unrepresentative. Apart from the grasses and the vegetation growing near the river deltas, it's your original barren wasteland. Or seems so right down to ten centimetres below the surface, which is as far as the sampler bots could dig.'

'You want the full spread here then?'

Lex might have shrugged but any such movement was lost in the bulk of his suit. 'It's as good a place as any.' He slid back a section on his armrest and turned a key. 'Thumpers armed.'

Cait made sure the craft was levelled. 'Launch at your discretion,' she said and the cockpit shook four times in quick succession.

She tracked the slim, cigar-shaped probes on the console monitor. Their casings were modified depleted uranium – no residual radioactivity but the same density. They sliced effortlessly into the grassy plain, throwing up a short-lived plume of dust, and buried themselves a good ten metres below the surface. The data signals came through loud and clear, but they could look at the telemetry later. It was time to go hunting.

A thrill ran through her again and she turned the dart-shaped lander away from the all but dead landscape and towards the promise of the ocean. The water was a clear blue with gentle waves unfolding themselves onto the softly sloping beach. It was a perfect day and a perfect location. Clear skies showed all around through the windshield bubble and on the rear monitors.

She pushed the throttle forward and they shot over the glistening waves, heading for deeper ocean.

The shoreline receded rapidly so Cait switched the monitors forward and maxed the focus, looking for the first glimpse of the storm. After ten minutes of near supersonic flight, a smoky blemish appeared dead centre on the screens. Five minutes later they could see it with the naked eye, and Cait cut back their airspeed in preparation. Both of them watched in silence as the storm swelled rapidly to dominate their vision.

The thing had looked awesome from orbit but approaching it now, side on, it was close to terrifying. A sheer wall of darkness, openly defiant of its surroundings, it looked alive – malevolent. Forked lightning crackled across it with such ferocity it seemed to form an eldritch outer membrane of transient light.

'How close are you going to get?' Lex asked.

The remark sounded offhand, but Cait was sure the sight of the elemental fury ahead was having the same effect on him as she felt.

'Not too much closer. I'm going subsurface now.'

The soft hum of the turbine dropped an octave as she reduced air speed further and the ship lowered towards the water.

'I think right about here!' she said, bringing the nose up and cutting the thrust. The ship dropped and there was a loud thud as it hit the water and bounced.

'Shit!' Lex grabbed at his restraining straps. The ship bounced again, then settled on the ocean's surface, rising and falling with the waves. 'Jesus, Cait, I almost lost my lunch.'

'Well, it's not exactly up with "one small step for man", but I guess it'll have to do.' She flipped a toggle on the control panel. 'You tracking us, Nadira?'

'Yes.' Nadira's voice came over loud and clear. 'We have good contact. We're also getting strong signals from the thumpers. I'm starting the prelim analysis now.'

'Well, we're going subsurface. I'll contact you again in three hours. No longer.'

'Okay. Good luck. *Magellan* out.'

Cait rotated the wings and nudged the turbines forward. As the inverted wing surface bit into the water and dragged the craft under, the bubble of glass surrounding them became slowly immersed and they passed into another realm.

The water was crystal clear below.

'Sonar's operational,' Cait said. 'Let's go.'

She increased thrust and trimmed the angle of the wings, and the vessel swooped into the depths.

As a child she'd spent a couple of months in the deepsea habitats of the Mariana Trench. Her mother had been offered a relief posting there, and Cait hadn't spoken to her for almost a week after she accepted it. The prospect of spending any time in an overgrown swimming pool instead of joining her friends at that year's mountain camp had appalled her. But going down for the first time in the transport she'd been amazed at how vibrant and varied the sea life was so far beneath the ocean's surface. After that she'd gone diving as often as she could to experience it again firsthand.

The oceans of Horizon were a different story. The flitting silvery shoals of fish, the swaying tendrils of kelp and sea grass clinging to the ocean rocks, the minute-by-minute dance of eat or be eaten were all missing. Instead, she was confronted with a watery desert.

Nothing lurked in the cracks and crevices of the rocks waiting to snatch breakfast; no drill-perfect battalions of fish turned as one and fled at their approach. There was nothing but them, the sea bed and the clear, clear water.

They carried on like this for half an hour and there was no change. The light from above was becoming more and more filtered as they descended further. Cait hit the lights and twin beacons speared out ahead of them. The water was so clear it might as well not have been there. Nothing was reflected in the beams. But as they went on a little further, she saw something up ahead. Closing on it, she realised it was a wall of churning silt, extending as far as she could see.

'What's that?' Lex asked.

She checked their position. 'We're nearly at the leading edge of the storm. It's possible the turbulence in this border area is circulating down and kicking up the sea bed. It's hardly registering on the sonar. It can't be very thick.'

She'd throttled the turbine back as much as she could. Any slower and the drag on the wings wouldn't be enough to keep them under. They'd shoot up like a champagne cork.

'I think it's safe to go on,' she said.

'I didn't come this far to wimp out now.'

She pushed the craft on towards the barrier of silt. There was a tension in her chest that wasn't wholly unpleasant: that feeling of expectancy that came with the promise of discovery. Everything they learnt about Horizon was equally unknown, of course, but this ... She felt it could turn out to be something very special indeed.

'This is going to change everything on a fundamental level,' Lex said, mirroring her thoughts.

But hearing the words forced Cait to consider the problem inherent in such a discovery: how they'd reconcile whatever they found down here with the needs of Earth. It was something she'd been happy to forget for the time being at least.

'Let's try and keep things in perspective,' she said. 'You know how many discoveries have been wrongfooted by sloppy work.'

'You miss my meaning,' Lex said, adopting a superior lecturing tone. 'You saw the sample. Whatever's down here, it's life. On a macro scale. It's not some microbe to be brushed aside for the greater glory of mankind.'

'I'm not missing anything,' Cait said as they plunged into the wall of silt. She gripped the control stick tighter and watched the depth gauge intently. 'The analyser identified a multi-celled organism that's differentiating. It's labelled it as an egg because that's the closest term it has in its lexicon to what it's seeing. But the system's not foolproof. What you found may not even have an Earth analogue.'

Lex snorted in disgust. 'Tap-dance around the issue all you want. It's my instinct that we'll come face to face with the real thing here. And it's going to blow this whole Compact deal right open.'

Cait remained silent. Everything they'd learnt about Horizon so far indicated it was the original tabula rasa – no animal life, nothing in the oceans or rivers, even the soil bacteria was functioning at a level below that found in Earth's Arctic tundra. Despite herself, she'd begun to think of it as a colonists' dream. Part of the tension she felt surrounding Earth's plight had begun to abate as a result, even though it meant her own dream of finding alien life was fading with it. Discovering that life now would complicate matters horribly. But it would also be wondrous.

'Instinct's a great thing,' she replied. 'But it can lead you into all kinds of trouble.'

'Okay, let's talk about something more concrete. If we find life down here, will you still recommend colonisation?'

'It's not that clear-cut.'

'Bullshit, it isn't.' Lex's voice rose in pitch inside her helmet. 'What is there that muddies the waters for you – how much life we find, how big it is, whether it has opposable thumbs or not? Seriously, I'm curious to learn what goes into your decision-making process.'

'Mature and rational examination and discussion of the facts is a good start.' A faint warning bell was ringing somewhere in the back of her head, but she was growing tired of the childish tack his questioning was taking. 'You should try it some time.'

'*Don't* push it!' he warned.

Something about his tone dragged Cait's attention away from the instruments. He was sweating heavily inside his suit and his skin was pasty. He looked sick, but he sounded so angry. Fear settled in her stomach.

'Are you threatening me?' she said.

His eyes swung away from hers. 'I'm trying to save you, dammit. I care about you, you know.'

'Save me from what?'

He faltered, looking unsure of himself. It was an expression that didn't sit well with him, Cait thought.

'From your own stupidity,' he said, focusing on the readouts, then out through the windshield again. 'How long till we get to the site?'

Cait punched up the trip log. She was glad the suit gloves were so thick; they concealed the fact that her hands were shaking.

'We're quite a way off. Maybe another half-hour.'

They were still moving through the silt, and visibility was close to zero.

Lex looked at his own instruments. 'Sulphide level's rising. The concentration is pretty high for this distance, although the sub-ocean currents could be driving the stuff this way, skewing the reading.'

Cait was only half listening. She was more

concerned about Lex. His mood swings were becoming worse. She'd been so caught up in his discovery she hadn't given a moment's thought to the fact they'd be alone in the lander. If he was working for the UNS, he couldn't have a better opportunity to get rid of a major barrier to whatever he was planning. A small equipment malfunction could leave her badly injured, or worse. And with no one else to see, they'd have to believe his explanation of events.

She thought hard, trying to come up with something in the cockpit to use as a weapon. Then she stopped. Did she really believe Lex could hurt her, even kill her? A couple of days ago, she would have laughed at the thought, but now … Had her universe tilted on its axis that much?

Lex obviously believed she'd made up her mind to agree with Bowen. But he couldn't be further from the truth. She wanted to do what was right by the people of Earth, but she also wanted to do what was best for Horizon. And despite any ties to the UNS, Lex's concern for the fate of Horizon must still be what drove him too.

Whenever she felt torn between opposites like this, she tried to let the moment flow; to not crystallise it with a decision. It seemed to short-circuit her desire to second-guess.

It was also something that had lost her more than one partner down the years, and nearly cost her the command of this mission before it was officially hers. For some, resisting making a decision equated to indecisiveness. But Cait thought this far too simplistic a view. The important thing was to know when the time to choose had arrived. Waiting allowed the dynamics of a situation to play out, maybe even allowed it to resolve itself without intervention.

She had to trust her instincts now to know when the time was right. But she could feel the pressure mounting: from Bowen and, more importantly, from Lex. If he acted before she was ready, it wasn't just her that would suffer. She had to handle his expectations, and believe that – given a viable alternative – he'd rather not hurt her or the others. That meant managing the dynamics to ensure he didn't feel forced into doing something stupid.

'We're coming out of it,' he said, and Cait focused her attention forward.

She could make out indistinct shapes, and as they left the last of the sediment behind, she caught her breath.

A forest of craggy columns lay ahead: black smokers, maybe twenty or thirty metres tall, topped with the billowing clouds that gave them their names – volcanic emissions from beneath the ocean floor, rich in sulphides and other trace elements. The whole scene was backlit in a dull red glow that gave it the appearance of something out of Dante's *Inferno*.

'What's that on the bottom?' Lex asked.

Cait looked at the feed from the sensors immediately below the craft, and turned up the sensitivity. The ocean bed looked slimy, as if it was covered with some kind of shiny gelatine. Now she saw it clung to the black smokers too, clearly visible in the forward beacons.

'I have absolutely no idea,' she said.

The navcomp chimed. It had plotted a course through the tangled gallery of smokers. Cait pulled her hands away from the controls and let it take over, even though the urge to regain control became almost unbearable as they headed straight for the nearest column. They swerved at the last minute, brushing past it and turning to head along a wide avenue lined with insanely twisted rock chimneys.

'The chemistry here is radically different,' Lex said, apparently happier to trust the navcomp over Cait with such close-quarter manoeuvres. 'Hydrogen sulphide's almost at saturation point. Very low in oxygen. Some other quite exotic stuff in small amounts. If I didn't know better, I'd say we were on a totally different planet. And then there's this.'

He touched a small screen in front of him and the cabin filled with a crackly drumming noise punctuated every so often by a loud pop.

'Sonar picked it up about ten kilometres back. Fairly erratic. It peaks at ninety decibels or so and ranges between a hundred and eight thousand hertz.'

'The volcanic activity?' Cait asked.

'The filters don't seem to think so.'

As the tiny ship turned again they caught glimpses of a dazzling line of brightness coiling off into the distance.

'That must be it,' Cait said, glancing down at the sensor display. 'The temperature gradient certainly fits for magma. God, it's bigger than we thought.'

'Can we get past the smokers? Parallel it for as far as it extends?'

'I think so. There's one final row up ahead. I think I can take it from here.'

She recovered control of the craft and aimed the nose for the largest gap between the columns, then jerked the joystick in shock as a huge shape surged out of nowhere and almost knocked them into a spin. She caught a glimpse of a giant wing, grey flashed with orange, covered with bumpy nodules and tapering into a devilish hook.

'What was *that*?' Lex yelled.

The proximity alarm bleated and Cait pulled at the controls half a second too late. The port side clipped the nearest smoker and a jet of black sulphide sprayed across the windshield as debris rained down on them, thudding onto the top of the bubble and making it ring ominously.

They cleared the smoke and Cait jerked her head around inside the clumsy helmet as she looked for signs of cracking. She started to apologise, but Lex wasn't listening.

'Never mind that. *Look*!' He was pointing dead ahead at a group of indeterminate shadows moving towards them.

The shapes entered the arc of the beacons and time stopped for Cait.

Bizarre combinations of colour and shape were all she registered at first. The creatures moved with a gentle grace that belied their travelling sideshow bodies. One translucent sphere glowed with a diadem of bright points waving on the end of tapered appendages. A nest of scilla below twitched and it surged towards them.

A collection of eel-like beasts moved to the centre of the beam, tangled around and over each other in a bird's nest of heads and tails – although it might have been one creature for all Cait knew.

A curling ribbon shimmered past, diffracting the available light in an oil-slick rainbow along its length.

And then all of them were gone.

The vessel lurched to one side as the first creature they'd encountered glided past the windshield again, this time in the opposite direction, its wing tips undulating as it too disappeared from sight.

Cait drew in a ragged breath, feeling as if she'd awoken from a dream. 'Christ,' she said, checking the readouts, 'did we get visuals on that?'

She turned to Lex, but his helmet was pressed to

the side of the cockpit bubble.

'Can you tip this thing a little?' he asked. 'Get a better view of the floor?'

She trimmed the wings and the nose of the craft dipped. The arcs of the lights swept down and across the floor. She turned back for another pass, and saw the sea floor was moving.

She dropped speed as much as she dared and tried to focus the beams on one spot. The silt was covered by large creatures that looked like elongated pumpkins with a clump of fronds around one end and dozens of long threads trailing along behind. Their bodies were brightly coloured in variegated yellow and blue chevrons and shone in the light from the beam. They were packed close, moving side by side in slow undulations.

'See the slime?' Lex said.

Cait nodded. 'It's all over the place. Do you think they're the cause?'

'A sample would tell us for sure. Bring us round for another pass.'

Lex opened a panel on his seat arm and pulled up a small lever. Cait anticipated the slight shudder in the craft's movement as its profile in the water altered. The cameras showed the flared nose of the sampling scoop extending smoothly.

'At least they move slow,' she said, and increased speed to bring the craft skimming along the bottom.

Lex was watching the feed from a camera mounted

at the business end of the scoop. 'Steady … steady … a touch left … steady …'

The creature was no match for the suction of the collector. It disappeared from sight, and a satisfying snapping sound rang through the ship as the unit closed over.

'This is unbelievable,' Lex said. 'Absolutely. Jesus! Just think – all of this hidden away. This changes things all right. No mistake.'

Lex sounded almost manic, but Cait couldn't blame him. She was feeling a little spaced out herself. There was a weird metallic taste in her mouth, and she felt slightly disconnected from her body, like it was responding just a little out of phase. The world had just become infinitely more complex, and with it the choices they had to make.

'I think I've seen all I need to see for now,' Lex said, leaning back in his seat. 'Take us home.'

## 23

Cait slammed the triple-glazed window with the palm of her hand and yelled. She knew shouting was useless but it made her feel better. Any harder and she was afraid she might crack the glass.

Thankfully, Lex finally looked up at her. She pointed to his PAL attached to the ceiling overhead. He nodded once and reached up to activate it.

She grabbed her own PAL and set it squarely in front of her. 'Link to Dalziel,' she said and the tiny screen flashed and made the connection. A different, smaller view of Lex appeared. He was looking up into the camera, which made his brow wrinkle.

'You've been in there thirty-six hours straight,' Cait said. 'Are you coming out or do I have to climb in there and haul you out?'

Lex's PAL detached itself and floated down towards him. He looked like shit, but she knew he wouldn't admit it, even to himself.

'I'm almost finished,' he said. 'At least on the first run. The biology of this thing is amazing. I just have a few more tests –'

'Wrong, you're finished now. You know when the meeting's scheduled and I want you alert. The specimen will still be there when we're finished.'

Lex didn't look like he was going to budge.

'Don't make me come in there to get you,' she warned. 'You know how that chemical scrub shits me.'

He hesitated a second longer, then thumbed a contact on the desk. The elongated pumpkin – the Morlock, as Lex had christened it, after it flipped out entering the glare of the lab lights – disappeared, along with its container, back into the specimen bank.

It took a lot less time to cycle out of the clean room than in, and Cait helped Lex through the final lock door. Red ringed his eyelids and there was heavy stubble on his chin, but his eyes were sparkling.

'Jesus, Cait, I've got the equivalent of three PhDs in there. You wouldn't believe what I've found.'

'Save it,' she said, raising a hand to head him off. 'I've read the early postings. I want you fed, showered and looking and feeling human again before the meeting, okay?'

Lex reached past her and grabbed the ladder to the web. 'You're taking your leadership role a little too far. You'll be organising my social calendar next.'

'Yeah, if you had one.'

She followed him up and through the tube to the ring, and saw him safely headed towards the shower stalls before she left him.

He was right, of course: she *was* orchestrating things. All part of keeping him from reaching crisis point. Besides, Lex would experiment and experiment, driving himself into the ground until he'd learnt all he could. Discovery was a drug to him and he was on a high right now. No doubt he was sure the rest of the crew would fall in line due to the sheer power and persuasiveness of his discovery. When he realised this wasn't necessarily the case, he'd get morose – imagine all the bad things that could and, for his money, would happen. That's when he'd most likely do whatever it was he was planning with Bren.

What they needed, Cait thought, was rational, well-balanced discussion. They stood at the threshold of a new epoch for humanity – and level-headed decision-making would make a nice change. She wasn't about to let emotion get the better of any of them. So, Lex would shower, and he'd eat. She'd even rub his tummy if it meant he'd sit still and really listen to someone else for half a second.

The sound of singing reached her from the showers. She pushed Lex out of her mind, or at least to some seldom-visited corner, and set out to find Nadira.

The Compact scientist was already at the worktable with a neatly stacked pile of flimsies in front of her. Nadira was the complete antithesis of Lex. She was very methodical in her work and she'd let the detail speak for her. Where Lex used wildly looping logic, entreaties to morality, ethics and so on, Nadira used flowcharts, trend analyses and time-lapse thermographic overlays. It was only when reason failed to be the undaunted champion Nadira felt it must be that her true fire was unleashed.

Lex had already annoyed her to the point where she'd be inclined to react badly to anything he said. Cait had to use the time before the meeting to let Nadira say what she wanted to say, and then edge her thinking onto a more consensus-driven track – one that each of them, perhaps even Lex, could live with for at least a while.

'Shouldn't be too long now,' Cait said as she sat opposite Nadira. The other woman merely nodded.

Cait ran an eye down the pile of flimsies. 'Quite a body of work you've compiled there.'

She could see Nadira's jaw muscles working beneath her skin. 'I hope it will be enough,' she said finally.

'What's the high end of your projections?' Cait asked, willing her to open up.

'The next twenty to fifty years,' Nadira said, glancing quickly at Cait before casting her eyes down to the flimsies again. Cait waited.

'It doesn't look good,' Nadira added. 'Not without some kind of intervention.'

Good, Cait thought. That's an opening I can live with. Something with the potential for movement. She settled back in her seat and let Nadira present her findings.

'The problems would have shown up sooner or later,' she said. 'The hypercane has merely speeded up a process that's been building for decades. The lack of variation in the plant life is a major factor.'

Cait leaned forward, steepling her fingers on the table. 'In what way?'

'The savannah grass is fairly innocuous. But the heavy-leafed plant, the one with the stranglehold on the waterways, is releasing a net surplus of $CO_2$ into the atmosphere. It's a small amount, but cumulative. Add to that the warming of the ocean and, as a consequence, the upper atmosphere, and we're looking at severe and sustained ozone depletion with resultant loss of breathable atmosphere through photodissociation.'

'You mean the overheated upper atmosphere will leak away into space?'

'Right. Lex may want his creatures protected, but whatever he's proposing is useless without a sustainable atmosphere.'

Cait nodded. 'So do the Compact scientists have the right answer?'

Nadira considered the question for a long while. 'I think the nukes are a last-resort strategy,' she said hesitantly. 'We could wait a year, look for other alternatives without seriously damaging our chances of righting the problem, but ...' Her voice trailed away.

'But the colony ships will need an answer before that if they're to get on their way,' Cait finished for her.

'Or,' she focused on Nadira's eyes, hoping to read her reaction, 'at least an assurance that we'll take that step if we absolutely have to.'

Nadira's gaze latched onto Cait's as she realised what she was proposing.

Come on, Cait thought, take the middle ground. We don't have to choose one course and one course only. Let's preserve our choices as long as we can until we're sure we know what the right one will be.

'I suppose ...' Nadira ventured.

'Pretzel, anyone?'

It was Lex, clean-shaven, hair still wet, and still buzzing from his work in the clean room. Bren was with him. Cait hadn't seen her for over a day and didn't know where she'd been all that time.

Lex dropped a bowl of pretzels onto the centre of the table and slumped into a chair at one end. Bren sat between him and Cait.

'Okay,' Cait began, hoping she'd had enough time to at least flag to Nadira that there were other approaches worth considering. She was glad Lex seemed happy and relaxed, but she wished he didn't look quite so pleased with himself. She knew how much his know-all attitude got under Nadira's skin. 'I think we all know why we're here. We've been working non-stop on Horizon for the past four days now and it's time to step back and take stock of where we are. Also, to consider how events back home may impact on us given our new insights into the planet.'

'Diplomatically put,' Lex said. 'You'd have made a good politician, Cait.' He laughed. 'Now, there's an oxymoron if ever I heard one. But if you'll permit – once I've shared the insight I've gained into Horizon, I think it'll make our decision much easier.'

Cait glanced at Nadira, who half shrugged.

'Okay,' Cait said, 'it's all yours.'

Lex interlaced his fingers and stretched his hands out in front of him. 'You've seen the live feed on our little Morlock hunt,' he said, looking at each of the crew members in turn.

Establishing a presence, Cait thought, drawing us in and setting the scene before he leads us all down the yellow brick road to his own private Emerald City.

'Living on the ocean floor smack in the middle of a cathedral of black smokers pumping out noxious hydrogen sulphide, among other things, barely a kilometre from an open sore in the planet's mantle that's weeping white-hot magma. An extremophile if ever there was one. Put simply, one tough son of a bitch. And yet not so very different from us. Old Morlock used to be an oxygen-breather.'

'You're sure?' Nadira asked. 'You didn't mention that in your postings.'

'A slight omission,' Cait said. 'No doubt withheld in order to create dramatic effect when the time was right.'

Lex smiled. 'You know me so well. Yep, an oxygen-breather. Fitted with a pretty standard set of gills. But one that found itself in an evolutionary dead end when the planet around it turned to shit. You know Earth's geologic history: it's strewn with cataclysmic events. Mass extinctions on a grand and only moderately lethal scale. Something happened on Horizon that forced this sucker's great-grandparents to up stakes and move to the only place on the planet that offered at least short-term survival. I don't want to tread on our Earth science specialist's toes,' he said with mock seriousness to Nadira, 'but I'm guessing some kind of widespread glaciation. That would account for the undulating landscape, the uniform aggregate strewn around the ground and the severely limited plant life we've found all over. Maybe so widespread that the entire planet was locked in ice for a while. A giant snowball.

'Imagine one small group of sea-going creatures seeking to escape the cold and taking up residence around the vents of an underground volcano. Pickings are slight down there, and what oxygen is available is badly tainted with smoker gases. The survivors are looking at slow, inevitable extinction. That is until something wonderful happens. Something totally unexpected. A symbiotic relationship is struck up between an extremophile microbe of the deep ocean and some of the surviving creatures, which allows them, through progressive generational mutations, to derive energy directly from a new source – the hydrogen sulphide cycle.'

'You mean the volcano?' Cait asked.

'Right.' Lex smiled. 'Not only does it provide the creatures there with heat, but they feed directly off the outpourings from the black smokers. You saw the slime that covers everything? Those are vast colonies of the microbe that makes the whole thing possible. We scooped some up with the Morlock. Plenty for a decent analysis.'

'Okay, so let me get this straight,' Cait said. 'This microbe is infecting the creatures in some kind of symbiotic relationship?'

'Right. The microbe oxidises the hydrogen sulphide, creating energy for its symbiont. It's a work of art!'

'But the ice has been gone for – well, long enough before Earth started making direct observations of Horizon,' Cait said. 'Why are the creatures still confined to this one spot? Why didn't the survivors spread into the vacant niches?'

'Because the same symbiotic relationship that helped the creatures survive has trapped them. They need a steady supply of hydrogen sulphide to live now. Countless generations have come to depend on it. But it looks as if they're about to get the break they need. The volcano's outpourings are on the increase, changing the chemistry of the sea water around it, and the habitable sphere is growing day by day. In geological terms, we're on the brink of watching a stampede of life across the whole globe.' He gave a short laugh. 'This "perfectly Earth-like planet" we found is simply in transition from one snowbound epoch to another, where a hydrogen sulphide cycle will support a form of life very different to anything we could possibly imagine.'

He sat back, his face flushed with excitement. 'Let's study it by all means. Let's learn from it, marvel at it, for fuck's sake. But let's realise Horizon is not for us, and never will be.'

Cait felt tempted to clap. Lex would have made a mesmerising orator.

'So you're in favour of protecting the fauna you've discovered?' Nadira asked.

Cait tensed, ready to jump in if things got out of hand.

'Of course,' Lex said defiantly. 'Any real scientist would.'

'Well, we can discuss "real science" another time,' Nadira said. 'But how are you going to protect your creatures if their ocean disappears?'

Lex stared at her blankly.

'Your volcano may be keeping the last native species alive, but it's having a much less welcome effect on the atmosphere,' Nadira continued. 'The hypercane is pumping greenhouse gases into the upper air at such a rate that your hydrogen sulphide oceans will boil away to nothing inside your lifetime.'

'So we nuke the creatures out of existence now?' Lex said bitterly. 'Kick over the nest and trample it into the dust like some deranged cuckoo. I've seen your projections and I'm not convinced. The greenhouse could still stall, reach a new equilibrium. A hotter world than your precious colonists might like, but still one where the indigenous creatures could prosper.'

'I couldn't have put it better myself.' Cait dropped into the conversation, stalling the threatened argument. 'The jury's still out. The projections are still projections, and the creatures still have a lot of science left to reveal. And, at least in the short term, it can stay out.'

Lex eyed her suspiciously.

'One or possibly two years' wait isn't going to make much difference in the scheme of things,' she continued. 'Time enough for us to amass a mountain of knowledge about the planet, refine our theories until we know what's going to happen without a shadow of doubt, and we're confident about any course of action we decide to take. The colony ships won't be here for another fifty-five years at least. All we need is a modicum of trust.' She hoped she sounded more confident than she felt.

'You know how I feel about what's happening back on Earth. You know I have my own particular views on what's possible and what's preferable. But I'm willing to put aside my own feelings and hopes if we can all just come together and work on a solution. A solution that will satisfy all of us here. If we can just get a little trust working, I'll state here and now that I won't support any actions that we can't all say in the final analysis we know to be the right and best thing to do.'

She paused for breath. The others remained silent, waiting. She hoped that was a good sign.

'Nadira, you wouldn't want to destroy the life down there if you could possibly avoid it?' she asked.

'Well, no,' Nadira said, although her tone suggested she felt she was being manoeuvred.

'And, Lex, no matter how much you hate your fellow man, you wouldn't consign the human race to extinction if there was an alternative you could live with?'

'I don't see what alternative could please us both,' he said.

'Come on. We're all intelligent. Who knows what we'll discover in the next couple of years. It's not an absolute impossibility, is it?'

Lex remained tight-lipped, but there was something in his eyes. She'd seen the same look when they were en route to the smokers, when he'd scared her. There's something more here, she thought. She remembered Phillips's inarticulate warnings in the core and felt the cold hand of failure on her heart. Her words nearly withered on her lips, but she pushed on, trying to convince herself she was imagining it.

'There's no reason we can't work together on this. There's a lot still to do down there and plenty of time for us to do it. But I must confess there's something I want too.'

'You mean apart from all of us loving one another?' Lex asked.

Cait ignored him. 'I want to push that trust out to include Earth too. They have to trust us to do the best we can for them, to guarantee that if the colony ships can't have Horizon on their terms, we give them viable alternatives, that we don't simply wash our hands. And I want the Compact to open up the colony ships to non-Compact citizens. If we're going to preserve the human race, I want every part of it represented. It's not worth going through all this heartache otherwise.'

'Knowing the human condition, I think that last wish will probably be the hardest one to accomplish,' Lex said. 'But it's a nice thought. I really mean that, Cait. I'd come on board in an instant. I admit I haven't trusted you. Not since we made it past Iota Persei F.'

Cait's jaw tensed. Here it comes, she thought.

'But you've surprised me with this. I believe you mean what you say, and I'm sorry it's not going to get a chance to work.'

'What is he talking about?' Nadira said, sounding confused and pissed off at the same time.

'I mean,' Lex sighed heavily, 'your friends in the Compact have already screwed us on the trust issue. They didn't trust us from the start. There are two armed cruisers, stripped down and fast, on their way. Coming to make sure Bowen gets what he wants.'

'You're lying,' Nadira hissed. Then, shouting, 'You bastard. *You're lying!*'

'I don't expect you to take my word for it,' Lex said. 'Get Bowen on the line. The ships are nearly here. He's probably ready to spring his little surprise. If I'm any judge of dramatic timing, it's the proper theatrical moment.' He sat back, arms folded.

The consequences of what Lex had just revealed were spawning in Cait's mind, spinning off in a thousand directions. In a dream, she reached for the hypercaster controls. Then hesitated. She looked at the others.

Nadira seemed as shocked as she felt, but Bren didn't seem surprised at all. This information must have come from the UNS. But was it the truth, or was it part of whatever Lex and Bren had been cooking up in the accessway?

Cait tried to think what advantage Lex could gain from telling her this now. Clearly he wanted her to challenge Bowen about it. But to what end? To force Bowen to show his hand if it was true; or to drive a wedge further between them if it was a lie?

Whatever Lex's intention, they couldn't move on until they'd cleared it up one way or another. She keyed the hypercaster channel open.

'Be careful,' Nadira said softly.

Cait managed a weak smile, but she felt sick as the walls of Bowen's office closed in around them.

# 24

Bowen was in shirtsleeves at the far end of the table, which melded neatly into his desk. His coat was draped over the back of his chair and he was studying a glowing panel floating inches above his desktop. He waved a hand and it disappeared as he sat back to regard the others who had appeared in his room.

'Commander,' he said. 'You have a response on our solution to the hypercane?'

'Not yet, I'm afraid, Mr Bowen,' Cait said, wondering how to bring up the cruisers.

He sighed. 'I fear that so far you have proved something of a disappointment to us. I hope now that we can put our relationship on a more positive track.'

'I think you'll find I've always been willing to cooperate,' Cait began guardedly. 'Perhaps not as quickly as you may like, but we're dealing with some very complex issues here, both scientific and ethical.'

'As you say.' Bowen picked a piece of lint from his cuff before looking at her once more. 'I have some more news on your family. Their arrival at our facility has been delayed. A road accident en route. But let me assure you, they are unharmed.'

'I'm glad to hear it,' Cait managed, even as a cold hard lump formed around her heart.

'So,' Bowen said, 'perhaps we can discuss our plans for Horizon.'

'Just a minute,' Lex said. 'We've heard we'll be getting some visitors of our own shortly.'

'Lex,' Cait hissed, but it was too late.

'Really? And where does this information come from?' Bowen asked.

'Oh, come on,' Lex spat. 'We know about the other two ships you sent. We know what their orders are.'

Bowen settled back in his chair and smiled. 'Very well, Specialist Dalziel. The *Brahma* and *Vishnu* will be rendezvousing with you in just under one hundred and forty hours. Their mission is to provide support and assistance in preparing the planet for the colony ships.'

'They'll be under my direction then?' Cait asked.

'You're ready to follow our recommendations concerning Horizon?' Bowen countered.

'I see,' Cait said. 'We're working on a proposal for you at the moment –'

'Let me be quite clear, Commander Dyson. You already have the proposal. We want the ocean rift sealed. *Now!*'

'There are other factors involved,' Cait said.

'There are no other factors. The only factor that

need concern you is the wellbeing of your family. Do I need to spell it out for you?'

Cait stood, her whole body tingling. She leant heavily on the table for support, part of her unable to believe she could gather the strength to say what she was about to.

'Mr Bowen, I can't place my personal concerns above what I believe to be in the best interests of my crew, of Horizon and Earth. And I can't commit to using nukes at this time.'

Bowen stood too, his face set and cold. 'Commander Dyson, you are not talking to some petty bureaucrat. I am the Secretary of Homeland Defence, and I speak for the Compact High Council. This has gone on long enough. You are hereby relieved of duty. Specialist Nadira Coomlah, by my authority you are now in command of the ship and this mission.'

Nadira's eyes widened, then she stood and walked to stand beside Cait, placed a hand on her shoulder. 'You will forgive me, Secretary Bowen, but I cannot accept the command. Commander Dyson has my full support, and I believe the safety of the crew and the interests of the colonists would be best served if she remains as commander.'

A terrifying calm descended on Bowen and he seated himself slowly. 'You have until our ships arrive in orbit to follow your orders,' he said. 'After that, I cannot guarantee your safety.'

He reached forward and the connection was broken.

Cait sat heavily, aware of Nadira's hand still resting on her shoulder. She took what strength she could from it, but still she felt sick. If her brother was alive, she'd just put him and his daughters in grave danger. But she couldn't see what else she could have done. She rested her head in her hands and tried to focus.

Lex whistled loudly. 'Good move, Nadira.'

'Shut up!' Nadira yelled. 'This is all your fault.'

'Jesus! How do you figure that?'

'Why is he waiting?' Cait said, sitting back in her chair.

'Huh?' Lex asked.

'Why is he waiting for the ships to arrive before he does anything? Why isn't he using the wyrm? Or at least threatening us with it?'

'It's past the time for threats,' Nadira said, sitting on the empty seat beside Cait. 'We've angered him too much.'

'There's nothing on the hypercaster channel,' Bren said. 'But if the wyrm trigger was being relayed from those ships as a conventional signal, it would still be on its way.'

'Lex,' Cait said, 'your informant. Did they give you any course information on the Compact ships?'

'No. Only that they're coming.'

Which could easily be another lie, Cait thought.

'We need to plot where those ships are, or at least guesstimate,' she said. 'They're a hundred and forty hours out. They'll be coming straight into Horizon's orbit, no doubt, so it's possible they haven't begun braking yet.'

'I can make a few projections if you like,' Bren said.

'What's on your mind?' Lex asked Cait.

'I don't know yet. But as long as that signal isn't broadcast, we still have some currency with Bowen and the Compact. And that means it's too early to give up hope.'

Cait knew it was a tenuous hope at best, but the alternative was unthinkable.

'Oh, come on,' Lex said. 'We're about to be attacked by hostile ships. How bad does it have to get?'

'That's your take on things. Those ships are coming to assist us – as long as we toe the Compact line. Besides, things wouldn't have got this bad if you'd shared your information with us a little earlier. Just what the hell were you thinking?'

'I should be getting on with those projections,' Bren said, and made to leave.

'No,' Cait said. 'You're in this too. It's obvious Lex told you about the ships before the rest of us. I want to know why neither of you thought the mission commander needed to be informed.'

'Oh, get off your high horse,' Lex said. 'This is bigger than you or Nadira. It's bigger than Earth even.

There's a planet down there about to be destroyed because of our innate greed. I didn't tell you because I knew you'd fall into line with Bowen as soon as you knew he was sending some muscle. I needed time to convince you Horizon is worth more than that. Under the same circumstances I'd do exactly the same thing.'

'Well, thanks, Lex. You've managed to achieve the exact opposite of what you set out to do. Luckily, we're not as shallow as you imagine. Bowen, you and armed ships notwithstanding, I'm determined to broker something we can all live with. Next time I suggest you don't sell your crewmates so short. And I'm talking to you too, Bren. We have a very difficult time ahead of us. If we're to get through it with more than our lives, I want a commitment right now that the team comes first. If we have a problem, *we* discuss it and *we* fix it. There's to be no more separate agendas.'

Lex looked sullenly back at her, but Bren seemed somewhat cowed.

'I suggest we all have a long, hard think about how we're going to handle this,' Cait finished, 'and we'll reconvene in twenty hours.'

Lex stood and saluted. 'Aye, aye, Commander.' He spun on his heel. 'Come on, Bren. I'll help you with those projections.'

They headed off together towards the command port.

'Do you think you can trust them?' Nadira asked.

'Lex?' Cait shook her head. 'About as far as I could throw him under double the g. Bren … I don't know. She seems so lost.'

She turned to Nadira. 'You're another matter. I know how much it took to stand up to Bowen. But I'm more than a little confused.'

Nadira smiled. 'It was less difficult than I thought. You mean what you say, Cait, and I respect that. Bowen's demonstrated he's the exact opposite. If he's a product of his culture, then the Compact is not the same nation I grew up in. Besides, threatening a person's family doesn't fit within my ethical framework.'

'Secretary or not, Bowen can't be representative of the whole Compact government,' Cait said. 'There must be others who'll listen to reasoned discussion and support a workable solution. Perhaps it's only a matter of being heard.'

'I hope so,' Nadira said. 'But humankind has a unique knack of disappointing itself. It's pessimistic, I know, but perhaps Lex is right. Letting humankind loose on Horizon could be like a cancer invading a body.'

'He's *not* right,' Cait said, feeling less hopeful than she sounded.

She lapsed into silence, staring at the benchtop. They needed help, and she could think of only one place to go.

'I have a little work to do in forward control,' she told Nadira. 'Meet you for coffee after?'

•

Lex hunkered beside Bren while she interfaced with the systems.

'That should do it,' she said, sitting back. 'There's only so much space in the probable approach route. As soon as we detect any movement or a change in doppler shift, we'll have them.' She focused on him. 'You didn't tell them about the UNS spies on the Compact ships. And what you're planning.'

'Because I still don't trust them not to try to stop me. And I have to go ahead with it. More than ever now we've found life. But I can't do it without you, Bren. We're getting down to the wire. I need to know you're with me one hundred percent.'

She examined him for a long moment. 'Horizon mustn't be touched, I know that. But I'm not sure how attacking the Compact ships is going to fix things. I'm only with you because I don't know what else to do.'

'That's not the answer I was hoping for,' he said. So much was going to depend on the next few hours.

'Well, it's the one you have to live with. Which means you're in exactly the same position as me.'

Cait settled the data helmet over her head and slid on the gloves. She was feeling more than a little foolish, but the sensation she'd had in the core after Phillips had finally left persisted. She knew she was acting on pure intuition, but either she was going crazy or there was more to this than she realised.

The data field appeared before her and she instantly plucked at the quickest route to the core. She was through with hiding her tracks. Bren could think what she liked.

The vast structures of information swept by and she dipped her fingers in to sample them, alert for any hint of strangeness. The bulk of the core seemed to swell until it towered above her. The column was in darkness again and she suddenly feared she'd reached another dead end.

'You're searching for something.'

She panned the helmet, trying to locate the sound. Phillips was standing a few feet away, behind her.

'You're not Phillips,' she said. 'You're the other one. The one from my dream. Why do you appear as him?'

The lines in Phillips's face rearranged themselves into a smile. 'I am as you make me. The dataverse is part information and part mediation. It allows communication, and ensures that communication is meaningful to those involved. It translates what I am, and presents me in an analogue that allows you to understand as much as possible of what I am. It even rephrases my speech in terms that will make sense to you.'

'So you're a computer program like Phillips?'

'It appears that is the closest analogue that gives

you a useful frame of reference.'

'So you're something else? Something I'd have difficulty comprehending. Are you alien in nature?'

Phillips grimaced. 'I think this part of the conversation is becoming increasingly redundant.'

'Okay. At least I know you're not a hallucination.'

'That, at least, is certain. I am here. To see what happens. Perhaps to help.' His stare was so intense it seemed to pierce her brain. 'Where I think such help is appropriate.'

'I take it you're not going to tell me what constitutes "appropriate"?'

Phillips remained silent.

Cait's head was buzzing. There were so many questions, but she felt she had to tread carefully.

'You know about the wyrm?' she asked.

'I've seen it,' was all Phillips allowed.

'Two Compact ships are coming. They'll be taking over our operation on Horizon. What I don't understand is why they haven't used the wyrm to destroy us already.'

'They need you. Or rather, your reserves, your air, your oxygen recycling plant. The only reason they've been able to travel so quickly is because they've been stripped down to the bare essentials. Less mass means more effective boosting. The crew won't leave deepsleep until they're closing on you. They don't have the safety margin for anything else.'

'So we still have something to bargain with.'

Phillips was starting to fade out.

'Wait,' she said, and he regained his former appearance of solidity.

'I need to know about Sharpe and Harris. How they died.'

Phillips shrank before her and his clothes shimmered on his body, changing into a pair of jeans and a T-shirt. As she watched, Phillips's head, arms and legs withered to nothing and his form changed to her brother Ben.

'I am a friend, Cait,' he said, and the breath caught in her throat.

He stuck his hands in his jeans pockets the way he always had and toed at the ground. 'That's why it's difficult for me to admit this to you. Sharpe was an accident. My first visit caused a malfunction in your systems.' He looked at her, his eyes pleading. 'I didn't mean it to happen. You have to believe me. I tried to restart his heart. But ...'

Cait shook her head. 'Ben – I mean, you, whoever you are. Why didn't you tell us?'

'I guard my privacy closely. I have to. When I reprogrammed Phillips to hide my visit, his algorithm was changed. It evolved in ways I couldn't anticipate. Phillips killed Harris when he found traces of me in the systems. The AI was acting to protect my anonymity, but not in a way I'd intended. When he realised what he'd done – I think that's what finally sent him over the edge.'

'But you're back now. You're revealing yourself to me. Why the change? Why are you helping us?'

'Horizon has become very important to me now. How you, your crew and the Compact intend to interact with the planet is being watched very closely. Your own actions have been potentially helpful. They deserve some encouragement.'

'And you'll continue to act when you think it's appropriate?'

Ben smiled his dazzling smile at her. 'I think you may be beginning to understand me, Cait.'

He took her hand in his own. She pulled back for an instant as she felt his touch – the gloves weren't meant to provide this level of feedback. It was as if her body was in two places at once. She felt the restraining straps of the acceleration couch. She felt the warmth of his hand, the calluses, the hardness on the tips of his fingers from years of guitar playing. Most of all, she felt his strength. And knew she couldn't stand to lose him again.

'My brother – is he all right? Can you know that?'

'They have him, but he's being treated well. And your nieces. I don't think they'll harm them. The arena has moved to Horizon now.'

A tear ran down her cheek, wetting the cushioning inside the hood. She placed her arms around her brother and hugged him tightly, feeling his strong arms around her shoulders and his stubble on her cheek.

'I have to go,' she said. When she opened her eyes there was only the blackness of the hood.

She pulled it off, wiping at her tears. She looked at her reflection in the blackened screen of the overhead monitor. God, she was a wreck.

Come on, she told herself. This isn't going to save lives. You have to think!

She wasn't sure what she'd just encountered, but more than ever she had to know the truth. If she was going to avoid any further deaths, she had to know everything. She had to hold it all, analyse it and make the right choices. If Bowen or Lex or anyone else took control of the situation, it would be a bloodbath.

It made sense that Bren must know more about the ghost in the core. If Harris had found traces of it, Bren couldn't have failed to do the same.

It was time they had a talk.

# 25

Cait descended the ladder from the access tube and saw Bren sitting alone at the worktable. She looked like she was asleep, but Cait knew better.

Bren's eyes snapped open as Cait approached the table and sat opposite.

'I've just got a fix on a doppler shift,' she said. 'Two ships, braking together. Bowen's estimate of arrival time appears to be right on the nose.'

'Thanks, that's very helpful,' Cait said. 'A lot more helpful than you've been recently.'

Bren's face froze.

'Don't go all sullen and pouty on me. I know what's hiding in the core. And I know you've known about it since we came out of deepsleep.'

Bren's eyes widened. 'You've talked to them?'

Interesting that she said 'them', Cait thought. 'Just a few minutes ago.'

Bren's focus shifted, then she looked at Cait again. 'I can't see them.'

She sounded sad and frustrated. Cait realised that

was why the specialist had been looking so lost.

Cait felt as if she was standing on the threshold of something important. All she had to do was find a way to take one more step.

'They're not talking to you any more,' she said.

Bren hesitated, then sat back. 'Not since we made orbit, and I don't know why. Did they say anything to you about me?'

'Nothing specific,' Cait said, feeling her way. 'The planet is very important to them. They're waiting to see what we do next. What do you intend to do?'

Bren's eyes narrowed. 'I'm going to do what they'd want me to do.'

'But you don't know for sure what that is.' And who the hell are 'they'?

'I know enough. I'm a lot closer to what they've become than you are.'

Cait smiled as one piece of the puzzle fell into place. 'Posthumans. The transhumans that chose exile from Earth. Are they totally uploaded? Do they have any physical presence at all?'

'You bitch,' Bren said. 'You don't know anything about them. You're using me again.'

'You left me no choice. Think about it. Maybe your judgement isn't as unclouded and augmented as you'd like to think. What do they mean to you? Do you want to be like them, is that it? You want to be one of them? Are you so unhappy being what you are?'

'You don't understand anything about me, or them. You couldn't even begin to,' Bren spat.

'We're not at war, you know. It's not us and them. They've spoken to me. They want to help.'

Bren just stared at her.

'Look, they've trusted me enough to reveal themselves –'

'Don't fool yourself, Cait. It doesn't mean they trust you, or that I should. It just means it suited them to intervene and point you in the direction they want you to go. You don't matter to them. How could you?' Bren stood and glared at her, red-faced. 'You're nothing. You're nothing but a puppet to them. So get out of my face.'

Cait stared at Bren's receding back. What would it take to get through to her? And was she right about the posthumans?

She felt frustration building in her again. She thought she'd come some way towards understanding what had happened. An explanation, finally, for the malfunctions and the deaths. Some insight into the Compact. What if it was all built on lies?

No. She couldn't go back down that path or she'd be totally paralysed, unable to act. She had to believe she was moving towards the truth. And Bren had done her a favour. It was important not to take what she'd been told in the core at face value. There could be motives within motives.

Some of it, she was sure, was true, especially about

the Compact ships. It explained Bowen's actions. The wyrm was to be his weapon of last resort. The ships would come alongside, look for a sign that Cait and her crew were willing to cooperate, and if they didn't get it, they'd try to kill her and the others and take what they needed. If all else failed, Bowen would threaten them with the wyrm. He'd probably trigger it out of sheer bloody-mindedness if he had to.

If the first malfunction hadn't occurred and alerted them to the wyrm's presence, they would be in a very different position now. Cait laughed to herself. Don't believe in dumb luck. The posthumans must have had a hand in that. The timing was right. Perhaps the wyrm's transmission even prompted their first visit. Clearly, they didn't want the Compact to have control over the mission.

She sat at the worktable and took stock. It made a certain kind of sense. Whatever changes they'd made to block the wyrm and cover their tracks had disrupted systems and caused Sharpe's death. Phillips had been affected, so why not Bren?

Cait shook her head. This was getting too weird, and there were more pressing things to consider. They had to place the ship in a defensive posture, ready for the Compact ships. She wasn't kidding herself they could achieve much against two armed vessels, but she wasn't giving up. Nadira would help. And Lex and Bren surely couldn't argue about that.

She looked at her PAL clamped onto the track on the nearby wall. 'Get me everyone.' The tiny tell-tale flashed green when the link had been made.

'Nadira, Lex – Bren, if you're not too pissed off with me – we need to meet. Discuss strategies for when our friends arrive in orbit. Five minutes, in the lounge.'

She hoped Bren would come, if only to find out what Cait was planning and how it might fit in with whatever she felt she had to do. It seemed to her now that Bren had been moving slowly towards a decision since they woke up. A decision about her very nature. She'd been so withdrawn from them all, non-committal. All along Bren had been struggling with a fundamental question: was she human, or something else, something more? She'd made up her mind now, it seemed. But was she truly becoming posthuman, or what she imagined the posthumans to be? Bren said they hadn't spoken to her since making orbit. What was the reason for their silence? Would it even make sense to a mere human?

Cait was going to have to get used to them, and so was the whole human race, if it survived. We've finally encountered alien intelligence, she thought, and it comes from Earth.

She pulled four bulbs of coffee from the servery and sat in one of the low armchairs in the crew lounge. Lex was first to arrive, then Nadira and, finally, Bren.

Cait handed out the coffee and they sat and drank in silence. It was astounding that they could actually enjoy a quiet moment together after all that had happened, she thought. Maybe everyone was as exhausted as she was; it was a relief just to sit still and focus on the moment.

Eventually, Cait sat forward and placed her coffee on the low table. 'There have been a few developments that everyone needs to be brought up to speed on.' She looked at Lex and Bren. 'And I think it's time everyone laid their cards on the table. Bren, how about you go first. Do you want to tell the others about our visitors, or do you want me to?'

Bren's eyes narrowed at Cait, and she took a sip from her bulb. Cait noticed that Lex was watching Bren with interest. Perhaps he didn't know.

Bren sighed and put her bulb down, then leaned forward, elbows on her knees, fingers interlaced. 'You read about the transhumans in the history files,' she began. 'The ones who were scapegoated by the Pax and exiled. Most of them ended up on an L5 station they bought together. Since then, as processing power and link technology increased, they've been evolving, augmenting themselves. They discovered the hypercaster years before the mundanes, and they've refined it beyond anything the Compact has. They used it to project their essence onto the ship.'

'They're here?' Lex looked around as if hoping to catch a glimpse of one. 'How long have you known about them?'

Bren smiled wryly; no doubt, Cait thought, at the

unasked portion of Lex's question.

'I wasn't sure at first,' she said, looking at Cait. 'I was in deepsleep. Honestly, Cait, I couldn't remember what was dream, vision or reality. They must have activated my link remotely, but it didn't function correctly. I got some kind of weird feedback from Phillips. Everything was pretty jumbled for a while.'

'The fugue state,' Cait said. She relaxed a little. It felt as if Bren was finally being truthful. 'Was that what caused your coma?'

'I think so. They were reprogramming Phillips, covering their tracks. I'd linked pretty deeply with him on the outward leg, before we went into the harnesses. It was only when we were approaching Iota Persei F that I knew for sure they were real. They helped me balance the drive and make orbit. I couldn't have done it without them.'

'And you decided to keep quiet about it?' Cait said.

'I didn't think it was any of your business.'

'So why did they come?' Lex asked. 'It wasn't just a social visit, I take it.'

'They were protecting me,' Bren said simply. 'They'd learnt about the wyrm, and they knew I was on board. They wanted to intercept it before it loaded into the ship's systems. What they didn't foresee was the effect their intervention would have on Phillips. Sharpe's harness malfunctioned. He came out of deepsleep and saw them.'

'He saw the posthumans?' Lex asked intently.

'He saw their manifestation. Fear response kicked in and his heartbeat soared. With AI systems compromised, the harness sensors overcompensated and caused a fatal arrhythmia. He was dead in seconds, before anything could be done.'

'But I checked the harness,' Lex said. 'There was nothing wrong with it.'

'Just another bit of track-covering.' Bren leaned forward again. 'It was a stupid mistake. They value their anonymity after all they've been put through. They didn't mean to kill him.'

'And was Harris a mistake too?' Nadira asked.

'That was Phillips,' Bren said.

'So I was right,' Lex said. 'I knew that nutty program was to blame.'

'The modifications the posthumans made had some unforeseen side effects on Phillips's personality. He felt he had to protect their anonymity at all costs. But he couldn't live with the guilt of killing Harris, or betraying us.'

'And yet he was trying to warn me at the same time,' Cait said. 'His weird behaviour and complaining about being crippled. I thought he was talking about Harris's modifications. He wanted to tell me, but he couldn't.'

Bren nodded. 'He got progressively more unstable. I did what I could to prevent it, or to delay it at least. It was a mental breakdown of sorts.'

'Something's changed now,' Cait said. 'The posthumans have contacted me too, although I didn't know who they were at first. They've offered some help.'

'Can you trust them after everything that's happened?' Nadira asked.

Cait thought about that. 'I'm not sure. Bren tells me they have their own agenda, although she hasn't told me what that is. Do you want to tell us now, Bren?'

'I think I've said enough.' Bren stood and walked over to the servery.

'Her account of Sharpe's and Harris's deaths tallies pretty much with what they told me,' Cait continued.

Lex's eyes followed Bren as she took another coffee bulb and sat down some distance away but still close enough to join in the conversation if she wanted to. Cait wished, not for the first time, that she knew what was going on in his head.

'They've told me one other thing that I'm inclined to believe,' she went on, 'because it explains why Bowen hasn't activated the wyrm yet. And why he won't until the ships have a chance to contact us. The *Brahma* and *Vishnu* were only able to get here so fast because they're totally stripped down. Their engines are better, but even so they had to shed every ounce of non-essential mass to reach the kind of speed necessary. When they finally arrive, they'll be in urgent need of food, air and water. Things we have, relatively speaking, in abundance. Bowen can't use the wyrm because he'd leave his attack force stranded without supplies, although he can still threaten us with it. But since we know it won't work, it means we still have a chance to broker a deal with the Compact.'

'You can't be serious,' Lex said.

'I've never been more serious about anything in my life,' Cait said. 'If we can control the *Brahma* and *Vishnu*, we're exactly where we were before you chose to tell us about them. We can study Horizon, firm up our theories and projections, and find a workable solution. Christ, it's even more urgent we agree on this if we want to preserve the life that's down there. No one's going to convince me we should call it a day so early in the game. Nadira, I believe you're willing to work with the team along those lines?'

Nadira nodded. 'I'm comfortable with the strategy you've outlined.'

'Jesus!' Lex said. 'You're both as mad as each other. Have you forgotten there's two armed ships coming? How are you going to stop them just taking what they want?'

'We'll need to work together on that,' Cait said. 'I assume you'd rather not be held captive or killed?' She was taking a sadistic enjoyment from Lex's discomfort. 'I don't want anyone to get hurt, but we need a total defensive strategy. I'm sure we can come up with a few tricks that will keep their crews on the right side of our hull. Once Bowen sees his tactics aren't working and the wyrm is inactive, he'll be more inclined to talk.'

'I agree we need to keep them out,' Bren said from the sidelines. Lex stared at her as if she was a traitor. 'I can think of a few nasty surprises we can build into the systems.'

'Okay,' Cait said. 'Let's get to work.'

## 26

Lex was fuming. Bren had come up with all kinds of proximity alert devices and hull security systems that she could program, as if she was a total convert. Then Cait and Nadira had moved on to how they would handle Bowen. That was when he'd excused himself. He'd been close to giving up and throwing in with them, but he couldn't see how they were going to stop two armed ships determined on getting their hands on vital supplies. And even if they did succeed, he was sure they were staring at a compromise that would doom indigenous life on Horizon. There was no way he was going to agree to anything that encompassed that kind of scenario.

He wandered aimlessly until he found himself staring in through the clean-room window at the specimen bank. It just wasn't right: to find what he'd been looking for all his life, and then to lose it.

'Lex?'

The voice rang out in the darkness. He looked at his PAL hovering overhead, but the screen was blank.

Then he caught movement out the corner of his eye as Bren swam towards him from the access ladder.

'Taking a break from plotting with your buddies?' he said.

She looked at him reproachfully. 'You've got a lot to learn about me. I'm not changing sides.'

He laughed bitterly. 'You've made it abundantly clear you're not on anyone's side except your own. And your posthuman friends', I suppose, now. Why didn't you tell me about them before?'

'Shit, I don't know. All sorts of reasons. Because it was none of your business. It still isn't. Look, when we reached the system I was ready to cut all of you loose. The only reason I didn't was because of what you said to me above the ring – how you feel about Horizon. It's exactly how the posthumans see things, and it was a shock. I didn't think a normal human being could put the protection of an alien planet ahead of their own life and the future of their species.'

'So will these posthumans help?' Lex asked hopefully.

Bren bit at the corner of her lip. 'They've gone quiet on me. They're so far above anything I've ever imagined; it's like I'm some distant cave-dwelling ancestor.'

'Which makes us what?' Lex said. 'Amoebas?'

She smiled. 'No, you're a lot more dangerous than an amoeba.' The smile vanished as she added, 'It's as if they're testing me. To see if I'm worthy of being one of them.'

This brought a new, complicating dimension to Lex's plans, and one that resisted any kind of useful analysis by the sound of it. He needed Bren so much if he was going to succeed in stopping the *Brahma* and *Vishnu* that he was afraid to ask his next question.

'So what does all this mean for you and me?'

She looked at him for a stretch of three or four seconds, and he felt sweat trickling down the hollow of his back. Three seconds was an infinite amount of thinking time for someone like Bren; he could almost feel the vortex of thought spinning through her, framing multiple scenarios, calculating probabilities, weighing competing factors, reducing everything, even himself, to a simple function in a subset of some grand logarithm. She really has gone beyond flesh and blood, he thought. She may look human, but in terms of her connection to humanity, her physicality's an artefact. A hangover to be shed when it becomes inconvenient. There could never be trust between them, only a fleeting mutuality of aims based more on serendipity than any shared understanding. But still he needed her.

'Cait doesn't have the answer, I'm sure of that,' Bren said. 'I just didn't want her breathing down my neck. Besides, if we can't destroy the ships, we'll still need ways to stop them boarding us. But there's something else you should know.'

Lex felt a band tightening around his forehead. He'd already sat through enough revelations to last a lifetime.

'I had a lot of help from the posthumans when I took over the burn sequence inbound to Iota Persei F. I'm not sure how well I'll be able to control the drive if you want to use it as a weapon. I mean, I don't think I'll get any help this time.'

He placed a hand on her shoulder. 'Then it's down to you and me.'

He tried to project an air of quiet confidence, but already he could feel a migraine building.

Cait stretched out on the sofa and closed her eyes for the first time in thirty-six hours. She'd set her PAL to wake her in fifteen minutes, not daring to rest longer than that no matter how much she needed to. Despite the imminent conflict, she was feeling relatively relaxed. Nadira was really coming through now, and Bren had been surprisingly helpful in developing defences, despite the fact she'd been so upset previously. Perhaps being in touch with the posthumans had given Cait some currency with Bren so she was willing to listen more. She hoped so.

Less predictable was what the posthumans intended. The knowledge that Phillips had been changed by them explained some of his behaviours. He'd been caught between two competing imperatives:

his desire, if she could put it in those terms, to help the crew achieve their mission; and the need implanted by the posthumans to keep their presence secret. But he was more than some simple calculating machine trying to reconcile two conflicting equations. He must have been party to the dialogue between the posthumans and Bren, and he'd witnessed their actions firsthand. He would have learnt a great deal about them, analysed their activities, reached conclusions about their motivations. Had he tried to communicate some of that knowledge to her in their encounters, to provide her with some insight even while trying to hide the posthumans from her? Her interactions with Phillips had been so intense, so weird, she felt there must have been some meaning hidden within them.

During the holographic hallucination, or whatever it was in the core, he'd shown her a trail of destruction leading outwards from Earth until the entire cosmos was engulfed in flames. But what did it mean? That the posthumans were going to destroy humankind wherever it spread? If that was true, *Magellan* and the rest of humanity were in deep trouble. Perhaps the posthumans hoped that provoking a battle between *Magellan* and the other two ships would start a war on Earth and do their dirty work for them. Which meant she should try to reach a truce with the ships before any unpleasantness occurred, perhaps offering them some supplies as an act of good faith. Once hostilities broke out, it would be too late for all of them. She'd been pushing for trust and cooperation. Surely opening dialogue with the ships couldn't hurt now?

The more people I can bring on side, she thought, the easier it should be to convince the rest, like a snowball gathering momentum down a slope.

She sat up, following her line of reasoning. The ships would be close enough now for direct communication. She swung her legs over the couch, walked quickly to the command port and punched the comms icon. She set up transmission for a localised contact and watched as the onscreen pictogram described a tiny arc and locked position.

She licked her lips and keyed for transmission.

'This is Commander Cait Dyson of the explorer ship *Magellan* to Compact ships *Brahma* and *Vishnu*. We understand you are in urgent need of supplies. If you will provide details, we can have them ready for you when you come alongside.'

A window opened on the screen relaying an image from Lex's PAL. Cait reached to mute the broadcast band.

'What are you playing at?' Lex asked.

She could see Bren beside him, but while Lex was obviously angry, Bren simply looked interested.

'Slight change of plan,' Cait said. 'I'd like to see if we can get things off to a civilised start with our new neighbours. It would make things simpler in the long run.'

'Oh, yeah? And what are we meant to eat and breathe?'

'Relax, Lex. At the very least it'll confuse them enough so they don't shoot first and ask questions later.'

'We're coming down,' Lex said, and the window disappeared.

'Fine,' Cait said to herself. 'I'll bake a cake.'

Nadira came up behind her and she swivelled in her chair to meet her.

'You're contacting the ships,' Nadira said, looking and sounding tense.

'If I can. I thought it'd be best to try to open communications with them, hold out the olive branch. It can't hurt.'

Nadira nodded and the lines across her forehead smoothed out.

Lex clambered noisily down the access ladder, followed by Bren, and almost charged across the ring towards Cait and Nadira.

'It would've been nice if you'd told us what you were going to do before you did it,' he snapped.

'Pots and kettles,' Cait countered. 'I'm still the commander here, and I judged that my actions fell within the parameters of what we'd agreed. If they stay hostile, there's no harm done. If they don't, we've gained a lot.'

'Bowen's going to be suspicious about how we

know his ships need supplies,' Lex said.

'He'll probably think your friends in the UNS told us,' Cait said. 'Okay?'

Lex sighed heavily. 'Okay. For now.'

'What needs to be done?' Nadira asked, concentrating everyone's attention, to Cait's relief, on the practical aspects of their situation.

'Well,' Cait began, 'we need to finish locking the ship up tighter than a drum. Bren, can you complete the software modifications in the time we have left?'

'Shouldn't be a problem.'

'Then I need you, Nadira, and you, Lex, to check all hatches are manually locked down and welded shut. Don't forget the access from the drive chamber. They could try to sneak in that way. I'll be in forward control.'

'What about your transmission?' Lex asked.

'We wait for a response. Rendezvous with me when you're done.'

Cait's body still ached for sleep. The acceleration couch in forward control was far too comfortable, and adrenaline could only keep her going for so long. Her mind roamed over jumbled images, making connections where no wide-awake person would. Phillips and Bowen. Harris and the posthumans.

The intercept chime brought her out of it in an instant, and the restraining straps cut into her shoulders as she tried to sit up. The screen above her was flashing an incoming message.

She keyed for intra-ship voice only. 'Better get up here. We've got company.'

Sensors showed the two ships closing fast on their position. Too fast, by the looks of things. She felt it best to meet the ships with everyone in forward control, just in case they had to do some quick manoeuvring.

Cait pulled on the data gloves and made sure the helmet was in reach just in case.

Bren, Lex and Nadira were with her in minutes, all wearing their vacuum suits.

'Software's running,' Bren said. 'We have full motion tracking in a twenty-metre sphere around the vessel and on any and all hull contact.'

'The hatches are welded tight,' Nadira added.

'Okay, we're ready.' Cait reached for the monitor. 'Let's see what these people have to say for themselves.'

She opened the broadcast and a man's face appeared onscreen He was dark skinned. Tiny hemispheres of sweat beaded his bald head. The eyes were in shadow beneath heavy brow ridges crested with thick black eyebrows, and his lips were thin. There was something odd about the camera angle; then she realised he was still strapped into his harness. The feeder tube was visible at the extreme edge of the picture.

'Am I addressing Commander Dyson?' he said, as if they'd bumped into each other at an embassy ball.

'I'm Cait Dyson,' Cait said. She was fully alert now,

looking for any hint that would give her a handle on this man's personality.

'My name is Shandra, commander of the *Brahma* and mission leader. It's nice to finally meet, Commander, after pursuing you for so many years.'

Softly, softly, Cait thought. 'Your coming is something of a surprise for us. But it's nice to see another human face so far out. We have a lot to talk about.'

Shandra looked at her for a long moment, his lips pursed so the top one all but disappeared. 'In a way we do have much to discuss. But in another way we don't.' His image grew as he leaned forward. 'You have your orders. And I have mine. We're coming up on deceleration. When we pull alongside, you will open your ship to us and turn over command to me.'

'I'm sorry, but I'm not prepared to do that,' Cait said.

Shandra shifted position and the shadow fell away from his eyes. Cait saw no hint of compassion there. They were the eyes of someone who got what he wanted, or took it and didn't mind how. The skin around them crinkled as he smiled humourlessly at her.

'Then you will be destroyed. Shandra out.'

The screen blanked.

'That didn't go so well,' Cait said, feeling the tension rise in the small chamber.

'They're going for a burn,' Bren said. 'Just an attitude change. Still coming in fast.'

Cait switched to external sensors. The bright flare of the drives was visible for an instant in the darkness.

'We're not going to get anything from these people,' Lex said. 'You saw what he was like.'

'I'm not giving in yet,' Cait snapped, wishing Lex would shut up for once. 'Strap in tight. I'm bringing the engines online just in case.'

'Here they come,' Bren said.

Cait pulled on the data hood and pumped up the magnification to the max. Two eruptions of light heralded the final braking burn of both craft. A pair of icy cones – white reflecting the sunlight of the primary – revolved slowly until they were pointing straight at them. Scale was hard to determine, but she thought they were smaller than *Magellan*. They were only about one hundred klicks out, on final approach, which would bring them alongside from the rear.

Seconds ticked by and soon she could make out tiny puffs of gas coming from the ships' nose-cones as they used conventional thrusters for course adjustment and further braking. They were ten kilometres out when she saw the missile.

'What the hell?' she yelled.

'It's the *Vishnu*,' she heard Bren say.

Cait pulled the helmet off as a tiny sun blossomed, and sought the monitors to check it wasn't a helmet malfunction. The *Vishnu* plunged through a halo of debris that could only be the remains of the *Brahma*.

Cait craned around to look at Nadira. Her face mirrored the shock Cait was feeling.

The chime of an incoming message pulled her attention back to the overheads. There was some static, then the screen cleared. Another man, black-skinned with tight red curls, stood there.

'This mission is now under the direct control of the Union of Northern States,' he said. '*Magellan*, prepare to be boarded.'

Cait punched at the buckle of her harness and crawled over her seat, grabbing at Lex's suit and pulling herself up until she was inches away from his face.

'What's going on out there?' she shouted. 'What have you done?'

Lex stared at her wide-eyed. At least he had the decency to look scared.

She heard a whine building behind them and turned her head towards Bren. The tiny woman was sitting rigid in her couch, eyes screwed shut. Cait could see a vein pulsing on the side of her head.

'Bren. Don't!' she screamed.

She reached for Bren, but Lex grabbed at her arms, holding her close.

'It's for the best, Cait,' he whispered.

'Let me go!' she screamed, struggling against him, trying to lever herself free.

She head-butted him, and his nose exploded in a burst of blood. Globules spurted across the cabin.

Some flew into her eyes and she blinked them away, still struggling, but still he held her tight.

Nadira was pulling herself out of her couch, reaching back towards Bren. The noise of the drive was becoming unbearable.

'Bren, stop it!' Cait screamed. 'Phillips, or whoever you are – stop her! Can't you see what she's doing?'

Lex kicked at Nadira and she fell backwards. Cait thrust her head into his busted nose again and his grasp loosened. She pulled herself free and grabbed onto Bren's arm, pulling herself over.

Bren's muscles were like rock. The scream from the drive was thrusting into Cait, through her, threatening to split her head apart. And then a giant hand pushed her over and onto Bren. She caught sight of the monitor as the aft of *Magellan* slewed around and flared for an instant. A jet of plasma flashed on the screen and was gone.

Cait's ears rang in the sudden silence as the afterimage of the flash cleared to show empty space. The *Vishnu* had gone the way of its sister ship.

# 27

Lex flinched as Cait applied a spray dressing to the bridge of his nose. 'Go easy, will you?' he whined.

She stepped back. 'There, you're done.'

The skin was puffy and discoloured, and he still had dried blood on his chin. She hoped it hurt like hell.

Bren was perched on a stool, leaning on the med-lab bench and cradling her head in one hand.

'Analgesics any good?' Cait asked, holding out a couple of tabs.

Bren glanced at her long enough to take the pills. 'Probably not, but thanks anyway,' she said, and dry-swallowed them.

Cait folded her arms and turned her attention back to Lex. 'So just how far in are you with your friends in the UNS?'

He prodded gingerly at his nose, trying to feel the extent of the damage. 'Not as far as you think. I knew they'd snuck some people on board the *Vishnu.*' He shifted uncomfortably in his seat, looking briefly at Nadira. 'I knew they were going to attack the *Brahma* and wanted my help. But they wanted to use Horizon just like the Compact – for their own benefit.' He tilted his head back slightly, staring Cait full in the face. 'I wasn't prepared to allow that.'

The mess of his nose detracted from the force of his statement, but Cait could see he'd known exactly what he was doing, and, given the same choices, he'd do it again.

She drew herself up. 'Well, it all stops now. No more secret plans and communications.'

Lex just stared at her with that same look in his eyes.

'Eight people are dead because of you,' Cait said. '*Both of you*. And you could have blown us to kingdom come into the bargain. This is *not* the way we are going to proceed. Both of you will get in line or I'll empty the nearest hopper and seal you in there.'

She could have said more – God knows, she was angry enough – but she had to rein in her anger and use it to drive on with what she knew had to happen.

'I'm going to explain this one more time. I am not prepared to sell out to the Compact. I *am* prepared to get a lot of good science done to pin down exactly what is going to happen to Horizon and its indigenous life, assuming everything is left undisturbed. If the news isn't good for the survival of that life, we can start looking at scenarios to save it; scenarios that may or may not include some kind of permanent human settlement on the planet. If it looks like indigenous life will survive without our interference, then we'll be looking at what that means for a human settlement. Would a settlement survive without environmental intervention? If not, what intervention would have nil or minimal impact on the life already there?

'All along the way I'm determined to balance scientific, ethical and humane concerns until we have the best possible outcome for everyone. This is something I won't compromise on. If you'll trust me on this, I believe that when we come out the other end, you'll find that trust was well-founded.'

She looked at Lex, then Bren. 'You've both got some thinking to do. And I need some rest. I'll see you in the morning.'

She walked off towards her harness.

Nadira followed Cait, leaving Lex and Bren alone in the med lab. Lex palmed a cabinet, pulling out two coffee bulbs and activating the heating element.

He passed one to Bren. 'Private reserve. If the caffeine doesn't help, the shot of cognac will.'

They sipped their drinks in silence, Bren staring at an active display, Lex watching her.

'Thanks,' he said after a while. 'Whatever Cait says, you came through. Horizon's safer now.'

'But was it the right thing to do?' Bren said, placing her coffee on the ledge.

'What?'

'Part of me wonders what would have happened if we'd let Cait do what she was trying to do. Would Horizon be any worse off? Did we really have to kill?'

'The UNS was ready to kill. They demonstrated that with *Brahma*. They weren't about to jump on Cait's bandwagon.'

'We might have had to fight, I agree, but Cait was right. We have supplies they needed. If we'd kept the others off *Magellan*, they'd have had to listen sooner or later.'

Lex turned away, not wanting Bren to see his expression. He knew he wasn't responsible for the *Brahma*, but the UNS crew ... Bren had destroyed them at his urging. Had he blinded himself to the possibility that Cait's ideas had a real chance of success? Had he really got it so wrong?

'You told me the posthumans want Horizon left untouched,' he said. 'Destroying the ships brought that one step closer.'

'You didn't do it for them.'

'No, but they want the same thing I do.'

Bren shook her head. 'I think they do, but ...'

'But what?'

'It's Cait,' Bren said. 'She cares so much, she's so ... human. She's found a middle way that could meet everyone's needs, even the planet's. It's not one I'd even imagined, which makes me wonder. I have all this power, but what has it got me? Am I more human as a result, or less?'

Cait woke feeling refreshed and well rested. Sleep, when it came, had been untroubled. Despite everything, she still felt they had a chance to succeed her way. She stopped by the servery to grab a quick bite before seeking out Nadira in the gym.

'It's time to talk to Bowen,' she said without any preamble. 'I'm sure he's realised by now that the *Brahma* and *Vishnu* are gone. It's time for him to face up to the reality of the situation.'

Nadira draped her arms over the oars of the rowing machine and wiped at beads of sweat on her brow. 'He's not going to like it.'

'Doesn't matter,' Cait said. 'He's not the one I'm trying to convince. His conversations are monitored. You've seen the way he looks sometimes, as if he's getting guidance from someone else. There's more to the Compact leadership than Bowen, and without control of our ship they're facing a real emergency.'

'So what do you want to do?'

'Get the Compact to cooperate with the other nations to at least try to alleviate what's happening on Earth. Force that cooperation if we have to at first, and trust that once they see the benefits it'll become habit. There's a lot of work that can be done to pool resources and seek solutions – even short-term – to the crop problem. With all their bickering and wars, I doubt there's been a concerted effort to fix things. If we can encourage that, it'll give us time to analyse exactly what's going on with Horizon and come up with a set of best-case recommendations. It may even be that they find a solution on Earth that negates the need to resettle on Horizon altogether.'

'And by "forcing" them to cooperate you mean …?'

Cait sighed. 'We threaten to withhold any and all information and assistance to investigate Horizon's continued habitability.'

She saw the look on Nadira's face. 'I don't like it either, but it won't have to come to that. The Compact leaders can't afford a crisis of confidence from their people. If they're not seen to be doing something constructive, the social fabric on Earth is going to break down very quickly. Which means it's time for them to make some sensible decisions.' She hesitated. 'I need your support, Nadira. And the support of the others if we're going to make this work.'

'I've come this far with you,' Nadira said finally. 'You're still the commander.'

Cait smiled. 'Let's go find the others.'


Lex seemed subdued; for once he listened in silence until Cait was finished. Bren was customarily quiet, but she looked comfortable with what Cait was proposing. Or perhaps that's just wishful thinking, Cait thought.

'There's one thing, if we can arrange it,' Lex said. 'We should try to hook the UNS in on the broadcast. That way the Compact can't bottleneck our proposal and keep it purely within their leadership.'

Cait almost laughed out loud when Lex referred to it as 'our' proposal.

'Is that possible, Bren?' she asked.

'I'll have to rearrange the software a little, but,' Bren glanced at Lex, 'at least we have the UNS frequency. Give me an hour and I'll see what I can do.'

'Fine,' Cait said. 'An hour should give me just enough time to prepare.'


Horizon floated below her as she wheeled slowly on the end of her suit umbilical, way out past the drive tubes. When she'd first seen the planet it had been exciting and mysterious, and it still looked that way to her even though it had given up some of its secrets. She marvelled at the distance they had travelled to be here. Despite everything, the thrill of their journey of discovery hadn't waned. She was glad she could still take such pleasure in it. She also felt a weight of responsibility to look after this world. They were all custodians of something much greater than themselves.

She heard the crackle of an open channel and pulled on the line to face back towards *Magellan*. Another space-suited figure was moving her way. As it came into sunlight, she could see it was Lex.

'Let me guess,' she said over the open channel. 'You missed my company so much you just had to come out here so we could be together.'

'Something like that,' he said. 'Although my nose might not agree.'

He reached out his arms and she grabbed onto him. They travelled together to the end of their lines and came to a halt: two tiny specks tethered to an icy cone floating above a pristine world. Horizon turned below them, and they watched in silence.

'I've been reassessing my place in the universe and trying to get some perspective,' Lex said finally. 'There's nothing like floating out here to remind you how insignificant you really are.'

'I don't believe I'm hearing this.'

'Well, enjoy it while you can because I'm not repeating any of it with witnesses. I know I was acting in the best interests of Horizon. I'm not going to apologise for that.' He hesitated. 'But I was too narrow-minded to believe anyone else feels as deeply as I do. I thought you'd bow to pressure, Cait. I see now that isn't true. I've decided to trust you. I hope you won't let me down.'

'I won't. You can count on that. But what about Bren?'

'I can't speak for her. I don't think she'll do anything without the direct intervention of her own people now.'

'And they're still very much a mystery,' Cait said.

'It's one variable I could do without.'

'They want to protect Horizon. That much I got from Bren.'

'Yes, but at what cost? Still, I can't try to second-guess them. I have to operate as if they aren't even in the picture.'

She took one last look at Horizon and let Lex go, pulling on her own line back to the drive accessway. Lex followed in silence and they cycled through the lock together.

'You know, you might start a war with this little broadcast of yours,' he said, pulling off his helmet.

'True. But I think war is inevitable if someone doesn't take a stand.'

They stowed their suits in the lockers and made their way back through the access tube into the ring. Bren and Nadira were waiting for them at the workbench.

Cait had a sudden sinking feeling, as if she was about to sit her finals all over again. Relax, she thought. Just don't tense up and you'll be fine.

She sat next to the hypercaster relay and looked around the table. 'Are we ready to do this?'

'The hypercaster's all set,' Bren said.

Lex sat beside Nadira and grinned at Cait. He thrives on conflict, she thought.

'Even if you fail, just seeing the look on Bowen's face is going to be reward enough,' he said.

'Thanks for the vote of confidence,' Cait said, but

before she could thumb the contact Nadira reached out across the table, took her hand and gave it a squeeze.

Cait activated the hypercaster.

## 28

Space seemed to extend around them, but in a different way this time. Looking straight down the table, Cait had the feeling that each of her eyes was receiving different information. She tried to blink the feeling away, but it persisted. Bowen's office was forming on her left, but on her right was an entirely different room: dark and windowless, the walls hung with flags, some tattered and stained – and, sitting alone in the centre, illuminated by a single ceiling spot, a grizzled old man. His face was crowned with a severe buzzcut of white hair and half in shadow, but Cait could make out one ruined eye and a criss-cross of scars on his cheeks.

Bowen had half risen from behind his desk and was staring from Cait to the other man. 'What is the meaning of this, Commander?'

The other man smiled, obviously enjoying Bowen's discomfort. 'Commander Dyson,' he said and nodded to Cait, then shifted his attention to Lex. 'You're still full of surprises, aren't you, Uncle? Let me save you the trouble of introducing me to your crew, Commander.

I am Alain Dalziel, Defence Minister for the Union of Northern States.'

'This is an outrage,' Bowen said. 'You have no right to break in on our transmissions.'

The old man raised his hands in mock defence. 'Don't blame me, Secretary. It seems I'm an invited guest of your commander.'

Bowen shifted his gaze to Cait. He seemed to be gathering himself for another onslaught, but she stepped in before he could get started.

'That's right, Secretary. I think it's about time we opened up a dialogue with everyone involved.'

'Dialogue!' Bowen spat. 'After they committed an act of war against our ships?'

'Your ships are gone,' Cait cut in, 'but the UNS isn't entirely to blame. I have to share some of the guilt.' She looked significantly at Bren and Lex. 'Elements of my crew took unauthorised action. It was ... regrettable. But it leaves you in an awkward position, politically speaking.'

Cait's last remark hooked Bowen as she knew it would. He sat back in his seat, still glowering at her but silent for the moment.

'I speak for the whole crew,' she continued. 'We renounce the authority of any sovereign nation over this ship. *Magellan* will act autonomously from here on as custodian of Horizon. We're prepared to cooperate with any and all nations who seek humanitarian assistance from us, and we assure you that our actions will be to the ultimate benefit of all people on Earth. The planet we're orbiting can sustain life, but it's undergoing violent climatic changes which we need time to study. We're willing to do this, and share our information with all of Earth. We may, after proper investigation, make recommendations for colonisation and even begin limited terraforming if that presents itself as both feasible and the best solution all round. But we won't do anything unless you – both of you – agree to two things. Firstly, if Horizon is suitable for colonisation, any ships you send must contain passengers chosen for their skills and fitness, not simply their nationality. And second, considering colonisation may not be feasible, you should pool your resources on Earth now. Do your people even realise that most of them will be abandoned to a lingering death? Work together on alternative solutions to the famine. Maybe the problem can be beaten without leaving Earth.'

'You will not dictate terms to me!' Bowen shouted. Cait felt he would have strangled her if he could.

'Don't you get it?' she said. 'Your ships are gone. It's time to stop fighting us and start working *with* us. When the truth about Horizon gets out – and I'm sure it will,' she nodded towards Minister Dalziel, 'how many of your people will commit to such a trip knowing the planet's atmosphere is degrading? How will they feel about what you've done so far to ensure their arrival will be a safe and comfortable one?'

Bowen swept his hand across the desk and a glowpanel appeared. He held his hand motionless above it. 'You will submit to Compact authority now or I will destroy your ship. How much do you value your life or the lives of your crew?'

'Your wyrm program was intercepted before it loaded,' Cait said simply.

She wasn't trying to anger Bowen further, just hold him up enough to let a few home truths sink in.

Minister Dalziel chortled. 'I think she has your measure, Secretary.'

But Bowen didn't hear. He was staring over Cait's shoulder, listening to some unheard speaker. 'No!' he said suddenly. 'No. *I* command.'

He thumbed a contact on the glowpanel. 'Bowen to *Shiva*,' he rasped. 'Attack plan Delta. Silent running. Execute.'

He sat back slowly in his chair, resting his hands on the desk in front of him. 'To hell with you,' he said quietly, and then looked once more past Cait. 'To hell with all of you.'

He smiled at Cait, in command again. '*Brahma* and *Vishnu* were not alone. *Shiva* is moving in on your position now, and her crew have their orders.'

'I'm not handing over supplies to a hostile ship,' Cait said. She sensed the tension rising in her crew. 'I'll destroy *Magellan* first.'

'My crew will do their duty even if it means their own death,' Bowen said, his eyes blazing at them. 'I've won, Commander Dyson. *Shiva* will destroy your ship, then turn its attention to shutting down the storm on Horizon. It will suck up the poisons of that world and cleanse it for the Compact.' He thumped the table and spittle flew from his mouth. 'Damn you, I will have my way!' he screamed.

A figure moved into view in Bowen's office, running towards him, and the room vanished in a wall of static.

Minister Dalziel looked at Cait with his one good eye. 'Interesting. We've streamed the entire broadcast to the globalweb. Perhaps if you survive *Shiva*, we'll talk some more.' He brought his hand up in a lazy salute. 'Adieu, Commander.' And the broadcast was cut.

'Long-range sensors are picking up a massive burn,' Bren said. 'I'd say *Shiva*'s locked coordinates and is making her move.'

'That bastard,' Lex hissed. 'He couldn't give up.'

'He's even more annoying than you are,' Nadira said coolly. She looked at Cait. 'Back in the suits?'

Cait forced her mental gears to start working again. Bowen had surprised her. Not only because he had *Shiva* waiting in the wings, but that he could hate her so much he'd throw rationality aside just to strike at her, regardless of the consequences.

'I think we have to consider abandoning ship,' she

said. '*Shiva* isn't going to slow down to parley. And I doubt even you could hit a fast-moving target, Bren.'

Bren shook her head almost imperceptibly. 'Unlikely.'

'The planet's big enough for us to hide on,' Cait said.

'You're not seriously considering going down there?' Lex said. 'We'd be four biological time bombs in that environment.'

Cait sighed. 'I understand that, but as long as we're alive we still have a chance of saving Horizon. We'll stay in the suits as long as we can. The alternative is sitting tight up here until we're blown to pieces.'

'What about your friends?' Lex asked Bren.

She shook her head again. 'Nothing. Maybe this is what they want.'

'The sooner we get moving the better,' Cait said. 'Time to intercept?'

'Three hours at current speed. They'll approach from starboard.'

'Okay. The lander hatch is to port. We launch in two hours. In the meantime, we cram supplies into every available corner of the lander.'

Suited up and trailing a net bag with her helmet and a toolkit, Cait made her way through the access tube to the clean-room section. She moved quickly past the triple airlock to the forward end, up to where the walls closed together at *Magellan*'s nose.

The emergency hatch was set into the internal bulkhead. Once she opened it, the accessway between the clean room and the lander would be sealed permanently. The hatch itself was only a metre in diameter. They'd need all the time they had to get the supplies through. But what then?

Right now, Earth might be at war as a direct result of her broadcast. After fifty-five years away she had no knowledge of what weapons they may be using, but even before she left, every nation had the ability to destroy the planet several times over. If that was still the case, what was the point of fighting on?

Jesus, she chided herself, you might as well open the external hatches and leave your space suit off. She reached out and yanked the manual release to the lander bay. She'd survived on faith this long. Either way, they'd all know whether it had been worth it very, very soon.

A warning klaxon blared in the darkness and she grabbed both hatch handles, turning them into the centre and pulling outwards. There was a hiss and a loud thump as the accessway to the clean room was explosively sealed, and the hatch cover floated free.

'You can start bringing down the supplies,' she said through her PAL. 'I'll be modifying the lander.'

The mass of tools in the bag tugged at her shoulder as she launched herself through the opening and aimed for the ship. She was headed not for the lander's cockpit, but for the cargo hold immediately behind. The hold was pressurised, which was a godsend. The engineers who'd designed it had intended it for transporting delicate, ground-based experimental devices that would have been severely damaged by exposure to vacuum and the cold of space. Cait felt sure they wouldn't have approved of the modifications she had in mind.

The hold door opened outwards at her touch, and she set to as soon as it was clear, cutting through cargo webbing and carving out a niche big enough for two bodies.

She reeled in her tool bag and grabbed the welder. Two additional passengers meant she'd have to attach two extra acceleration harnesses. It wouldn't be comfortable – in fact, it would be downright claustrophobic with no light once the hatch closed over – but hopefully it would keep them alive until they made it down to Horizon. *If* they made it to Horizon.

## 29

Cait pulled off her mask and ran the suit's glove sensors over her work. The weld seemed strong enough. She planted her feet on the hold floor and pulled at the harness with all her might. It didn't show any signs of shifting. Not the most scientific testing, but it would have to do.

There was a shout and a muffled curse behind her. Lex was wrestling an improbably long line of meal trays through the hatch.

'Could they have made these openings any smaller?' he said when he caught sight of Cait. 'You should have seen the fun we had getting this lot through from the other hold. You can get it moving easy enough but the road-handling is zero.'

He managed finally to push his baggage train through the hatch, and Nadira appeared with another line of trays.

'Bren says the *Shiva*'s still on a steady intercept,' she told Cait.

'Shove this stuff aft of the harnesses and suit up,'

Cait said. 'You and Lex will have to share. I need Bren in the cockpit with me. We leave as soon as the lander's prepped and Bren's here.'

She clambered out of the cargo hold, moving hand over hand along the sleek hull to the cockpit.

'Open,' she said to her PAL, and the cowl lifted. She swung her legs round and slipped inside. The controls came alive at her touch and she pushed for comms.

'Bren, where are you?'

Bren appeared on the monitor in front of her. 'Just laying a few booby traps in case the *Shiva* crew decide to board. Explosive decompression can ruin your whole day.'

'Well, finish up and get down here. I want some distance between us and *Magellan* before *Shiva* gets much closer.'

Cait switched to diagnostics. The lander was powered up and fully fuelled. They could survive inside for three days if they didn't move around too much. After that, their suit reserves would give them another twelve to fourteen hours. Assuming they lived longer than that, they'd either suffocate in their suits or crack them open and expose Horizon to several billion alien bacteria. Perhaps we'd kick off a whole new evolutionary line, she thought. But it wasn't very likely.

Bren slid into the seat beside her. 'What's up?' she said.

Cait shook her head. 'Nothing. Get strapped in.'

Tactical plot had the *Shiva* pegged now. The distance between them was ticking down uncomfortably fast.

Cait locked her helmet shut, fired up the sensors and chinned her suit mic. 'We have one hour to intercept. Lex, you finished down there?'

'All stowed and we're strapped in.'

'I'm closing the cargo hold,' Cait said. 'Helmets on, everyone – we'll use the suit air till we're well clear.'

The cowl above her head locked down and she twisted her helmet into the neck ring. She looked over at Bren to check she'd done likewise. The younger woman was staring at her awkwardly.

'I'm not sorry about a lot of things you might be mad at me for,' Bren said. 'But I am sorry I lost you as a friend. I'm sorry what had to happen got between us.'

Cait's eyes were stinging. 'We all choose our own paths, and we have to live with the consequences. But that doesn't mean we can't become friends again.' She placed a gloved hand on Bren's shoulder. 'Let's promise each other we'll live to see that happen.'

She turned her attention back to the controls. 'But first – we have to get out of here.'

She keyed the launch sequence and a large section of *Magellan*'s outer hull slid back. Chunks of ice, displaced by the sudden movement, floated in the blackness, and then the planet loomed through the widening gap. They'd be exiting on *Shiva*'s blind side, which was the first bit of luck they'd had for a while.

'Goodbye, ship,' Cait said. 'Thanks for getting us this far.'

The launch cradle deployed, lifting the lander and extending it forward through the opening.

'Hold tight,' Cait said into the suit mic. 'I'm going to fire the thrusters while we're still in the bay. It'll get our orbit vector moving and shield the engine flare from *Shiva*'s sensors. Might buy us some time. That's the plan anyway.'

She took a sudden kick in the chest as the engines fired. There was a terrifying sound of metal tearing as the cradle bent under the stress, and then they were falling free from the ship, angling down towards Horizon.

Cait checked the readouts. 'Fifteen minutes to atmosphere. Everyone okay?'

There was a chorus of yeses.

'I'm still linked with the ship,' Bren said. '*Shiva*'s course is steady. Looks like they didn't – oh, shit!'

Cait felt her heart jump. She looked at Bren. The colour had drained from the young woman's face.

'*Shiva*'s accelerating again,' Bren said through clenched teeth. 'On an intercept with us. I'm trying ...' She fell silent.

Cait heard Lex shout, 'What's happening?'

She keyed the monitor to aft view. *Magellan* was beginning to spin, the maw of the drive section turning towards them. Bren was shaking violently in her seat. Flecks of foam sprayed from between her clenched lips and stuck to the inside of her helmet.

'Bren, stop it!' Cait reached for her own harness release, but a warning ping from the nav system made her hesitate.

Tactical showed *Shiva* coming in fast, tumbling as it came. The aft view showed *Magellan*'s drive section pointing straight up, the entire ship balancing on its endpoint.

Bren screamed.

The drive fired for an instant, spewing out a blinding stream of plasma. Cait screwed her eyes shut but the radiance still hurt. Then everything was black and she blinked away the afterimage. *Magellan* was gone from view. The sudden thrust would have sent it careening into the void.

There was another plasma blast directly over Cait's head and something flicked past, too fast to see, then more fire directly in front of them.

'M'sorry, Cai'.'

Cait was startled by Bren's slurred speech. The systems specialist was slumped back against her seat, panting. Her nose was bleeding freely, staining her lips and chin bright red.

'Missed 'em,' she said. She raised a finger and shakily pointed forward.

A sleeker, somehow meaner version of *Magellan* was settling down dead ahead, floating between them and the planet.

'Can someone please tell us what's going on?' Lex's voice came through again, sounding pissed off and scared at the same time.

'I think our options just narrowed considerably,' Cait whispered.

A small port was opening in *Shiva*'s front section. As the ship drifted slightly into sunlight, she could clearly see the warhead inside.

Bren sat bolt upright, grabbing the console for support. 'They're here,' she said, lips pulled back over her gums. Her teeth were stained red with blood.

Cait looked back towards *Shiva*. The ship hung in front of them, blocking their path to Horizon. But there was something happening behind it. It was as if she was seeing Horizon through a heat haze that made the sphere of the planet bulge to one side. An incandescent pinpoint of light appeared, bending the planet's image further around itself.

There was a silent puff of vapour from *Shiva*'s launch tube. The pinpoint of light grew rapidly to a bright disc, like a small sun.

Cait moved her hands towards the controls, instinctively wanting to take evasive action. The light in the cockpit dimmed and strobed strangely. The missile emerged, creeping free and moving towards them at a leisurely pace. Cait's own movements seemed to slow to the same speed. The air around her felt viscous, pushing against her. Then she saw what was happening and froze in fascination.

The rear half of the attacking ship was bending strangely, distending and twisting. It elongated and spiralled in a lazy arc towards the brightness behind. There was a flash as it touched the disc, which began to suck hungrily as more and more of the ship bulged and twisted towards it. It was like watching toothpaste being forced back into the tube. *Shiva*'s nose was still pointing towards them, but the rest of her was fast disappearing.

The missile had covered half the distance between them, but was slowing even further, as if tiring of the effort. Cait watched as the last of *Shiva* became a distended pretzel and was sucked into oblivion. The missile was next, stretching and then visibly losing ground, accelerating away from them until, with a flash, it had gone the way of its ship.

The disc flared again, and then it was gone from sight.

They were alone once more, and time resumed.

Cait's hand gripped the throttle and then withdrew as her brain caught up with her body.

'Now what?' she wondered aloud, and looked over at Bren. She was hunched forward in her restraints, eyes glassy.

Cait reached out a hand to shake her shoulder gently. Nothing.

Cait smacked her own harness release, pushed Bren back in her seat and straddled her, fumbling for her helmet latch. She cursed and tore off her own gloves and helmet, trying again and this time getting Bren's helmet off easily. She pressed two fingers against her carotid. Nothing.

Panicking now, she lifted Bren easily in the zero-g and laid her flat across both seats. She tilted her head back, wiped slick blood from her face, pinched her nose shut and forced air into her lungs. Four breaths, then she placed her hands over Bren's breastbone and pushed down, counting off as she did so. She repeated the process. Again. And again. Breath, push, count. Breath, push, count. The movements became everything to her, the counting like a mantra.

Lex's shouts finally broke through and Cait fell back against the console. Bren's skin was waxy pale and stretched too tight over the bones of her face. There was no spark in her eyes.

'Cait!' Lex shouted again, joined by Nadira now. Their voices sounded tinny, coming from her discarded helmet.

As Cait bent once more to force air into Bren's lungs, the contact to the cargo hold suddenly died. There was an audible click, and her eyes tracked the slowly floating helmet.

'Go home, Cait,' a voice said. 'Horizon's off-limits to humanity now. It's not to be touched.'

It was Sharpe's voice.

Movement aft caught her eye. *Magellan* slowly

reared up behind them like a huge white whale. The nose jets fired and it slowed its upward climb.

Cait reached a hand out behind and activated the docking pilot. The lander began to move, turning back towards the now stationary ship.

# 4 DEPARTURE POINT

IN MY BEGINNING IS MY END.

# 30

Lex pulled the Mylar blanket a little tighter around his shoulders. He seemed about to speak, but instead shook his head and pulled a decent draught from the coffee bulb in front of him. Cait sat beside him and opposite Nadira on the low lounge. Behind her she could hear the steady murmur of the med-lab machines hooked up to Bren.

Bren had sacrificed her life to save them. Cait had seen the strain the woman was putting herself under, but had done nothing to stop her. I should have found an alternative, she thought. Something that wouldn't have ended like this.

She'd replayed the scene in the cockpit so many times her brain hurt. It was the worst of all possible worlds: lose–lose all round.

'She might still come around,' Nadira said, without any real hope.

'To what?' Lex said. 'The embolism caused major damage. She'd be little more than a vegetable if she did regain consciousness.' His eyes dropped to study the backs of his hands. 'We have to face it: there's nothing more we can do to help. The harness can breathe for her, remove her waste, but in the long term she'll be a drain on resources. Resources that are definitely finite now.'

'You really are a heartless bastard,' Nadira said.

Lex rose from his seat. 'I've had all I'm going to take from you.'

Cait stood too and shoved him hard in the shoulder, sending him sprawling back into his seat. 'Just shut up! Both of you!' she shouted.

'Not heartless,' Lex said angrily. 'Practical.'

'This is getting us nowhere.' Cait sat again, rubbed at tired eyes. It was an effort just to focus. 'We have to look at our options.'

'What options?' Lex said. 'We've got no drive control, and the posthumans have embargoed Horizon. We're stuck.'

'There are six other planets and countless moons we can reach on thrusters alone,' Nadira pointed out. 'The supplies will last years. We have time to complete a lot of good science.'

'If we don't kill each other first,' Lex said, then looked guiltily at Cait. 'You'll forgive me, but the thought of spending my remaining years cooped up here with both of you leaves me cold.'

Cait rested her head on the seat back and closed her eyes. At least they'd stopped shouting at each other.

Personality aside, Lex always knew the right questions to ask. Just what could they do now? She had no answer.

Since she'd woken to find Sharpe dead, she'd been driving herself and the others towards a tangible endpoint. There'd been doubts along the way, but there'd always been a goal, whether it was reaching Horizon, unlocking the planet's secrets, or trying to negotiate a lasting deal with the Compact. All of those goals had been removed now. Horizon was embargoed, and she'd been unable to raise anyone from Earth on the hypercaster. For all she knew, the planet had been blasted to radioactive rubble.

Nadira's suggestion was practical as always. They had food and air. They could manoeuvre easily in-system. There was a lifetime of discovery in whichever direction they cared to look. But what would it ultimately get them, and was it worth the price they'd paid? It certainly wasn't worth the destruction of Earth, the death of her crew or the murder of her family.

She felt a rigidity descending over her. The pattern of her life had been fluid, responsive, up until the destruction of *Shiva*. Now it seemed set in amber. Fossilised. They were alone now. They'd run their race and lost.

'There is an alternative.'

The voice cut across Cait's thoughts and she was on her feet before she knew it.

Bren was standing on the deck outside the lounge

area, looking better than ever. And Sharpe was standing beside her.

Cait heard Nadira gasp and her own words froze on her lips. Over the shoulder of this new Bren, she could still see her old body lying motionless in med lab. Was it just more tricks, Cait wondered.

'It's us,' Bren said, reading her mind. 'As much as the term "us" can have any meaning any more. We've both been uploaded.'

Cait stepped towards them. Her mind grasped what Bren was saying but still she held out a hand towards her, watched it pass right through Bren's body. She looked up towards the access tubes and saw that the holo-projectors were working.

Lex was on his feet beside her. 'For once I don't know what to say. Bren, can you get back into your body?'

Bren chuckled, and the sound seemed to double and redouble until it reverberated around the ring. She stopped and glanced at her other self in med lab.

'It's just meat,' she said. 'And damaged meat at that. It's a prison cell compared to what I can do now. I'm with them now, my family. They've accepted me.'

She flashed them a brilliant smile, the careworn exhaustion gone from her face.

Sharpe stepped forward and Cait resisted the impulse to back away. He looked so healthy: his strong, open face relaxed, his kindly eyes watching her. He reached a hand out to her, stopping just before they touched.

'It is me,' he said. 'I was dying and they took me. I had no other choice.'

'How did it feel?' Cait asked quietly.

'Terrifying,' he said, and smiled. 'We always talked about pushing back the boundaries, but this is one border I'd never imagined crossing. I'm sorry I wasn't there for you, Cait. I could see what you were going through and I wanted to help. But the posthumans do things their own way.'

Cait's mind was reeling. It was too much to take in.

'That's why we're here,' he went on. 'We're willing to pilot you back to Earth. I can trim seventeen years off the trip time, and subjective time will be even less. If that's what you want.'

'What's happening there?' Cait asked. 'We can't raise anyone.'

'There's been fighting,' Bren said. 'They're talking now. You started something, Cait. But it's too early to tell if it's enough.'

'The posthumans – did they plan all this?' Cait asked.

'Not in the way you mean,' Bren said. 'You surprised them, Cait – with your resolve, your strength, your way of looking at things. Shit, you surprised me. With a little help from the right people, Earth may still have a future.'

'And what about Horizon?' Lex asked.

Bren grinned again. 'You don't give up, do you, Lex?' She paused for barely half a second as her gaze shifted away from them and into somewhere unimaginable. 'The storm will stall, but Horizon will have a much hotter and chemically different climate. One where the life you found will have a real chance to flourish.'

Bren looked at them again, and there was such certainty in her, unlike anything Cait had seen. She shook her head. Could she return to Earth? However long the trip took, there was no telling what they'd find. If the posthumans couldn't foresee it, she certainly couldn't.

But she couldn't deny the thrill that ran through her at the thought of going home. It was the same electricity that had brought her this far, but subtly different. She'd come to Horizon for the scientific pursuit, for the chance to push back the borders of knowledge. It was a cerebral thing. But as she'd travelled further and further from Earth, she'd realised what she'd lost in the bargain. The chance to be a part of humanity. To create something that might persist long after she was dust. Nothing out here could offer her that now. Perhaps it was time to pass over the horizon again, back to where she'd started.

Bren stood quietly, supremely patient. Cait wondered how many thousand other places she was right now.

'What do you say, Cait?' Sharpe asked. 'One more trip into the unknown?'

Cait turned to Lex. 'What do you think?'

Lex folded his arms. 'I don't know. I don't doubt Bren's friends can get us back to Earth, but I'm not sure I'll like what we find. Part of me would take a lot of satisfaction in Earth being a smouldering wreck so humankind can't screw anything else up. But then there wouldn't be anyone around for me to say "I told you so" to. Horizon has a future now. That's all I really care about.'

'There has to be a reason for all this,' Nadira said. 'I think Earth needs all the people of good conscience it can get. It needs people like you, Cait.' She bit at the corner of her lip. 'And if there's a chance I can help things along the way, the journey will be worth it for me.'

Cait's skin was tingling. She felt on the threshold of something exciting again. Something that would change her, Lex and Nadira in ways they couldn't possibly imagine. It was a good feeling.

'When do we leave?' she said.

'As soon as you're harnessed,' Bren told them, and was gone.


The harness tightened, inflating around her, and Cait felt the pinprick of the deepsleep drugs in her fingertip. Behind her, the drive was building for a prolonged burst. Newly augmented and free from the limitations of her physical body, Bren was going to boost them to maximum speed while still in-system.

Lex and Nadira were already asleep. They'd said their farewells over a strained meal, during which the conversation had faltered and lapsed into awkward silence.

Cait was alone now, and the decision that had seemed so right was under assault from her private demons. Nothing remained between her and the void, and beyond that an uncertain future. She was naked before it, and it seemed more terrible, more impenetrable, than ever before.

For a split second adrenaline coursed in her veins, pushing back the deepsleep and threatening to overwhelm her. Her muscles tensed, preparing to pull her free of the harness. She'd rip the tube from her throat and scream at Bren to abort the countdown.

There was an almost masochistic pleasure in not giving in to the impulse. It's okay to be scared shitless, Sharpe had told her in training. Just don't let it ruin your whole day.

The scream of the drive faded as the drugs claimed her. Cait stared into the darkness ahead. Endless possibilities beckoned.

# MAGELLAN PRE-LAUNCH TIMELINE

| YBIP[1] | Event |
|---------|-------|
| 110 | Nuclear bombardment of selected targets in the Middle East and Asia by the United States of America, Australia, and the United Kingdom. |
| 109 | War on Terror officially declared 'at an end'. |
| 107 | Compact of Asian Peoples formed. Compact petitions for UN membership. United States of America exercises its veto. |
| 104 | Pro-EU factions win UK government in landslide election. |
| 96 | Significant shrinkage of polar icecaps recorded for the fifteenth successive year. Effect of rising sea levels felt worldwide. |
| 94 | Fuel-cell boom sees formation of the Union of Northern States to protect sensitive patents. |
| 94 | Kyoto III finally ratified. |
| 93 | Compact coalition cuts all trade ties with Australia. |
| 90 | EU governments consolidated under a single body. |
| 88 | Hurricane Iago lays waste to the eastern seaboard of United States of America and a large part of Central America. |

---

1    YBIP – years before wake-up near Iota Persei

| | |
|---|---|
| 87 | United States and Australian governments ratify creation of Pax Americana, effectively merging the two countries into a consolidated trade, defence and diplomatic entity. The wastelands from Florida to Pennsylvania are officially excluded from the Pax. |
| 85 | The first fully fledged Pax election sees an increase in pro-Green elected candidates as a result of increasing environmental degradation and the legacy of Hurricane Iago. |
| 84 | Pax Americana vetoes the Compact's petition for UN membership. |
| 79 | To meet its Kyoto III targets, Pax Americana switches exclusively to fuel-cell technology for all public and an increasing percentage of private power utilisation. |
| 78 | The Pax oversees a massive retooling and retraining effort to gear its industries for the new information economy. The need for a larger skilled workforce prompts employment lotteries in the marginal eastern seaboard colonies. Thousands of former USA citizens are resettled in the Pax. |
| 74 | The UNS develops second-generation fuel-cell technology, halving cost and mass and doubling output of the new cells. |
| 72 | The Pax economy takes off on the crest of the fuel-cell revolution and the rebirth of Silicon Valley. |
| 66 | First bio-jack experiments yield amazing results in quadriplegic subjects. |

| 64 | The UNS uses its voting bloc to force Pax Americana to approve the Compact's petition for UN member status. Compact granted member status of United Nations. |
|---|---|
| 63 | Pax Americana Space Administration (PASA) formed, with its headquarters at Woomera, Australia. Near-Earth asteroid mining commences. Limited trial and use of deepsleep for asteroid-belt mining sorties. |
| 63 | UN aid program to the Compact finds health infrastructure is 'primitive' and in need of immediate assistance. Pax, UNS and EU pledge six billion U-dollars to build and equip fifteen hospitals and train over three hundred doctors. |
| 61 | EU scientist Earnhard Godel develops the picopulse black-box propulsion system. Wins Nobel Prize. |
| 60 | Environmental studies conclude that the depletion of the ozone layer has halted. |
| 60 | PASA announces the Explorer Ship program. International Space Station brought out of mothballs to coordinate the search for a target star. |
| 57 | Testing of *Magellan* prototype explorer ship complete. Crew selection includes Pax, EU and UNS members; however, the UNS representative is injured in training. The Pax government requests a replacement and UNS suggests a Compact citizen. |
| 55 | *Magellan* launches from Earth orbit. |

# ACKNOWLEDGEMENTS

Writing is a solitary art, but you need a lot of help from others on the way. In particular I'd like to thank my teacher from long ago, Ray Mooney, who helped me form the basic shape of *Horizon*; Jack Dann and Marianne de Pierres, who gave me early input and helped me connect with possible publishers; Deonie Fiford and Rochelle Fernandez at HarperCollins for recognising my story had something worthwhile in it; and my partner, Nicola O'Shea, for helping me pull it all together at the end.

I'd also like to acknowledge the many authors who filled my head with visions of the future as I was growing up, and made me think I could do the same.

# ABOUT THE AUTHOR

Keith Stevenson is a speculative fiction writer, editor, publisher and reviewer. His short fiction has appeared in *Andromeda Spaceways Inflight Magazine*, *Aurealis Magazine*, *Oceans of the Mind* and the Agog! Press anthology *Agog! Fantastic Fiction*. He was editor of *Aurealis – Australian Science Fiction and Fantasy Magazine*

from 2001 to 2004, hosted the Terra Incognita Speculative Fiction Podcast, and edited and published *Dimension6*, the free Australian speculative fiction electronic magazine from 2014 to 2020. *Horizon* is his first novel.

Photo: almcphotography

WWW.KEITHSTEVENSON.COM